THE FROST CHILD

EOIN McNAMEE

THE FROST CHILD

illustrated by Jon Goodell

WENDY
LAMB
BOOKS

Text copyright © 2009 by Eoin McNamee
Illustrations copyright © 2009 by Jon Goodell

All rights reserved. Published in the United States by Wendy Lamb Books, an imprint of Random House Children's Books, a division of Random House, Inc., New York.
Wendy Lamb Books and the colophon are trademarks of Random House, Inc.

Visit us on the Web! www.randomhouse.com/kids

Educators and librarians, for a variety of teaching tools, visit us at www.randomhouse.com/teachers

LIBRARY OF CONGRESS CATALOGING-IN-PUBLICATION DATA

McNamee, Eoin.
The Frost Child / Eoin McNamee.—1st ed.
p. cm.
Summary: Owen the Navigator is once again called on to marshall the Resisters and beat back the enemy Harsh in their attempt to take over time.
ISBN 978-0-385-73563-6 (trade)—ISBN 978-0-385-90551-0 (lib. bdg.)—
ISBN 978-0-375-89104-5 (e-book) [1. Space and time—Fiction. 2. Adventure and adventurers—Fiction. 3. Fantasy.] I. Title.
PZ7.M4787933Fr 2009
[Fic]—dc22
2008036220

The text of this book is set in 12-point Galliard.
Book design by Trish Parcell Watts
Printed in the United States of America
10 9 8 7 6 5 4 3 2 1
First Edition

For Róise

The procession moved in silence. At its head, the body of the great Harsh king was borne along on a black wagon. The wagon was drawn by six horses, if they could be said to be living horses. Their coats gleamed in a way that suggested health, but the gleam came in fact from a coating of frost, and their hooves appeared to be of ice. The horses' heads were the same shape and size as that of a normal horse, but their eyes were dark and lifeless, and icicles hung from their mouths.

Behind the wagon came the Harsh in procession. Ice kings and queens, princes and dukes of frost, their gorgeous icy raiment shimmering as they moved. And behind them, carried aloft, the small solitary figure of a Harsh child, the only one of his kind.

The procession was silent, because the Harsh did not need to speak among themselves. But for those with ears to hear, conversation moved among them like leaves whistling in the wind, and the subject of the conversation was always the same. Revenge. Swift and merciless retribution against the boy who had caused the death of their great king. The boy who had thwarted their plans. The Harsh were haters of warmth and life, and twice already they had attacked the very fabric of time in an attempt to destroy all living things. They had wreaked great destruction on the earth, but each time Owen the Navigator had stood in their way. After the king was buried the boy and his world would be crushed for once and for all.

And so it was that when the great frozen doors of the king's tomb had clanged shut forever and the terrible funeral rites of the Harsh had been observed, the frozen kings and queens gathered in conference, standing in their hundreds before the tomb. They fell silent as the dead king's wife raised her hand. The Harsh could change their appearance, and she appeared to them as a young girl, cold and beautiful, the better to persuade them.

"We have waited too long," she said, "and have given our enemies the chance to escape. I say no more!"

"What is your proposal?" A tall prince spoke.

"We still control most of time. We should unleash a flood of time, and upon that flood we can launch our ships."

"The fleet," the prince murmured, "you are talking about the fleet."

"We should set sail on time itself," the queen said, "hunt down this boy, slayer of my husband."

"The fleet is ready," he replied. "It is time to take our revenge on this boy."

"Revenge!" the queen shrieked. The young girl faded and her real face appeared, that of an ancient and terrible crone.

"Revenge!" The word ran through the crowd.

"Launch the fleet!" The queen's voice rose in command.

"The fleet! The fleet!" The crowd chanted the words, although they made no sound that could be heard by human ear. The queen smiled grimly and bowed. The Harsh were going to war. Only one small child standing to the side of the throng did not raise his voice in acclaim.

Perhaps they should have been watching the grandfather clock. Owen and his mother had taken over a little house that had belonged to a woman called Mary White. To the rest of the town Mary had been just a simple shopkeeper. But Owen and his mother knew her as one of the links between a secret world and the world they lived in. More than that, she was the keeper of a secret. The grandfather clock was not just a timepiece. When you opened it you found a gateway into time itself, known as an ingress. Owen and Martha, his mother, knew the clock was important, but even if they had been watching it, they might have missed the sign, or not have recognized it for what it was. And besides, it was growing ·dark.

Owen lit the oil lamp and placed it on the table. The electricity supply was better than it had been but was still unreliable, and they were grateful for the wood-burning stove in the sitting room. It had been ten months since the moon had almost crashed into the earth, and the rebuilding was still going on. All over the world, power stations had been damaged, roads and bridges destroyed.

Owen was one of three adventurers who had traveled across time to the great City of Hadima in order to save the world. They had brought back a tempod from the City. The tempod was a rare hollow rock containing a quantity of time, enough to repair the fabric of space and time and send the moon back to its proper orbit. The Harsh had drained time from the world, disrupting gravity, and sending the moon plunging toward the earth. The adventurers had succeeded in stopping the Harsh, but the damage wrought on the earth had been terrible.

Even now the school in the nearby town was only open for three hours a day, and half the people had not returned, giving the streets a strange deserted feel. But still, the little house they had moved into after Mary had died was cozy, and Owen's mother was stronger than she had been for years. They both knew that there were battles to come, and that Owen's friends, the Resisters, would wake once more to defend the fabric of time, but these days they were happy with simple things, such as the pie his mother now set on the table, steam rising from the crust. Martha cut into it and put a slice on Owen's plate, the oil lamp casting shadows on his pale face that made him look serious and grown-up, until he reached for his knife and fork and dove greedily in.

"Take it easy," she said, laughing. "Leave some for me."

Perhaps that was the moment they should have looked at the clock, but they were content in each other's company, and in any event, it was nothing. Just the hands of the clock hesitating for a brief moment, trembling as if they bore a huge weight, and then moving on as normal. The only sign that something had changed.

A mile away Cati leaned on the parapet of the Workhouse, eating a supper of cheese and hard biscuit. She could see the light in Owen's window and wondered what her friend was doing. She shifted restlessly. She was one of the Resisters, fighters dedicated to protecting time. All of the other Resisters were asleep in a place beneath the Workhouse called the Starry, bound to remain there until there was a threat and they were called. Cati's job as Watcher was to guard them and wake them when needed. She lived in the shadows of time where no one could see her, and was only allowed to contact Owen in an emergency. Someday, she thought, she would get used to the loneliness of it.

She sighed and stretched. Every evening before she went to bed she patrolled the Workhouse, the ancient building above the riverbank that was the headquarters of the Resisters. To the outside world the building was a ruin, but Cati knew that it stood on an island in time, and had on many occasions served as a bulwark against chaos when the normal smooth flowing of the hours and years had been interrupted.

She knew every stone and every passageway and longed for the days when, instead of being empty and cold, the rooms were thronged with men and women. She walked through the great silent kitchens, then went to look at the Skyward, their friend Dr. Diamond's laboratory, which was hidden deep underground for the moment. Inside its glass walls the Skyward was dark and still, but she could imagine the doctor at work in it, inventing and studying. She half smiled at the thought—you were as likely to get a permafrozen rose as a cake from the battered old oven by the door, or find yourself seeing backward in time through a contraption made from what looked like old vacuum cleaner parts.

Her final task was to check on the sleeping Resisters. She went round the side of the building and carefully unlocked the hidden door to the Starry, the chamber under the earth where the adults and children waited for the call to rise. Beneath the domed and star-flecked ceiling, the Resisters lay sleeping, row after row of them on beds with their hands folded on their breasts, breathing gently. Her heart warmed as she saw familiar faces. Dr. Diamond, a smile on his face. Pieta, the brave and proud warrior, her strange mocking eyes closed for now. Cati shook her head, feeling the sleep of the Starry wash over her. If she stayed there long enough, the sleep would overcome her. With a wistful grin, she stepped back out into the fresh air and locked the door behind her.

If she had stayed another minute, she would have seen what happened. But perhaps she would not have known what it meant. It was only a small thing. For a moment everyone in the room held their breath, and then they breathed normally again.

Cati went down to her small room deep inside the Workhouse. She lit the fire she had laid and curled up in bed with one of Dr. Diamond's books—a history of the Workhouse. After a few minutes she put it aside. She was glad that everyone was safe again, and was proud of the part that she and Owen and the doctor had taken in bringing back a tempod from Hadima and using the quantity of time it contained to save the world. But, proud and glad as she was, she wished that something would *happen*. She didn't want the moon to come close to the earth again, or anything dangerous like that—just something to break the monotony of the days. She pulled the sheets over her head and tried to sleep.

In a forest far away—the distance measured not so much in space as in time—another girl about the same age as Cati would have given anything for five peaceful minutes in a warm bed. Instead she crouched at the base of a tree in the snow, drawing great shuddering breaths. She had lost her pursuit for the moment, but there was a long way to go and she was cold and hungry. The tree branches had raked at her skin, and her clothes were filthy and torn. Wearily she got to her feet and felt in her pocket for the last of the dry bread and cheese. She wolfed down the food and forced a handful of snow into her mouth to follow it. Then she crammed her battered hat onto her head and gathered her torn black shawl around her, a look of determination on her face. It might be too late to save her birthplace, the great city of Hadima, but perhaps her friends Owen, Cati, and Dr. Diamond could do something. And if not, she could at least warn them of the great danger they were in. Moving lightly in her high-heeled shoes, Rosie ducked under a branch and plunged into the trees. In a moment she was gone.

Owen walked home from school, signs of the damage caused by the out-of-control moon still visible everywhere. Some shops had reopened—many of them in buildings that were only half repaired. He went into what used to be a sweetshop on the corner below the bus station. Now the elderly man sold anything he could, from old car batteries to secondhand shoes. But today, the man smiled through his cracked glasses.

"The first delivery this year!" He beamed, indicating a full carton of chocolate bars on the counter. With the little money he had, Owen bought two bars.

As he left the shop he met a group of children coming from the junior school that had been set up in the old town hall after their school had been destroyed. They were chatting happily, but Owen thought that they looked thin, and some didn't have coats to protect them from the cold east wind blowing up from the harbor.

"Hey!" he called. "Come here." The children ran over and stared at him curiously.

"Sit down on the wall," he said. He distributed the chocolate between them, keeping two pieces for his mother.

They examined the chocolate carefully before putting it in their mouths, and Owen realized that some of them might not have tasted chocolate since before the moon had swung off course.

"You live in that shop out beyond the river," a solemn-looking little boy said.

"That's right," Owen replied.

"Out where Johnston lives," the boy went on.

"Used to live," Owen corrected him. Johnston had been the Watcher for the Harsh, as Cati was the Watcher for the Resisters. He had been the Harsh's ally and spy in the human world, and a formidable foe. On their journey back from Hadima with the tempod Owen had seen Johnston swallowed up by time itself. Since then Johnston hadn't been seen in the town. But the child's next words made his blood run cold.

"Lives," the boy said. "I seen smoke coming from Johnston's chimney." Owen stared at the child. He had kept an eye on Johnston's house and had seen nothing.

"You couldn't have," Owen said at last.

"I did so." The boy stuck out his chin. "Smoke coming from the chimney."

Owen watched the children walk off down the street. Surely the boy was mistaken. For a moment he considered going down to the Workhouse and calling Cati from the shadows to talk about it. He was permitted to do that if he thought there was a threat to time. Better, though, if he went to Johnston's and looked first. There had been many times in the past months when he had gone to his private hideaway, the Den on the riverbank, and thought of calling out to Cati so that she would appear and they could talk about everything that had happened. But he knew that she took her position as the Watcher very seriously and would be furious if he broke the rules by calling her just to chat. No. He would go alone and report back to her if he found anything.

He hid his schoolbag in a hedge and went up the hill. It took fifteen minutes to walk to Johnston's gate, the landscape changing as he approached—trees and fields giving way to wasteland where trees had been uprooted and ancient hedges bulldozed. There were oily puddles on each side of the road, and the grass was withered and brown.

The gateway to Johnston's house had once been gracious, but now the railings were caked in rust and the gate hung drunkenly from its hinges. Empty oil drums lay about the place. Looking nervously up and down, Owen stepped onto the pitted drive. Lime and chestnut trees lined the driveway, but they were each and every one lifeless, their bare and crooked branches arching over the drive. Owen could see the outline of the house up ahead, and forced himself on. A solitary raven croaked a single note from the black branches over his head.

Owen had been to Johnston's house before when it had been an armed camp, and had been held hostage in it, but somehow it was more intimidating in its deserted state. It had once been a great mansion, but now it was surrounded by scrap metal and barren ground. Some of the tall windows were broken, and torn curtains hung from them.

Owen crept closer. Johnston's old scrap truck was parked at the side of the house, one of its tires flat. A door creaked in the breeze. Owen went around the side of the house. Rubbish was piled everywhere. He made his way toward the back door. It was open. He stepped into the rear hallway. An old mattress lay against the wall, and there was some kind of liquid on the floor. A broken light hung crookedly from the ceiling. Owen edged his way around the foul-smelling pool on the floor. He could see the doorway to the cellar where he'd been held prisoner.

That's far enough, he thought. *The house is deserted.* He had seen Johnston's ship being sucked down into time. The scrap dealer was gone. Relieved, he turned to go, the sunlight at the back door beckoning to him. And then, just as he reached the threshold, he heard a sound that made him feel as if someone had placed a cold finger on his spine: a single piano note from somewhere inside the house.

Owen froze. The note hung in the air, then was followed by another and another, a melody being picked out. A slow and eerie music, as if a ghost hand wandered lightly on the keyboard.

As suddenly as it had begun, the music stopped. Owen spun around to face the hallway. He remembered that there had been a piano in the front room, Johnston's room, where the scrap dealer would listen to opera. And as he watched, a huge shadow was cast on the hallway wall. Owen shrank back against the stained wallpaper. He hadn't really thought that he would find Johnston alive and in the house, and he felt paralyzed with shock and fear. The shadow grew massive, full of menace. He forced himself to think coolly. No purpose would be served by a confrontation with Johnston. The man was strong and cunning and Owen could not win. Better to retreat and leave Johnston to think that his homecoming was a secret.

Steeling himself to move, Owen slipped out of the back door. As he emerged into the daylight, a flock of rooks burst from the dead trees and wheeled into the sky, the air filling with their cries. *They'll give me cover,* Owen thought. He lowered his head and ran. In half a minute he had cleared the gate and was running down the road, while behind him the rooks cawed as though jeering.

Johnston moved slowly down the hallway. He looked older. His massive sideburns had grayed, and he was limping heavily. But the same cunning light still shone in his eyes. He had been sucked into the maelstrom in time, as Owen had seen. But the distortion in the fabric of time that had enabled Owen and his friends to put the moon back into orbit also allowed his escape.

Johnston limped to the back door and knelt slowly to examine the footprints in the dust. A mirthless smile showed his huge yellowing teeth like tombstones.

"The Navigator has run home, has he?" Johnston said softly to himself. "He thinks Johnston is stupid. But winter is coming, little boy, winter is coming."

Martha was peeling potatoes in the kitchen when she saw Owen running down the road. The radio was on in the background—the television networks and satellites had been destroyed and still had not been rebuilt. The presenter's voice was crackly and distant as he talked about expanding ice caps, but Martha was only half listening. The world had been so changed by what had happened that the unusual appeared almost normal.

She went out to the little grocery shop and ran her hand along the dusty counter. The shop had been owned by her neighbor, Mary White. On the surface Mary had appeared to be just a normal countrywoman, but in fact she had been the Resisters' contact in the world of ordinary people, and had been wise and knowing. Martha had been pursued by the Harsh when Owen was a baby, and her mind frozen by their deadly cold breath. It was Mary who had eased her, had put Martha's mind to sleep to allow it to heal, leaving her barely able to look after her young son. When Martha was needed, Mary had awakened her. But Mary had died in the end. She had been weakened by age and the effort of waking Martha's mind again, but it had been an attack on her by Johnston that had done the real and final damage.

There was a crash, and she turned in alarm as Owen burst in through the door.

"What is it?" Martha asked. "Why were you running?"

"Johnston is back," Owen gasped. "Dr. Diamond was right. He wasn't lost."

Martha would have fallen if it was not for the support of the counter. She gripped Owen's arm. Her voice was hoarse.

"No! It can't be starting again so soon."

"It's all right," he said, "it's okay." Martha shook her head. Owen shouldn't be allowed to face this responsibility on his own. She straightened herself.

"It is time to contact Cati." Her voice was firm now. "The Watcher needs to know that Johnston is back."

Owen looked at her. "You're shaking."

"It will pass," she said, "it was just the shock." She gripped his arms and looked into his eyes. "We'll beat him this time as well. Besides," Martha went on, forcing a smile, "I know you're dying to see Cati again! Go and call the Watcher!"

But as she watched him run across the field, her heart was seized with dread. Twice Owen had been the key to defeating Johnston and the Harsh. What burden would fall on him in this new struggle?

Owen ran across the fields and straddled the tree trunk that formed a bridge across the river. The sun sparkled on the surface of the water and the wind gathered leaves against the low river wall. Owen jumped off the other end of the log and called.

"Cati?"

No answer. He called and called, but she did not respond.

"Come on, Cati!" he shouted, impatient now. "It's important!"

In the end he gave up. He walked down the river path to his Den, pushed aside the bushes that he used to disguise the entrance, and went in. Everything was as he had left it. Greenish light from the clear perspex that acted as a skylight showing the old sofa and table with the stove on it. A truck wing mirror, dusty and forgotten on the wall. Under the table was the wooden box with his grandfather's maps, and on another wall something that looked like an old boat propeller but was in fact the Mortmain, an object of great power.

He threw himself down on the sofa.

"Where are you, Cati?" he said to himself.

"Here, you dimwit."

He looked up to see Cati standing in the doorway in her faded uniform, which she had studded with brightly colored badges. She looked a little older than he remembered, but then again so did he. But she still had the same restless movements, her green eyes dancing in her freckled face, quick to anger and quick to forgive.

"Dimwit?" He jumped to his feet, not knowing whether to hug her or shout at her.

"Blundering about the Workhouse calling my name. Did you want me to appear there and then, in front of whoever might be passing by? The outside world doesn't know about the Resisters and I'd like to keep it that way."

"Good to see you too, Cati," he said.

"Of course it's good to see you," she said, her face transformed by a smile, "but we have to be careful. There are still enemies out there."

"I know," Owen said. "Johnston's back!"

"What?" She looked at him in dismay. "We saw him—"

"I know! We thought he was lost, but I think that in some way we turned back time when we sailed from Hadima in the *Wayfarer* with the tempod."

"The *Wayfarer* rescued Johnston?"

"I'm afraid so. We didn't mean it to happen, but there was no other way . . ." The *Wayfarer*! Just hearing the name of the slender vessel made his heart jump. At its resting place behind his house, it looked like a battered little schooner, but in fact it was a boat that could sail on the currents of time.

"I went up to his house," Owen said. "It is him, Cati."

"I believe you. I thought I heard opera music one night coming from that direction, but I put it out of my mind. You know the way Johnston loves opera." Cati's ears were very sensitive since her time in Hadima when she had temporarily joined up with a pack of children known as the Dogs who wore dog masks and sometimes seemed half canine. A bite from one of them had left Cati with more acute hearing, and a keen sense of smell.

"Did he see you?" Cati went on.

"I don't think so. . . ."

"At least that gives us a little time to think."

"So what do we do now?" Owen asked. "Is it time to wake the Resisters?"

Cati shook her head reluctantly. "Johnston was always here, even when they slept."

"It's our job to keep an eye on him," Owen said.

"You're right," Cati said. She had a strong sense of duty, and he could see that she knew it was the right thing to do.

"Are they all okay, the Resisters?"

"Yes," she said, "all sleeping peacefully."

"Why is it that when something happens, I want Dr. Diamond to be here?" Owen said.

"I miss him too," Cati said, "but we have to be able to make our own decisions without him." She smiled. "I wouldn't mind a bit of his cooking though."

"His apple tart," Owen said.

"His scones with butter," Cati said dreamily.

"Jam tarts, pear flan . . ."

"Stop!" Cati leapt to her feet. "I have to go back to cured ham and hard biscuit."

"It's not really his food you miss, is it?"

"No," Cati said glumly. "I could do with a bit of company. And there's always something happening when he's around."

"Do you remember the jet-propelled rucksack?"

"He rescued you from the Harsh with that. And the silly glasses he got in Hadima."

20

"It's hard here too sometimes. I can talk to my mum about stuff, but it isn't the same."

"I know. You know, I don't think I was really made for rules," Cati said sadly, "but I have to follow them. It's time for me to go now."

"Stay awhile."

"I don't know. . . ." She frowned.

"We need to talk," Owen said slyly, "pool our knowledge. There may be some small bit of vital information that the other has missed."

"I suppose you're right," she said. "It might be useful. . . ."

"I'll make some tea,' Owen said, springing to his feet and grabbing the battered kettle.

They had tea and some of the dried biscuit Cati carried in her pocket. They talked until nightfall of journeys through time, and great cities, and battles with the Harsh. They talked about the Yeati, the mythic beast that had helped them in Hadima, the City of Time, and of Conrad Black, the crooked keeper of the Museum of Time there, and of Rosie, the streetwise and clever girl who had been their guide.

"I'd love to see the Yeati again," Cati sighed. "He was like something out of a book."

"You remember how vain he was," Owen said, "always combing his fur? I'll never forget the night you and Rosie rescued him from Black's museum. He must have spent two hours in the bathroom looking after his fur."

They talked as old friends do when they haven't seen

21

each other for a long time. But finally Cati looked up and saw that they were sitting in near darkness.

"My rounds!" she cried out. "My inspections!" She leapt to her feet, and before Owen could say a word, she was racing through the door. Owen followed her out, but she was gone. He shook his head.

"Good night, Watcher," he whispered, then he pulled the bushes across the gap to hide the Den and started home across the fields.

Half a mile away, a small exhausted girl crouched in the mouth of what looked like an old drain. Rosie's body ached from top to toe. She couldn't remember the last time she had eaten, and her hair, which once had been glossy and piled high on her head, hung in filthy hanks about her face. The last few hours had been the worst. Unseen creatures in the forest lining the roads, then a dark tunnel and a strange crossing point. The directions pieced together from what she had heard around the City and what Owen and Cati had told her about the journey they had undertaken to Hadima. Now she had retraced their path and had reached her destination. She looked over her shoulder. The drain was no ordinary drain, but an opening into another world, the world that Rosie had left behind to undertake a long and dangerous journey.

She looked at the drop below her—how would she

get down? *Come all this way and then break my neck at the last of it,* she thought gloomily. She scrambled over the lip of the tunnel and grasped the edge, trying to lower herself over. But she was weak with hunger and her fingers did not have the strength. With a low moan she slipped from the mouth of the pipe and plummeted toward the edge of the river that flowed below.

She landed in a patch of thorny bushes on the bank, winded and sore, but none the worse for the fall. She tried to disentangle herself from the bushes, ripping what was left of her coat in the process. She cursed as she struggled, using terms that would have made one of the Resister soldiers blush.

With a final volley of swear words she tore herself free. As she did she heard a low chuckle above her head and shrank into the shadows.

"Who's there?" she demanded.

"You've got some tongue in your head for a youngster," a man said. Rosie peered suspiciously into the dark. She could just make out a figure leaning over an upstream bridge.

"None of your business what I say," Rosie snapped. The man chuckled again.

"You're right, of course. But I saw you fall and wondered if you were all right."

"I'm fine," Rosie said stiffly.

"That's good. There is one thing I have to remark upon—you coming out of that pipe up there."

"If I want to climb into a pipe, then that's my business," she said.

"Of course, of course. I was going to remark on . . . how do I put it? A certain navigation took place through that pipe. . . ."

"Navigation?" Rosie lowered her voice. "You mean you know about . . ."

"The Navigator? Of course. A brave fighter."

"Anybody could know the name," Rosie said.

"That's true," the man said, "but who knows that his name is Owen and that his companion is Cati, the Watcher?"

"You do know them!" Rosie said.

"Friends of mine, in fact."

"Can you take me to them?" Rosie said eagerly.

"Well now," the man said, "how do I know I can trust you?"

"Of course you can trust me. I came all the way from Hadima to find them!"

"I suppose you're right," the man said. "There's something about your voice that I like. Come on up, I'll take you to them."

Just below the bridge there were footholds, and Rosie scrambled up, her tiredness forgotten. When she got to the final part of the climb the man leaned over to help her. Rosie reached up and grasped Johnston's hand.

Rosie felt warm and sleepy. The inside of Johnston's truck was untidy. Springs poked through the seats and there was rubbish everywhere. But the heater was on and opera music played softly on a stereo that looked home-made. Johnston talked as they drove. He really did know a lot about Owen and Cati and the Resisters, Rosie thought, and he was delighted to know about how Rosie had met them—the search for the tempod in particular. He wanted to know what else Owen had found at Hadima, and when Rosie told him that Owen had found his grandfather's old maps, Johnston laughed and slapped his leg as though he had heard a great joke.

But when Johnston asked what news Rosie had for Owen, she fell silent, her mind dwelling on the scenes she had left behind in the City of Time, and Johnston did not press her.

The truck bounced up a driveway overhung by crooked tree limbs.

"Where are we?" Rosie looked about her as the truck jolted to a halt.

"My house," Johnston said. "I just want to get a few things to give to Owen and Cati. And maybe a bite to eat for you. How does steak sound? With potatoes and peas and gravy?"

Rosie thought she would faint at the idea of steak and potatoes. Johnston took her by the arm and led her through the big front doors, talking about apple pie with hot custard followed by ice cream. They were halfway through the house before her mind, dazed and exhausted with the long and dangerous journey, started to focus on the dereliction all around her—wallpaper hanging off the walls, old machine parts stacked to the ceiling.

"Where . . . ?" she said as he led her down a narrow staircase, the steps gleaming with damp.

"You'll like it down here," Johnston said, his huge teeth shining in the gloom. "It's a very special place where we keep . . ." His hand shot out and wrenched a door open. "Where we keep the rats!" he snarled, shoving her through the door.

Rosie fell down the steps inside, skinning her hands and knees, then landed with a splash in brackish water. She looked behind her just in time to see Johnston's wolfish grin as he slammed and locked the door, plunging the room into semidarkness. She felt something slimy beneath her fingers and snatched her hand out of the water.

She was in a cell, with one barred window high on the left-hand wall through which came a dull gleam of moonlight. The floor was covered in water, and in a far corner something slipped or fell into the water with a plop. Feeling her skin crawl, she backed onto the staircase, which was at least dry. What a fool she had been, she thought bitterly, to trust the first person she came across. And now she was alone and hungry and a prisoner. Worst of all, she had let her friends down. Rosie almost never cried, but she could feel tears of blame prick her eyes now. Crossly she brushed them away. She looked around as best she could in the dim light. The only ways in or out were the high barred window or the solid-looking door. The cell reminded her of the damp cellar where she had found the Yeati imprisoned the previous year. The Yeati, the mythical beast whom she had helped escape in Hadima and who had given the Resister children a ring of immense power that had healed her damaged hands. She rubbed her hands, thinking. She had picked the lock then; could she do it again now? But no. When she examined the door she found no lock on the inside.

She felt a new wave of exhaustion sweep over her. She had last slept in the forest, and that was many hours ago. Ignoring the rumbling in her stomach, she made herself as comfortable as she could on the step, and curled up to sleep in the very spot where Owen had also slept a fitful sleep while a prisoner of Johnston.

Owen went out to the *Wayfarer*, as he did every night before he went to bed. The little boat lay tilted on her side in the orchard behind the house. He touched her timbers and could feel a shudder run through her, how the boat was eager to be aloft and sailing on the currents of time. But he knew that he could not take her out.

"Think about it," his mother had said to him. "You might be seen, or picked up on radar. Anything. The next thing the government would track you down and take the *Wayfarer* away. They'd tear the boat apart to get at her secrets."

"But that means I can never sail her," Owen said.

"No. When the time comes, when you are needed, you can risk taking her out, but not until then. The *Wayfarer* isn't just a sailing boat."

I know she isn't a sailing boat, Owen thought, climbing on board and taking hold of the tiller, which jumped in his hand. Dr. Diamond might have all sorts of complicated explanations to explain how the *Wayfarer* sailed on the sea of time, but Owen felt that if there was such a thing as magic, then the boat was magical.

His grandfather had first owned the *Wayfarer,* and had left maps that would guide her as she sailed through time. In the evenings Owen would bring the maps and the Mortmain up from the Den. The Mortmain fitted onto a spot below the wheel, as a type of compass, and Owen would spend hours trying to understand how it worked. The maps were very old and covered in strange symbols, but he knew that none of it would work when the boat was sitting on the ground. He *knew* that if he could sail the *Wayfarer* she would show him the way, as the boat had done the time he had brought her from Hadima. More and more he understood that he had an instinct that enabled him to work out directions and distances. That was what made him the Navigator.

He gripped the tiller hard and imagined her billowing sails, which appeared to be made of time itself, rather than cloth, if that was possible. He ached to sail her, but his mother's warning stayed in his head. He pictured men in white coats going through the little cabin, sinking instruments into the delicate timbers, ripping up her decking in search of something that could not be measured by any instrument.

He had never forgotten the first time he had held the tiller of the *Wayfarer.* She had lain, dusty and forgotten, in the Museum of Time in Hadima, but Owen had found her. The moment he touched the tiller he had known that she was a living thing and that somehow they were bound together. And the first time he had sailed her into the sky and out onto the ocean of time, his heart had leapt.

Owen ran his hand over the space where the Mortmain would fit on the hatch in front of him, then let go of the tiller regretfully and swung over the side, giving the *Wayfarer* one last glance as he walked back toward the house. He went in and closed and locked the door behind him.

His mother was sitting at the table, an accounts book open in front of her. She didn't hear him coming in, and he heard her sigh and say, "Oh, Owen."

"What is it?"

"Nothing—well, not nothing. We just don't seem to be making very much money from the shop."

He told her about meeting Cati. His mother thought it over.

"I think you did the right thing. It was very sensible of you both. I think the best thing is to keep a close eye on Johnston. It's true that he was always here causing mischief, but his reappearance is suspicious."

Owen hesitated. "When I came in, you said, 'Oh, Owen.' Why did you use my name?"

"I didn't. I was thinking about your father. He was Owen too, as was your grandfather—the first Navigator."

"I wish I'd met my grandfather."

"He was quite a man. He made and lost fortunes,

learned how to sail on time, invented and discovered all sorts of marvelous things. Everybody looked up to him, but . . ."

"But what?"

"He didn't have time to bring up your father properly," Martha sighed. "Your dad missed that. I think he was always trying to live up to your granddad."

They were both silent for a moment, each thinking about the moment Owen's father had been lost.

"Am I like either of them?"

"You are just yourself, Owen." She smiled and ruffled his hair. "That's all you have to be in order to be the Navigator. I don't think your father ever realized that."

Owen's father had been the Navigator before him, but had died when his car had crashed into the harbor. Owen, a baby, had been in the car too, but his father had saved his son's life by throwing him from the car. Some of the Resisters had been suspicious of Owen's father. They had accused him of taking the Mortmain, and of opening up the road to Hadima when it would have been better left closed. And for those Resisters, such as Samual, the son was not to be trusted either.

Owen fished in his pocket now, bringing out the last two pieces of chocolate. He held them out to his mother.

"Here. I nearly forgot—it's not much . . . ," and he told her about the children. She smiled at him and took a piece.

"You see, Owen? You're just yourself."

And you are yourself as well, he thought. There had

been long years when, as a result of being attacked by the Harsh, his mother had been vague and forgetful, barely there. But now she was strong. He noticed that people from the town would come out to the shop to buy some small thing, then spend half an hour asking her for advice. There were questions about rebuilding part of the hospital, or setting up a fire brigade. They were subjects she knew nothing about, but she had a way of giving people confidence and sending them home full of hope. She caught him looking at her now, smiled, and yawned. Behind them the grandfather clock chimed.

"I still don't understand how the clock—the ingress— works," Owen said.

"Goodness," Martha said sleepily. "That's a big and complicated subject. An ingress, well . . . it lets you into the engine of time, like lifting the hood of a car. When you look into it, you're looking at the machinery of time. Does that help? Now, unless you've any more difficult questions . . ."

"Okay," Owen said, "I'll go to bed."

Down at the river all was quiet, save for the stir of a sleeping moorhen and a gentle splash in the shallows as a late-migrating salmon drove up the river toward its mountain birthplace. Through the town the river flowed, under the bridge and past the entrance from which Rosie had come, and on toward the sea. But Rosie was not to be the only person to pass through the entrance that day. If Johnston had been leaning on the bridge he would have seen another figure standing in the mouth of what appeared to be a drainage pipe. He would have had no trouble picking out the long white hair shimmering in the moonlight, the violet eyes ringed with black mascara, a pale and cold and beautiful creature poised without moving above the river, moonlight glinting from the chrome talons attached to her nails. No one in this world knew her name, although she had led an attack against Owen and Cati and Dr. Diamond, and had hunted Rosie through the dark forest. She was Agnetha, the leader of the Albions, guardians of the forest that stood at the other side of the gate, and she had never dared to pass through the tunnel to the other side. But this time the Harsh queen had told her that it was allowed. The Harsh queen had told her what to do.

She turned and gave a signal. Other Albions appeared out of the darkness, all with the same white hair and violet eyes, though none as beautiful as she. Thin ropes snaked down into the darkness below. Agnetha caught a rope and slid gracefully downward, followed by the others. Above them another Albion rolled up the ropes, leaving no trace of their passage. They crossed the river, jumping lightly from stone to stone. Suddenly Agnetha turned her head to one side and listened. She gestured to the Albions. They ran to the other bank and melted into the shadows under the bridge.

Cati's nightly round took her along the front of the Workhouse and down along the riverbank. Strictly speaking, she should have stopped at the boundaries of the

Workhouse, but she often went as far as the opening in the wall that led to Hadima. She told herself that it was important to inspect it, but really it intrigued her, seeming to reek of mystery and of the strange lands beyond.

As she approached she thought she glimpsed movement in the mouth of the opening. She took a quick look around to make sure there was no one watching—she was supposed to be invisible to ordinary people, hidden in the shadows of time, but there was no point in taking chances. Then she clambered up the wall beside the bridge, unaware of the Albions on the other side. She put her hands on the parapet and stared hard into the opening, but nothing moved. Probably a bird roosting—or even a rat, she thought with a shudder. If she had looked down just then she would have seen a circle of violet eyes looking up at her from the darkness, and the gleam of cold chrome talons within striking distance. Cati was invisible to ordinary people, but the Albions' violet eyes saw much that ordinary people did not.

A gust of cold air struck her. She shivered. It was a long way back to her warm bed. She crossed the bridge again and climbed down to the riverbank, setting off for home at a fast pace. One of the boy Albions gave Agnetha a questioning look, showing his scimitar-shaped talons. For answer she jumped onto the riverbank and started to follow Cati.

They were skilled trackers. Within minutes Cati was walking, unknown to herself, within a deadly circle of the pale-skinned creatures. Four moved silently through the fields at either side of the path. Two more had circled on ahead and glided along the path in front of Cati, with the rest following behind. At times they drew close enough to touch her, and yet she did not know they were there, although she was uneasy, and more than once stopped and looked around her. They stopped too, starting off again at the exact same moment as she did.

They had the gift of moving silently. Cati's ears were extraordinarily sensitive due to her time with the Dogs of Hadima, but she did not hear them. And though her sense of smell was acute, she did not smell them, for the Albions were entirely odorless.

Encased in their deadly cage, Cati walked all the way back to the Workhouse, the Albions almost toying with her—one of them would get close enough to touch her, then duck back into the shadows so that she thought that she had brushed a moth or a cobweb.

At last she stood in the shadow of the Workhouse, silent presences all around her. She looked up at the crumbling walls, while violet eyes gazed expectantly at Agnetha. Agnetha stood without moving. Moonlight gleamed on steel. Agnetha pondered, then shook her head. They would leave the girl alone. They had got what they came for, and there might be others who would miss the girl and raise the alarm. The Workhouse was silent and unmanned. They would tell the Harsh queen, and await further orders. The girl could wait, for a greater prize was at stake: the queen had promised them what they longed for most. She had promised them that once the Workhouse had fallen, that they would relish the thing that they now found intolerable—they would be able to stand in the sun without pain. She had promised them light.

Without even the faintest of rustles the Albions faded into the night. Cati was alone again, without ever realizing that she had been surrounded. She yawned and trudged up the stairs and into the Workhouse, leaving the night to its wild and scurrying creatures.

Rosie woke feeling stiff and frozen. The cell didn't look any better in the daylight than it did at night, and it certainly wasn't any warmer. She crawled to the top of the steps and examined the door. She remembered again how she had freed the Yeati by picking the lock of his cage in the basement of the Museum of Time. But that trick wouldn't work here. The door was padlocked on the outside. She sat down on one of the lower steps and tried to think. She was a prisoner. The man who held her must have had some purpose. Why did you keep a prisoner? Perhaps to question them? (Rosie tried to push the notion of torture out of her mind.) Or as a hostage or some other kind of pawn? If she found out, then perhaps she could turn the situation to her advantage.

The door at the top of the stairs flew open.

"Good morning!" Johnston boomed.

"Not so good from down here, fatso," Rosie said, but her voice quavered, more from weakness and hunger than from fear. Johnston roared with laughter.

"The little squeaker has spirit! Come on up and have

some breakfast. Sorry about putting you down there, but I had to check you out. The Resisters are suspicious folk. Anyway, the Navigator wants to see you in an hour!"

"Not taking any breakfast from you," Rosie muttered as she made her way up the stairs. Johnston took hold of her arm lightly, but she could feel the strength in his huge hand. Her resolve faded as she went along the corridor and smelled good things cooking. There had been little food in Hadima, and none on the road, otherwise she would have been more cautious.

Johnston led her into the kitchen. In contrast to the rest of the house, it was spotless. A table was laid with an oilcloth cover, and pots and pans gleamed on the wall. Johnston went to the oven and took out a platter laden with bacon and sausages, fried mushrooms and tomatoes, and hot buttered toast. He put the platter down in front of Rosie.

"Eat up! I've had mine." And he watched as Rosie overcame her suspicions and started to eat. The food was delicious and it was a full ten minutes before she had enough.

"Wonderful." Johnston beamed. "Excellent! Have some tea. Sugar?"

Rosie took the mug of hot, steaming tea from Johnston, feeling warmth creep back into her body, the feeling of well-being so strong that she had to remind herself that the smiling man had in fact kidnapped her and locked her in a freezing cell.

"When are we going to find my friends?"

"In a little while."

"In a little while? What does that mean . . . ?" Rosie was feeling light-headed. Johnston swam in and out of focus.

"It means that I'll let you go when I'm finished with you," Johnston said softly.

Fell for the oldest trick in the book, was Rosie's final thought before her head hit the table.

Late the following morning Cati went back to the Hadima entrance and scouted around, but could find no tracks on the riverbank. It was cold and the sky was a strange silvery gray color. The movement in the mouth of the entrance played on her mind. She had brought a rope and a grappling iron with her, and she stood for a long time looking up at the entrance. Before he had gone back to sleep, Dr. Diamond had made it plain that he did not want her going anywhere near the entrance.

"It is far too dangerous, Cati," he said. "We don't know enough about it." Cati thought about what he had said. *But I am the Watcher,* she said to herself, and she took the grappling hook from her pack.

It took several goes before the hook gripped. She tested it with her weight, then climbed rapidly upward. She grabbed the slimy edges of the entrance and pulled herself in. The tunnel smelt of mud and algae, and she wrinkled her nose before climbing upward, slipping several times on the slimy floor.

In a few minutes she had emerged into a courtyard. She'd been here before, when she and Owen and Dr. Diamond had opened the wooden doors of the shop with the sign *J. M. Gobillard et Fils* on the window, and had found the tunnel that led to Hadima. Little did she know then who Gobillard would turn out to be—a friend of Owen's grandfather, maker of an amazing trunk that could enclose a deadly whirlwind of time, a trunk that used the Mortmain as a lock. Owen had met Gobillard in the prison in Hadima and had got his grandfather's maps from him. But Gobillard had died there.

Then, the first time Cati had entered the courtyard, it had been an empty, sleepy place, the row of shops closed and almost derelict, weeds growing in the center. But something had changed. Cati's eyes narrowed as she moved cautiously forward.

Someone had been here. On every surface—the walls and fronts of the shops, and even the dusty glass—words had been scrawled in red ink. They were words in some strange language that she did not recognize, but their jagged forms spoke of hate and envy and bitterness so strongly that Cati gasped and took a step backward.

She forced herself to move forward toward the wooden double doors that led downward to Hadima. The graffiti was concentrated there, an almost continuous scrawl. One of the tunnel doors was slightly ajar, as though someone had passed through in haste. Cati stared at it. The Hadima entrance was no longer intriguing. She dreaded what lay beyond it.

Instinctively she reached out to the open door and closed it. She made her way back down the tunnel, casting nervous glances over her shoulder. When she got to the end she cast the grappling hook onto a branch of a tree growing out of the bank and, using the rope as a swing, descended to the opposite side. It was only then, as she loosened the grappling hook from the branch, that she noticed something different. The sky had gone from gray to a sullen zinc color, with a dull red at the edges, and the cold was biting. Something was terribly wrong.

I need to contact Owen, she thought, and set off up the river as quickly as she could.

Owen too had seen the sky from the kitchen. He went outside. Without thinking he leaned on the thwart of the *Wayfarer,* and as he did so he felt a shock through his sleeve, a bolt of anxiety from the boat itself. He looked at the sky again. How ominous it was! He knew that it was time to contact the Watcher. Without stopping to tell his mother, he set off for the Workhouse.

A few minutes later Martha, who had been in the shop, became aware of the odd light. She went to the back door and looked up at the strange, dull color. Her first impulse was to find Owen. She called him but he wasn't in the house or the garden. Then she saw his red jacket, two fields away, moving toward the Workhouse. She drew breath to call to him, but the sound never left her mouth. There was a great howling, like the cry of a terrible beast, and, almost instantly, Owen disappeared as if he had never been, as a curtain of needle-sharp sleet swept in front of her. The storm had struck.

Cati had never heard anything like the shriek of the wind as it drove sleet and snow horizontally across the town. Blindly she made her way upriver, using the water underfoot as her guide. Soon she was soaked to her hips. There was some shelter from the wind in the trees and bushes along the river, but there was no hiding from the terrible cold that tore at her exposed flesh. She rubbed at her nose and cheeks. *You can't get frostbite that quickly,* she thought, but still she rubbed at the exposed parts.

Through eyes narrowed against the cutting sleet she could see that the water at the edge of the river was starting to freeze, and the water that flowed around her knees was a milky color, as though just about to turn to ice.

But it wasn't the air searing her lungs that caused the sudden pang of fear, or the weariness in her limbs as the cold sapped her strength. It was what she could hear, carried on the storm, faint and far away, yet still terrifying. Voices crying out without words. Voices that she had heard before. Harsh voices. Cati tried to run, but she had been frozen by the Harsh before, and their cries drained her of energy and hope. Grimly she put her head down and battled upstream. The snow and sleet whirled around her, so she could only see for a few feet, but she could feel the Workhouse nearby. Its old stones called to her. She stumbled and found herself in the center of the river, the icy torrent up to her waist now. The water threatened to sweep her downstream. Her feet were too numb to gain any purchase on the slippery rocks. Frantically she looked up and saw that she was just under the tree trunk that served as a bridge. But her hands wouldn't reach. Three times she tried, and three times she failed. Fatigue had her in its grip now. She could close her eyes, she thought, and let the river carry her away, floating gently downstream . . .

"Quick!" a voice snapped from above. "Grab my hand!"

Without opening her eyes, she responded. A strong hand gripped hers.

"Help me," Owen panted. "I can't lift you on my own!"

With one final effort, Cati grasped the stub of a branch with her free hand and heaved herself upward. Between them they managed to get Cati onto the log. She lay there panting.

"What happened?" Owen shouted above the noise of the storm. "Where did this come from?"

"I heard voices," Cati said, her voice weak. "I heard voices in the storm."

"What voices?"

"The Harsh . . ." Her voice was shaking. "A long way away. But they sent the storm, Owen. They're behind this."

He knew that she was right. The storm was unnatural. He touched her cheek. Her skin was icy—frozen not just from without by the storm, but also from inside. Once you had been frozen by the Harsh, a sliver of ice always remained within.

"Come on," he said, "we need to get you warm."

It was easier to go along the riverbank and use the cover of the trees, but still it was half an hour before they reached the Den. As Cati pulled off her wet clothes and climbed into the sleeping bag, Owen lit the Primus and put water on to boil. The little stove helped to warm the Den as Owen lit candles. Snow had gathered on the sheet of perspex in the ceiling, blocking out the light.

Owen made soup from a packet and gave a mug to Cati. She gulped down the hot liquid gratefully.

"In a minute," she said, "I might be able to feel my toes."

Owen went to the entrance and looked out. Even in the most sheltered part of the riverbank, the wind howled like a demented thing, and snow had started to pile against the wall of the Den.

"We're not going anywhere for a while," Owen said.

"I felt them," Cati said.

"What?"

"The Harsh. Like the time they caught us on the riverbank. The way the cold gets inside you."

"You said they were far away?"

"That's what it seemed like."

"Then maybe it is just a storm. The weather's been strange since last year."

"I heard them!" She stared at Owen.

"Sorry. Every time I think about the Harsh I get worried they'll come after me for killing their king." Owen stared moodily out into the snow.

"They were there, Owen."

"I believe you."

He made tea and found some biscuits in a tin under the table. They were a little bit stale but Cati and Owen ate them anyway. Then they sat in silence, listening to the wind outside.

"Owen?" Cati's voice seemed to come from under the sleeping bag.

"Yes?"

"Do you know a terrible thing?"

"What?"

"Even though the Harsh are coming, I'm kind of glad."

"Glad? About the Harsh?"

"But it means that there'll be a few people about the place—we'll have to wake the Resisters. There'll be things happening. Do you ever get lonely?"

"Lonely? I kind of like being on my own, but it's not like being the Watcher. Besides, I'm at school, and there's my mother. . . ."

Owen suddenly realized just how solitary Cati's life as the Watcher must be—looking after the sleeping Resisters and the Workhouse on her own day after day.

"Tell me what you've been doing all year," he said hesitantly. And she started to tell him about the patrols, and the long nights when she stood guard on the Workhouse battlements because something had told her there was danger nearby. How she would wake fearful in the night and hold conversations in her head with the Sub-Commandant, her father, pretending that he was alive again. He had been the Watcher before her.

Owen didn't interrupt. It was rare for Cati to admit to fear and loneliness. Since her father had been lost following the Harsh's first attack, she had been more and more driven by her sense of duty. She talked on while the snow fell on the perspex over their heads and the stove hissed gently. Owen found himself talking about the years after his own father had gone missing and his mother had been in a fog, so he'd had to look after her. How he'd been treated as an outsider at school and had always felt different.

Afterward they would both think of that evening, the storm raging outside and darkness falling, two friends poised on the cusp of great events, sharing simple things until, at the last, the candles guttered and went out and they fell asleep, Cati in the sleeping bag and Owen with his head on her knee.

Owen woke before Cati. The first thing he noticed was the silence. The storm had passed. Somehow during the night he had pulled a blanket over himself, but he was still cold. He was sure that something else had woken

47

him. Slipping out from under the blanket, he went to the entrance and stepped out.

The world had been transformed. Stars glittered, hard and cold, in a black sky, and moonlight fell on a landscape turned white, trees and walls outlined in snow, with wind-sculpted drifts piled against banks and hedges. He breathed in and the air seared his lungs. And as he looked up toward the distant mountains he saw great bands of color, shimmering and eerie, high in the northern sky. The northern lights!

Then he heard a voice, carrying across the snowy fields in the clear still air—his mother calling him. He felt a pang of guilt. He could hear the anxiety in her voice. He felt a movement beside him. Cati had come out of the Den.

"She must be worried sick," Cati said. "We'd better go to her."

"We?" Owen said.

"The time for hiding in the shadows has passed, I think," Cati said, "if the Harsh are back. Besides, your mother is from Hadima. I don't think anyone could get mad at me for consulting her."

"Consulting her?"

"On whether I should wake the Resisters immediately and get the Workhouse ready for war."

It was as if the lonely, uncertain girl of the previous night had never been. Cati set off determinedly through the snow. Owen ducked back into the Den. When he emerged the Mortmain and his grandfather's maps were tucked safely in his jacket.

The snow was deep and powdery and hard to walk in. It had drifted chest high in places. Their breath came in great plumes that dissipated in the night air. Once they had crossed the river Owen shouted to tell his mother that he was safe.

"That'll tell any enemy where we are," he said, panting with effort as they plowed through the drifts.

"All they have to do is follow our tracks anyway," Cati said, turning to look at the furrows they had made in the pristine snow.

They were both panting when they got to the top of the field. Owen's mother was waiting there, worry etched on her face.

"I saw you disappear in the storm," she said.

"All I had to do was follow the slope of the hill." Owen stamped his boots on the stone step. "I was bound to hit the river sometime."

But you reached the river exactly where the bridge was, Cati thought. *You navigated your way to it.*

"Cati!" Martha said, the real delight in her voice changing almost instantly to scolding. "Look at you! Soaked. And you're out in the snow! Quick, inside."

Martha ushered them in.

"I'm not being an old hen," she explained, chasing Cati into the bedroom with some of Owen's clothes. "It's more than just a cold night out there. Those aren't normal temperatures. It feels like . . . like the Harsh."

"I think they're coming." Owen watched his mother

carefully. Like Cati, she had been attacked by the Harsh, and had a trace of cold in her bones.

Owen told her what Cati had said about hearing Harsh voices. When Cati came out of the room, Martha quizzed her at length. Owen couldn't keep the grin off his face at the sight of the Resister girl out of uniform in jeans and a sweatshirt. But Martha's face was full of concern.

"Perhaps the storm has only happened here. . . ."

She turned on the radio and they listened to the news. The signal was much fainter than usual. It seemed that the storm had struck all over the world. Power stations had closed down in some places. There were reports of seas freezing and of whole cities being cut off. Some roads and airports were closed, although locally roads remained open. Farther north, whole regions had not been heard from. Martha turned the radio off and they sat in silence. Then Owen stood up.

"What are you doing?" Cati asked.

"Going out to the *Wayfarer*. I have to find out what's happening."

"Should we not wake the Resisters first?" Martha looked at him with raised eyebrows.

"But we don't know that the Harsh are actually coming."

"There were voices in the storm, Owen," Cati said grimly. "They're coming."

"When we wake the Resisters we need to tell them what they're facing. We need to know what the danger is," Owen said stubbornly.

"I don't think it's a good idea—" Cati began, but Martha interrupted.

"No. You should go, Owen. The Resisters will appreciate anything you can do for them. But you must take Cati with you."

"Right," Owen said. "Cati can come." A light shone in his eyes at the prospect of sailing the *Wayfarer*.

"I'll go put the Mortmain in place," he said, and raced out the door.

Cati frowned as soon as Owen was gone. "I still think we should wake the Resisters."

"Perhaps you're right." Martha looked after Owen. "But I don't think that caution alone will win this battle with the Harsh, nor force of arms. But perhaps out there in time something may be learned that will give us the key to victory. And if we are to win, Owen must be confident at the helm of the *Wayfarer*. Besides," she said, smiling, "I trust you to bring him back safely."

"But I'm the Watcher," Cati protested. "I should stay."

"There is more to watching than just guarding the Workhouse. You must go with him."

Half an hour later they were standing beside the *Wayfarer*. Owen could feel a tight knot of nervous excitement at the back of his throat. The first time he had sailed the craft he hadn't really grasped the enormity of what he was doing, but this time he knew what lay ahead.

"Come on," Cati said, shaking him, "standing around worrying isn't going to help." She clambered over the gunwale and stood on the deck, looking as if she owned the craft. That was enough for him. He jumped over the rail. When he landed he could feel a little shiver of recognition in the boat's timbers. He took out the Mortmain and slipped it into the hole where it belonged. The dented brass ring lit up. The faint markings on its surface that had looked like scratches now appeared as deeply etched symbols.

"Does anybody have a plan, by the way?" Cati said.

"I don't think we can plan," Owen said. "We just go out there and see what we can find."

The *Wayfarer* trembled, then slowly and breathtakingly rose from the ground.

"The boat isn't going to let us hang around," Cati said. Owen looked down at his mother. She was already ten feet below.

"Take care," Martha called out. "I will keep watch." Owen waved in response and grabbed the tiller. The *Wayfarer* forged through the air, rising steadily over the snowbound landscape. Nothing could be more beautiful, Cati thought. She turned to look at Owen. The worry in his eyes had been replaced with excitement. With a flick of his wrist he turned the *Wayfarer* so that she was heading straight into the heart of the northern lights.

Martha looked after them for a little while, then fetched her coat. She had work to do. She walked into town, slipping on the frozen path in her hurry. If the

Harsh were going to invade, then the people had to be got out. The Harsh would not allow civilians to stand in their way.

She feared that she might have to persuade the people of the town to leave, but when she reached the square she was met by a motley convoy of old buses. The buses were already full of old people, and children were running around in delight, throwing snowballs at each other.

Martha caught sight of Mr. Mulligan, the head of Owen's school. He looked tired and worn, but his face brightened when he saw Martha.

"The government ordered us to evacuate this morning," he said. "There's more snow on the way, and they can't guarantee food for us if the roads are cut off."

"It's probably for the best," she said. "Where will you go?"

"There's an old army camp up the coast. They're putting us there."

"You're doing the right thing."

"Do you think so? The town's a bit of a ruin right now, but I'm fond of it. I hope we won't be gone long."

"I hope so too." She smiled.

Martha spent the day helping the townsfolk load up the convoy, offering a smile, soothing a crying child, or helping a frantic parent. She chatted to grandmothers about things that happened long ago and to teenagers about things that were yet to come to pass. And when at last the convoy pulled out, there was a cheerful atmosphere, the townspeople full of strength and hope for the future. She waved at the last bus, then stood alone in the square, the snow around her reddened by the setting sun.

"Unfurl the sail!" Owen shouted. Cati scrambled over the deck and stood on top of the wheelhouse. Above her was the great wheel of the northern lights, and far, far below she could see mountains. For a moment she was paralyzed. One slip and she would be gone, tumbling into space.

"Cati!" Owen shouted. With frozen and trembling fingers she began to unfasten the ties that held the sail to the mast. After what seemed like an age, the sail opened out. She stepped back in wonder, almost forgetting that she was far above the ground. The sails were shimmering and translucent, much larger than the sails of any yacht. They appeared to reach out in front of the *Wayfarer* for hundreds of feet and to billow far above her. It seemed to Cati that the sails were made of the same magical substance as the northern lights themselves, if that was possible.

"Cati," Owen shouted again, and leapt forward,

grabbing her jacket and pulling her back. In her wonder she had stepped to the edge of the wheelhouse roof.

"Sailing was never really my thing," she muttered, picking herself up from the deck, but Owen did not answer. He was absorbed in the movement of the *Wayfarer*, the way she rose and pitched and responded to the slightest movement of the tiller. He looked over the stern and saw that the land had disappeared and that they were now sailing over a great lake of time itself, the little tiller carving a trail of phosphorescence in the surface as they went.

For a while Owen delighted in the *Wayfarer*, feeling almost at one with the boat. If he wanted greater speed, he leaned forward and the sail grew even larger. If he leaned back, the boat slowed. The *Wayfarer* skimmed lightly along, but Owen could see that a less able craft would soon be in trouble. They started to scud up the sides of huge waves of dark matter and plunge down the other side. It felt as if they were sailing on an ancient and perilous sea.

"This is different from the first time, on the way back from Hadima," Cati said. It was true. Then, time had seemed shallow, like a river in the dry season, and they were always in danger of running aground. Now they could feel vast quantities of time to either side, and beneath their feet enormous depth.

"I think . . ." Owen spoke hesitantly. He didn't really understand time, certainly not the way their friend Dr. Diamond did, and he was always afraid of being laughed at. "Well, do you remember the way the Harsh had hoarded time so there wasn't enough to go around? Well, it looks as if they've released all that time back where it should be."

Cati looked around in wonder. "So this is what it is meant to look like?"

"Yes. But what are they up to? That's the question."

A mighty wave crashed down, sending spume leaping high into the air. The spume swept over the boat, stinging their faces like shards of ice.

"Get the suits!" Owen said. There were suits of a kind of chain mail hanging in the cabin, and Cati fetched two. Quickly she pulled hers on.

"Take the tiller," Owen said, struggling into his suit. Cati's hand closed on it, but he could feel the boat hesitate slightly, then veer as Cati moved the tiller nervously.

"Just hold it straight!" Owen said. "She can feel that you're nervous."

"I can't help it," Cati snapped. "I'm a land girl."

"Look out!" Owen shouted. Cati had not been watching what she was doing. They were driven across the side of a giant wave. The wave broke on the foredeck so that they were almost buried in the stinging spume. Cati was knocked to her knees and Owen fell back against the side of the boat.

"Keep her pointing straight into the waves," Owen said, correcting the tiller, "and don't look away for a moment."

With a doubting glance at Cati he pulled the maps out from under his jacket. He picked the one that looked like the master copy of them all and pinned it to the hatch beside the Mortmain. Then he stood up and took the tiller.

"I couldn't help it," Cati said, looking crossly at him.

Owen grinned at her.

"I know. You're a landlubber. Next thing you'll be seasick. Tell you what, you want to do something useful?"

"What?"

"Make a cup of tea. Go on. Everything's in the galley. I stocked up."

Cati opened the hatch and slid down into the cabin. She closed the hatch and breathed a sigh of relief as the storm sounds were shut out. It was roomier than she would have thought, with a table at one end surrounded by soft benches that could be turned into beds. Cupboards lined the walls and at the other end there was a little kitchen.

Must be what he means by galley, she thought. She looked around. There were small copper pots and pans that fitted neatly into each other, drawers full of beautifully shaped knives and forks and kitchen implements. There were silver platters and pewter mugs, everything made to be stowed away in stormy weather. In front of her was a small cooker on gimbals, and a sink beside it. She lifted the kettle from the cooker and put it under the tap. The water boiled quickly and within minutes she was back on deck with two mugs of steaming tea.

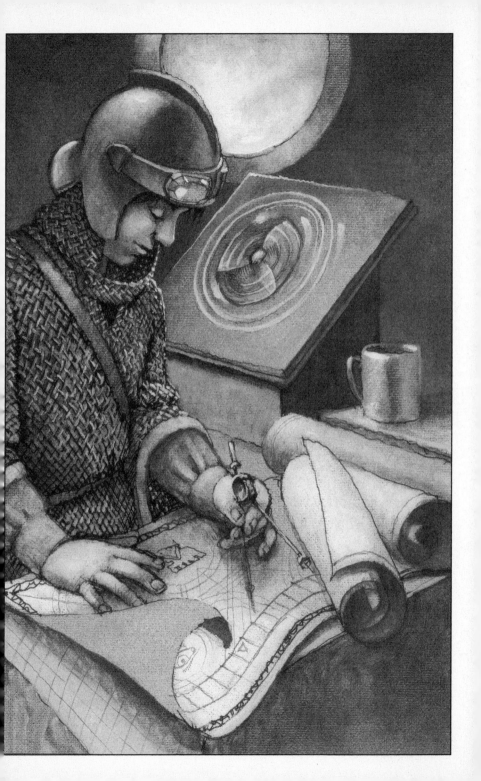

"Thanks," Owen said, setting his mug down on a shelf that seemed made for the purpose. He was engrossed in the maps, his eyes moving from the spinning Mortmain to the old parchment.

"I need to look at these," he said. "Would you go into the bow and keep a lookout?"

Cati, grumbling a little, made her way forward, expecting to be exposed to the waves. But she found it was cozy, crouched in the bow, as long as you ducked sometimes. The weather, if it could be called weather, went straight over your head. She munched contentedly on a chocolate biscuit, beginning to feel a little at home on the *Wayfarer*.

At the tiller Owen puzzled over the symbols. The place with the tower was obviously the City of Time, Hadima. And the Workhouse was obvious as well. There was a plain, almost shapeless white symbol on the map, and if you touched it, your hand burned with searing cold. So that had to be something to do with the Harsh. But what or where was the pillar, and the silvery knife? The pair of sightless eyes, the elegant glass flask, the delicately shaped woman's ear, or any other of the dozens of symbols on the map?

He sighed, wondering if he would ever master the map, or the secrets of the Mortmain, which moved precisely in its mounting, reacting to each movement of the tiller under his hand.

He was tempted to steer the *Wayfarer* toward one of the unknown symbols—the red hand, or the fiery horse—

but in the end he decided to sail toward the place that he knew: Hadima. Apart from anything else, it was the last place he had come across the Harsh. He moved the tiller until the signs for the Workhouse and Hadima were aligned. The bow came around until the boat was on course. Owen wasn't sure if he should go all the way to Hadima, but it would be good to see Rosie again.

Rosie awoke on the stone step in her cell. She had a headache and her head felt fuzzy. Her side ached where she had lain on the stone, and as she felt her body gingerly there were bruises and sore patches, as if she had been dragged back to the cell.

She sat up, vague memories running through her mind. Johnston had taken her to the kitchen and fed her . . . then she'd collapsed—a drug of some sort in the tea, perhaps. After that there was . . . something . . . just out of reach. . . . As she searched for it a snatch of music drifted through her head, then a stab of pain drove it away.

She shook her head impatiently. She was cold and hungry and a prisoner. It was about time she did something about all three. She took a little mirror from an inside pocket and looked at herself. She was also grubby, and her hair was a mess. Then an idea occurred to her. There was a large crack under the locked door, more than enough to slip the mirror through. Rosie crawled to the top of the stairs and pushed the mirror under. There was just enough light to see the big padlock that held the door. Rosie barely dared to breathe. Her captor had made a mistake! He had put the lock through the two rings that held the door, but he hadn't bothered to close it. If she had something that could reach it, she could knock it off. She looked around. Perhaps underneath the foul water . . .

Despite the cold she took off her shoes and stockings and hitched up her skirt. She gingerly put her bare foot into the water and shuddered at its oily, unclean touch. Resisting the urge to jump back onto the step, she put the other foot in, then bent down and started to run her hand along the floor under the water. She groped around for a few minutes until her hand touched something slimy, which seemed to squirm momentarily in her grasp. With a shriek she jumped back. Her heart hammered in her chest. *Come on, Rosie,* she said to herself. *Who knows what else old sideburns has in store for you?*

Gritting her teeth, she got back into the water and swept the floor with her hand. Her hand brushed against all sorts of strange things, hard and soft. Near the bottom of the steps she touched an object that rolled away from her. Instinctively she reached out for it and found her fingers gripping the eye sockets of a skull.

She didn't know how she kept searching, her hands blindly sweeping from corner to corner, but in the end her hands touched something metallic, fumbled, lost it again, then brought it out of the water. She held it up. A long slender piece of wire, shining in the moonlight. She yanked her stockings and boots back on and ran up the stairs to the door. She slipped the mirror under the door so that she could see what she was doing and worked the wire through the jamb, level with the padlock. Forcing her frozen fingers to move, she got the end of the wire under the hasp of the lock. Time and again, the wire slipped from her numb and aching fingers, but in the end, agonizingly, the rusty old lock relinquished its grip on the door and fell to the ground with a thud. She put her weight against the door and it swung open.

The corridor outside was flooded with moonlight. She stopped and listened. Somewhere in the house a man snored loudly. She slipped down the corridor. The back door sagged on its hinges and she had no trouble ducking past it and out into a world changed beyond recognition. The snowfall had made even Johnston's yard look magical. Old cars and truck chassis and piled scrap metal took on strange and fantastic shapes. With a nervous glance over her shoulder Rosie ran into the yard and took cover behind one of the snow shapes. She was used to cold weather. Perhaps, for all she knew, it snowed all the time in Owen and Cati's world, although they had never mentioned it. She listened. From an open window somewhere in the house she could still hear the snores.

The only way out that she could see was the tree-lined avenue, so she ran into the eerie shadow of the dead trees. She waited for a moment, then ran to the next. On she went down the avenue, through the broken gates and out into the road. *Free at last,* she thought. *Now to find*

Owen. She set off, her feet barely denting the surface of the snow.

In Johnston's bedroom, the snoring stopped for a moment. Johnston's great head rested on the pillow. One eye opened and stared without blinking into the darkness. Then it closed again and the snoring resumed.

They had been sailing for several hours when Cati
pointed over the bow.

"Look!"

About a hundred yards from the bow a shape rose
above the water, slick and black like a whale's back. The
creature sank below the waves again and the next time it
rose it was facing toward the *Wayfarer*. In shape it was
somewhere between a seal and a dolphin, with two fins on
its back. It had a drooping mouth with long supple lips
and great elegant whiskers that arced into the air. There
were round markings around its small black eyes that
made it look as if it was wearing old-fashioned glasses.

"What on earth is it?" Cati said, looking on the
strange creature with delight.

"It's a schooner, I think," Owen said, remembering
the skeleton of the beast that hung from the ceiling in
Hadima's Museum of Time.

"Oh, I remember!" Cati said. "Doesn't it feed off time or something?"

"I think so."

The schooner stared at them in a mournful way as if it was thinking sad but dignified thoughts, then, with a flick of its tail, it was gone. Cati stared at the spot where it had appeared until it was out of sight behind them.

The waves died down and soon it was almost flat. The *Wayfarer* slowed to a gentle pace. They sat on the hatch cover, eating the rest of the chocolate biscuits, lulled into a sense of security by the calm—that is, until Owen looked behind them.

"We should have kept a better watch," he said quietly. Thirty yards behind them, and closing fast, was a vast bank of silvery fog.

"I hope it isn't poisonous!" Cati gasped as the fog bank swept over them.

The fog wasn't poisonous, but it did bring a strange sensation, half a smell and half a feeling.

"It smells . . ." Cati's sensitive nose was twitching. "It smells like . . . like stars!"

"Do stars have a smell?" Owen asked.

"I suppose they must. It's the only description I can think of. Kind of cold and beautiful and far away. What do we do now?"

"Keep on sailing, I suppose. We're moving slowly enough and there isn't anything out here to run into, as far as I know."

The *Wayfarer* sailed on soundlessly through the silver

mist. Owen could barely see the mast, and every sound they made seemed to be muffled. After a while they started to notice a strange thing. When they spoke to each other the words took a long time to cross the distance between them, so for a second or two after their mouths stopped moving, the other still had not heard what had been said.

"What do you expect from a fog in time, I suppose?" Owen said, and waited for his words to reach Cati.

"Kind of funny, all the same," Cati said. "And look at this." She moved her arm swiftly through the mist in front of her face as she spoke. Her words distorted as they passed through the swirling fog, the vowels elongated, as if someone had slowed them.

"Let me try that," Owen said, doing the same thing. Cati heard his words in a deep, slow version of Owen's voice. She giggled, and the sound wavered as it struck Owen's hand. Then, as if in reply, there was another sound, right beside the *Wayfarer*, a long, mournful cry full of the sorrows of the vast ocean they sailed upon. Cati edged a bit closer to Owen.

"It sounds like the schooner," he said. "I don't think it's dangerous."

"No, I don't think so either," Cati said, peering nervously into the mist.

They didn't hear the schooner again. Owen could see Cati yawning.

"Why don't you go below and get some sleep?" Owen said. "I'll take the first watch."

Cati was going to argue, but then she thought of the cozy beds in the cabin, and she found her feet moving toward the hatch.

"Just for an hour, mind," she said, opening the hatch and climbing through.

Down below, all was calm. She was quite glad to be out of the swirling mist. The cabin was warm, and in a quiet way there was a welcoming feel, as though the *Wayfarer* herself was glad to have a crew again and wanted Cati to feel at home. Slipping off her boots, she climbed into one of the beds and pulled the blankets up around her. The bed was narrow but comfortable, and she lay staring at the ceiling and feeling the movement of the hull beneath her. She saw that the ceiling was engraved with symbols like those on the Mortmain. Then she closed her eyes and drifted off to sleep.

Owen studied the maps, but it was difficult to see in the mist and he gave up. Instead he stood at the tiller and abandoned himself to the rhythms of the vessel. He felt as if the *Wayfarer* was trying to tell him things, if only he could understand.

After another hour his own eyelids grew heavy, the gentle motion of the ship rocking him. He tried to fight it, but gradually he slipped into a doze, the *Wayfarer* sailing onward, carrying her sleeping crew.

Owen didn't know how long he had slept, but he woke with a start. He looked down at the tiller, his hand still resting on it. Had he dreamed it, or had the tiller given an urgent jerk? The hatch opened and Cati leapt out, pulling on her boots.

"What is it?" Owen said.

"I don't know," she said, scratching her head. "One minute I was sleeping and the next I was on the floor." She looked down at the deck in disbelief. "I think the *Wayfarer* threw me out of bed!"

Then, as if a curtain had been drawn aside, the bank of fog lifted, and they were sailing in a clear silvery light. But it wasn't the sudden emergence from the fog that drew the sharp intake of breath from Cati, or the gasp from Owen. They were no longer alone. All around them, and towering above them, were great white ships moving silently and swiftly, their ranks of sails billowing, a ghost fleet sailing through time.

"What is it?" Cati said in a whisper. A familiar chill started to creep through her bones.

"I don't know," Owen said. One of the ships was bearing down on them, and he moved the tiller so that the *Wayfarer* passed just under the bow. As they passed under he saw that the ship was nameless but bore a figurehead on her bowsprit of a haggard queen. And as the ship swept past them, he saw the gun ports on the side, and how the masts towered far above the *Wayfarer*'s little spar.

"Look!" Cati said, her voice trembling. At the helm of the ship stood a gaunt figure in white, cold eyes fixed on the horizon.

"The Harsh!" Owen said, weaving in between two more ships coming behind the first. Cati shivered and hugged herself tightly.

"Why can't they see us?"

"They're not looking," Owen said. "They don't think that anything can harm them, so they don't have any watchmen, and the Harsh at the wheel look like they are wrapped up in steering the ships. Still, better to be safe."

He put the tiller hard over and brought the *Wayfarer* just in under the stern of the last ship.

"They won't see us here."

"That's why they put all the time back," Cati said. "They wouldn't be able to sail their ships—it's like water that is too shallow. The *Wayfarer* could do it, but they're far too big."

"The real question is, where are they going?" Owen said. They looked at each other.

"The Workhouse!"

"Not just the Workhouse. Our whole world! They sent the storm on ahead to clear the way," Owen said.

"They're invading!"

"Yes, but why now?" Owen said. "Why like this?"

"The king," Cati said, her voice shaking. "You killed their king."

"You think that this . . . this armada is for me?" Owen looked incredulous.

"Maybe not all for you. They always wanted to crush the world, to destroy heat and light. There are so many of them, Owen. There have never been so many. What will we do?"

Owen put his arm around her shoulders.

"We'll find a way to stop them, Cati."

"How do you know for sure?"

"I can . . . I can feel it." Owen turned to look at her. Her face was pale and when he touched her hand, it was freezing. Any time she was close to the Harsh, it affected her. His gaze swept over the ghastly fleet. He tried not to let Cati see what he was thinking: there were too many of them, far too many.

Cati's voice broke the silence. "If they are heading for our world . . ."

Sudden realization dawned on Owen. He grabbed the tiller. "We need to get there ahead of them! We need to wake the Resisters!"

Owen eased the *Wayfarer* from the side of the ship and sailed away from the fleet. The fleet seemed to stretch off into the distance, each ship with three or four towering ironbound masts, from which sails were stretched. Cold, glassy lanterns hung on the decks and from the masts. The ships appeared to be made from timber, but a timber that was frosted and cold, and ice hung from the rigging. Cati had to turn her eyes away from the ghastly captains who stood at the wheels.

When they were almost out of sight, Owen reset the Mortmain so that they were now on a course for the Workhouse.

"I'm not sure how to set the time," Owen said. "I could turn it back so that we arrive just after we set out, but I don't want to miss. If I get it wrong, then we could arrive in three weeks' time instead. We have to rely on the *Wayfarer* to do it for us."

"Can she do it?" Cati said dubiously. As if in answer the boat leapt forward; Cati staggered back and sat down suddenly on the deck. Owen grinned.

"You shouldn't doubt her. All right, *Wayfarer*, let's get back to the Workhouse!" He leaned forward and the *Wayfarer*'s sails billowed until they filled the sky. Owen could feel the frame of the boat tense as she picked up speed.

Rosie made a forlorn sight as she trudged down the snowy road. She was even dirtier and more disheveled than she had been when she emerged from the tunnel. Her clothes were torn and stained and provided scant protection against the biting cold. A mile from Johnston's she passed a little shop on the side of the road. She stole a look through the window. The shop was low-ceilinged and cozy and beyond it through a doorway she could see a blazing fire with armchairs to either side. She stood at the little door for several minutes, uncertainty tearing at her. The inhabitants might be friendly, but could she take a chance? Owen and Cati and Dr. Diamond had never mentioned such a place. In the end she decided she couldn't risk an encounter with a stranger. She sighed and walked on, not knowing that Owen's mother, the one waking person in this world who would have known about Hadima and the Harsh and would have welcomed her, sat at the kitchen table, unable to sleep.

On Rosie walked, and this time she came to a gate where she could see down a slope toward a river running through a line of trees. Just beyond the river, a dark shape loomed. She squinted, trying to see more clearly. Her heart leapt. Owen and Cati had told her that the Workhouse stood beside a river! Climbing the gate quickly, she ran down the field. When she got to the riverbank she could clearly see the gaunt, lifeless building beyond. Puzzled, she stared at it. Owen and Cati had told her about the Workhouse when the Resisters were awake. She had no idea that it was disguised as this crumbling ruin when the Resisters slept.

There was no way to cross the river except by an old tree trunk. Rosie climbed on and gingerly made her away across. But the bark was slippery with ice and Rosie was weak. Halfway across she lost her grip and tumbled off. She braced herself to hit water, a fleeting thought crossing her mind that she could not survive the night in the open in wet clothes. She landed with a bone-numbing crunch—the river was frozen solid.

She picked herself up and made her way to the far bank, her whole body aching. She clambered up the bank and looked around. The Workhouse loomed above her, silent and forbidding.

"Owen!" Her voice echoed in the trees. She climbed the bank toward the Workhouse. There was ivy growing through the windows, and it was roofless. She called out,

"Owen! Cati! Dr. Diamond!" time and again. For an hour she explored the Workhouse, calling as she went. In the end she sank down on a stone.

Her mission had been in vain. She was shivering uncontrollably and knew that if she did not find some shelter for the night, she could die in the snow. Wearily she rose to her feet and walked to the river. Downriver, the town lay sleeping, but instinct forced her away from it. She was a traveler in time, a refugee from a great city whose presence the people of this world had not even guessed at. Even if people could see her through the shadows of time, she could not risk contact with them.

Finally she had her first piece of luck since she had stepped through the Hadima gate, if luck it was. Rosie wandered off the snow-covered path along the river and found herself floundering on a hillside, forcing her way through snow-covered bracken. Suddenly there was something slippery underfoot. Her feet shot out from under her and she fell flat on her face in the bracken. Her eyes pricked with tears of self-pity. Angrily she wiped them with her sleeve, then blinked and blinked again. She was looking down through the scratched sheet of perspex into a room that was dimly lit by the glow of a piece of magno. There was a battered old sofa, and a table with a little cooker on it, and she remembered Owen talking about a place he went to be on his own. She had stumbled on the Den!

It took another half an hour of casting about before she found the entrance. Then, swaying from exhaustion, she fell into the cozy little room. She saw the sleeping bag on the sofa. With one last effort she pulled the bushes across the entrance, then without another thought climbed into the sleeping bag and closed her eyes. Once more a snatch of music drifted through her head before a sharp pain drove it away. The pain faded and she fell into a deep, deep sleep.

Dawn broke clear and cold over the Workhouse and over the snow-covered town. A few birds sang, but only to keep warm, and the others saved their energy in the hope that a thaw would reveal some food. There were few other sounds—sometimes the sharp crack of the sap exploding within a frozen branch or the rustle of snow sliding from a roof to the ground, but otherwise it was quiet. There was no one to hear the faint whistle of a streamlined hull cleaving the air as the *Wayfarer* appeared in the sky, and swooped downward.

Cati had lowered the sail at Owen's signal. For several hours the *Wayfarer* had skimmed across time, never faltering, while Owen stayed at the helm and Cati stood anxiously in the bow. They had moved much faster than on the outward journey, but time was still short. Owen worked the tiller so that the craft swooped low over his own house.

"To the Workhouse! To the Workhouse!" he shouted as loud as he could, and as they sped away he saw his mother's bedroom curtain move. The *Wayfarer* crossed the fields and the river, hit the ground hard in front of the Workhouse, and slithered to a halt in the snow. Before the boat had stopped moving, Owen and Cati leapt over the side and ran toward the Starry. With trembling fingers Cati took the key from around her neck and unlocked the door.

Inside, after their frantic dash across time, the quiet struck them like a blow, and for a moment they stood looking down at the rows and rows of sleeping Resisters. Then Owen broke the silence.

"Come on," he said, "you start on that side."

Owen moved toward the first Resister, a young soldier in red who was smiling in his sleep. Owen tapped him sharply on the shoulder.

"Wake up!"

The soldier stirred in his sleep and after a moment sat up, rubbing his eyes. But by this time Owen had moved on. Cati hesitated as she realized she was standing beside Samual, the angry, suspicious leader of a group of Resister soldiers, who was no friend to her, or to Owen. She touched his shoulder.

"Wake up, Samual," she said. "The Watcher calls you."

Samual's eyes snapped open and he sat up, studying Cati as if she was up to no good. Cati moved on to the next sleeper, a man in a red coat, another of Samual's soldiers.

As fast as they could, Owen and Cati moved through the Sleepers. They tried not to stop too long at old friends. Owen woke Contessa, and the wise and gracious head of the Workhouse kitchen smiled gently at him on opening her eyes. Cati woke Rutgar, the leader of the Resister army and a grizzled veteran of many fights.

"Wake up, Rutgar. The Harsh are coming!"

"Are they indeed," Rutgar said, rubbing the great scar on his cheek, sitting up and swinging his feet over the edge of the bed. "I'll be ready, Cati!"

Owen woke Pieta, the subtle and dangerous warrior.

"Time to fight, Pieta," he said. But as he started to walk away, her hand closed around his wrist in a grip of iron. With the grace of a panther she rolled out of the bed to stand beside him.

"Call my children next, Navigator," she said.

Hello would have been nice, he thought, but in his heart he knew why she asked. Her children had once not woken when called because the Harsh had been interfering with time.

"Aldra, Beck. Wake up!" he said. And this time they woke easily and stood, a tall, quiet boy and girl who took up their stations at their mother's shoulder.

Owen was tiring as he reached Dr. Diamond. He touched his old friend's shoulder gently and the doctor's strange blue eyes opened. He stretched his lanky frame and smiled at Owen.

"Owen, you see to Good," he said, and grinned apologetically. "I have to stop speaking backward."

"times old like Feels," Owen replied with a smile. When the Harsh had turned time backward, Dr. Diamond had sometimes got mixed up and started speaking in reverse.

"Very clever," Dr. Diamond said, "and you have grown, Navigator. But why are you waking us so soon after we went to sleep?"

"I'll explain at the Convoke, but there's a Harsh fleet close by."

"What? Why didn't you tell me?" Dr. Diamond said, leaping to his feet. But before Owen could answer, Dr. Diamond had darted off through the crowd.

After an hour the Starry was thronged with just-wakened Resisters, making their way out to the snowy Workhouse. Owen had called a Convoke, which was what the Resisters called their gatherings. It was to take place immediately in the Workhouse.

"Give us time to shake the sleep off, boy," Samual snapped.

"There is no time," Owen said, and something in his voice made Samual stop and stare.

So they gathered in the still roofless Convoke hall, the last of the Resisters straggling in as Owen began to speak. Contessa, Rutgar, and Samual sat on the dais. Pieta took her usual seat by the fireplace. Owen wondered where Dr. Diamond was. Contessa motioned for Cati to get up onto the dais.

"You are the Watcher," she said. "It is your entitlement." Then she clapped her hands sharply.

"It is my privilege to address you first. I hope you are all refreshed after your sleep," she said. "It is wonderful to see your faces again, and I would like time to dwell on each one. But the Navigator tells us that danger is close by, so I will let him speak." She motioned to Owen, who got up onto the dais.

"I'm also glad to see all my friends again." There was a murmur of greeting from many of the Resisters—apart from Samual, who folded his arms and didn't look in Owen's direction.

"But we don't have time for saying hello," Owen went on. "Cati and I have seen a Harsh fleet of many ships, and it is, I think, almost on us."

The murmur turned to an agitated babble.

"What size of fleet?" a voice called.

"Many ships," Owen replied. "They are sailing through time. I saw them from the *Wayfarer*."

"We'll never raise the defenses in time," someone else shouted. The level of noise in the room rose. Some of the fighters got to their feet.

"Open the armory, Rutgar! We need weapons!"

"We had trouble enough dealing with four or five Harsh," a woman said. "How are we going to deal with a whole fleet?"

People were arguing and gesticulating. Owen put out his arms to try to calm things, but he was ignored—until one man in red rose to his feet and pointed at Owen.

"It's your fault. You opened the Hadima gate when it was forbidden."

Owen said nothing. It was true. He had opened the gate.

"None of you would still be here if he hadn't," Cati shouted, but no one heard her.

"Good way to open a Convoke, boy," Samual said with an unpleasant grin. "See what you've left for Rutgar and me to make a fighting force from?"

Contessa stood up, white-faced and dismayed at how things had gone downhill so quickly.

"Sit down!" she called, but she was ignored as well. Rutgar gathered his lieutenants about him and looked as if he was about to knock a few heads together to restore order. Then there was a rumbling noise deep in the bowels of the building. The ground under their feet shook, and fragments of mortar fell from the walls. The noise grew louder, and everyone fell silent. Was it an earth tremor, like the ones that had come with the last Harsh attack? Owen looked at Cati and saw that she was grinning.

The earth seemed to erupt. Owen jumped back as a huge column of brass shot from a half-hidden hole in the floor. On top of the brass column was perched a structure that looked like the top of a lighthouse, with glass walls. Owen watched as the brass column continued upward, divided into sections and unfolding like a telescope, the sections screeching against each other as they moved. The whole thing, swaying alarmingly, rose to roof level, and beyond.

"If the whole world doesn't know that we're awake, then it does now," Samual said.

"If there is a Harsh fleet on the way, then it doesn't really matter what the world thinks," Contessa said.

The brass column halted its ascent with a tremendous

bang, accompanied by groaning from the brass segments. There was a pause, then a glass door in the top section slid open and Dr. Diamond stepped out onto the walkway that encircled the top. The glass top of the column was the Skyward, his laboratory. The whole thing was known as the Nab.

"Friends," Dr. Diamond said, "we are all confused after our long sleep. Do you not remember, we are the Resisters? The odds are against us, it is true, but we have good people here, and I may have a few surprises for the Harsh. All I need is a little time. So go, prepare what defenses you can. All is not lost. The world knows nothing of you, and you will fight and give your all without anyone knowing. But we are the Resisters. That is our work."

The Resisters turned to each other, embarrassed at how they had panicked. Some shook hands and grinned. Others patted Owen on the back as they passed him. Pieta came toward him.

"Diamond can say what he likes," she said, "but we're helpless without defenses."

"I know," Owen said. Pieta gave him a long look, then strode off, her deadly magno whip hanging at her side.

Everyone was busy. Contessa was organizing food supplies. Gangs of men and women were working at lightning speed rebuilding the Workhouse. Watching them, Owen realized that the tumbledown look of the building wasn't completely an illusion—parts of it had been removed and hidden away. Even now, men were lowering huge sections of the roof into place. But Pieta was right—as fast as the Resisters worked, they could not have the defenses ready in a couple of hours.

"Cati," Owen called.

"What?"

"If anybody's looking for me, say I've gone to the Den," he said.

"What's going on?"

"I've got a plan. But I'm not sure everyone will go along with it. Besides, it would take two hours talking about it, and we don't have two hours."

"Right," Cati said. "I'll cover for you. Good luck."

Owen slipped and slithered down the path to the *Wayfarer*, dodging out of the way of people carrying timber and stones and ropes. Down at the frozen river Rutgar was distributing weapons to his men at a frantic pace, while Samual strode up and down barking orders.

When Owen got to the *Wayfarer*, he saw a familiar, long-legged figure perched on the bow. Dr. Diamond stood up when he approached.

"Going somewhere?" the doctor asked.

"If I told them, they'd try to stop me."

"They might and they might not. At the moment, you're their only hope."

"So you're not going to stop me?"

"You have to make your own decisions. But haven't you forgotten something?"

"What?"

"No one has wakened the Raggies."

"The Raggies! How could I have forgotten! But I don't have time . . ."

The Raggies were a branch of the Resisters who lived in a warehouse at the harbor. The warehouse was an island in time like the Workhouse and had its own Starry. The waiflike appearance of the Raggies, all children, belied their toughness. They had been cruelly abandoned in time by a sea captain who had been supposed to look after them.

"I will take Cati to do it. But go now, Owen. We're depending on you."

As if to underline his point, a gust of icy wind blew snow into their faces.

"What is your plan?" Dr. Diamond asked.

"To get them to chase me away from the Workhouse."

"And will they?"

"I think so," Owen said grimly. "I think so."

"Go, Owen," Dr. Diamond said. "Buy us as much time as you can, but a day will do a lot."

Owen scrambled on board the *Wayfarer,* which rose off the ground. He adjusted the helmet, which he had pushed back on his head, so that the chain-mail visor covered his face, but as he put his hand on the tiller his mother ran up.

"You don't understand," he said. "I *have* to do this. For all our sakes."

"I know you do," she said. "Pieta isn't the only warrior among the womenfolk around here." His mother's eyes flashed in a way that he hadn't seen before. "I brought you this," she went on, placing a magno gun and ammunition inside the boat. "Take care of yourself," she said. "Use your speed and maneuverability. Trust the *Wayfarer*. And remember, we don't need that long."

Owen looked at his mother standing straight and tall with the wind blowing her hair back, and felt a rush of pride. He grasped the tiller firmly. The *Wayfarer* pointed her bow toward the sky. Within seconds she was speeding upward. Martha stared after her son.

"Take care," she said faintly.

"That can't have been easy," Dr. Diamond said, putting his arm around her shoulder.

"It was hard, but he is ready," she said, her eyes still fixed on the distant craft.

High above the Workhouse Owen lashed the tiller so that it wouldn't move, and clambered forward to unfurl the sail. As it billowed out, catching the winds of time, the *Wayfarer* surged forward. The scene below faded from view. Owen felt both nervous and exhilarated. For the first time he was alone on the *Wayfarer*.

"Let's find some Harsh," he said grimly, and the *Wayfarer*'s bow appeared to rise in response.

It didn't take long to come upon the enemy ships. Within twenty minutes Owen had spotted the tops of their masts on the horizon. He felt a thrill of fear. Even from this distance the Harsh fleet was impressive. He examined the chart and the Mortmain. They couldn't be far from the Workhouse, and as he came closer, he saw that there were Harsh standing in the rigging of the great ships. *Ready to take in sail,* he thought, and when they did, they would emerge at the Workhouse.

As the *Wayfarer* rose and fell jagged fragments of spray struck the chain-mail armor and his face mask, but still he urged her on. On the first ship, a sail was run down and then another, but he was still too far away to attract their attention. He looked around wildly, then saw the magno gun. He grabbed it and fitted one of the glass missiles. Shooting one-handed from the bucking deck of the *Wayfarer,* he wasn't likely to do much damage, but he might attract their attention. He put the gun to his shoulder and fired. The missile arched into the air and exploded. As the magno spread in the shimmering sky, it pulsed a deep blue. The Harsh stopped what they were doing and looked up. It bought Owen a precious minute. By the time they bent back to the sails, he was within hailing distance.

"Hey, you!" he shouted. "Hey!"

The *Wayfarer* sailed under the bow of the lead ship. The Harsh were high above him, but he could see a group of them clustered round the wheel. They were in their true shape of ancient kings and queens, haughty and evil-looking, but the Harsh in the rigging were in the form of teenagers—young men and women with spoiled faces.

The *Wayfarer* tossed wildly in the bow wash from the massive ship. The dark planks of the ship's bow reared above him, and Owen could see that there was ice between the planks, as though it held the ship together. Fighting to keep on his feet, he reached for the magno gun again. He fitted a missile and fired wildly in the direction of the ship. The bolt glanced harmlessly off the ship's planks and exploded in the air. Three of the younger Harsh ran to the side and looked over.

"Come on, frostface!" Owen shouted, wheeling the boat around. "Come down and fight!"

Above his head, a gun port opened and the muzzle of a cannon appeared. Owen barely had enough time to turn away before a bolt of ice flew over the top of the *Wayfarer*'s mast with a vicious buzz.

I don't want to be shot at, Owen thought. *I want to be followed!* As far as he could see, the rest of the ship's crew were ignoring him. In fact, more sails were coming down, the fleet slowing as they did so. He needed something more.

Easing the *Wayfarer* back around the bow of the lead ship, out of range of the cannon, he found himself looking up at a group of the Harsh. And in the middle of them stood the Harsh queen.

"Down here," he shouted, "down here!" His voice sounded shrill and small, but the wind died a little and the queen looked down. Owen lifted the mask so that she could see his face. The queen gave a silent bellow of rage, sending an icy blast of air downward, spinning the *Wayfarer* around and heeling her over so far that she almost capsized. Owen was thrown against the rail, cracking his head. He tried to stand up but swayed. The pirate queen turned to the helmsman. He spun the wheel. Owen looked up and saw the massive bow of the ship turn toward the *Wayfarer*. She had righted herself, but he couldn't reach the tiller and the boat was sailing right under the Harsh ship's bow! With a sickening crunch the iron bow of the ship struck the *Wayfarer*'s rail. The wood buckled but held, though great splinters flew off into the air. As Owen finally reached the tiller, he thought that he could feel the *Wayfarer*'s timbers shiver and flinch.

The *Wayfarer* leapt free of the ship and within seconds she was a hundred yards ahead. Owen looked back. The fleet was turning slowly to follow him. His plan had worked. He had a good start, but then the entire Harsh fleet was on his tail. They were raising sail again. The chase was on.

Shortly after Owen left, Dr. Diamond called Cati and told her, "I need you to come with me to wake the Raggies."

Cati was delighted at the prospect of some time alone with Dr. Diamond, but he went so fast that she was running to keep up with him and didn't have enough breath to ask questions as they raced along the river to the harbor.

When they got to the warehouse, Dr. Diamond led her straight to the Raggies' Starry. He looked in at the sleeping children.

"Wake Wesley first," he said. Wesley was their leader—a freckled, tough-looking boy. Cati touched his head and called him. He opened his eyes and looked at her, puzzled.

"Cati!"

"Wake up, fish boy," she said teasingly, and smiled. He sat up.

"Wesley," Dr. Diamond said urgently, "I need to talk to you."

While the two of them talked in low voices, Cati went among the Raggies, waking them. Some of the children jumped straight up and gave her a hug. Others looked dazed. She recognized faces: the marksmen, Mervyn and Uel; the kind and practical Silkie, who set about organizing the smaller children.

When Cati finished, Dr. Diamond called her.

"It's time to go," he said. She opened her mouth to object but realized that he was right. There was too much to do.

"Never mind, lass," Wesley said. "There'll be time and plenty of it for a chat at the Workhouse."

"At the Workhouse?"

"The Raggies are coming to stay there for a while. Doctor reckons we should all be together when them Harsh come. So go on and get working!"

Once again on the way back, the doctor was preoccupied. Cati didn't dare question him. When they reached the Workhouse he went straight back to the Starry.

"Come on, Cati," Rutgar yelled from the walls. "The Workhouse won't rebuild itself."

Cati had never worked so hard in her life. All day they hauled timber and stone from hidden storepits and the riverbank, strengthening the walls of the Workhouse and the defenses in front of it. Everyone worked at the defenses. Even Contessa left the kitchens after making enough warm gruel to keep everyone going. Cati looked to where Contessa worked beside her and saw that her hands were bleeding from handling the rough stone.

Cati was pushing a barrow of sand when she heard a commotion down below: an angry girl's voice, and men cursing. She put down the barrow and slid along the snowy slope to find a group of Samual's men surrounding a small figure. Cati broke through the ranks of men. To her absolute and complete amazement she recognized the ragamuffin.

"Rosie!"

"Cati! These big galoots won't let me go."

"She's a spy," one of them said. "We caught her sneaking about down at the river."

"I'm not a spy," she said angrily, "and I wasn't sneaking about. I was looking for someone."

"If she's that innocent, then what is this?" a familiar drawling voice said from behind them. It was Samual, and he was holding a long, razor-sharp hairpin in his hand.

"That's mine!" Rosie said. "Give it back."

"I don't think so," Samual said.

"There's been a mistake!" Cati said. "She's a friend of ours—from Hadima."

"Then what is she doing here?" Samual said. "Sent to spy, no doubt."

"What I'm doing here," Rosie said, "is trying to warn

you about the Harsh. There's a fleet of them on their way."

"There, you see?" Cati said. She stepped forward and took Rosie's hand in hers.

"We know that already," Samual said. "You could have heard that from anybody around here."

"And what is she doing with Johnston's symbol pinned to her?" a woman called Moorhead, one of Samual's lieutenants, asked. There was a single red rose pinned to Rosie's lapel, and the red-faced woman tore it off.

"I never saw it before! I didn't even know it was there!" Rosie looked at the ring of faces around her. "I can't believe I went through hell and high water to get here to warn you," she burst out, "only to be told I'm a spy!"

"Exactly." Cati glared at them.

Rosie embarked upon a stream of cursing that caused Rutgar's men to look up from what they were doing and grin to themselves.

"When you are quite finished," Samual said coldly. Rosie subsided.

"I don't believe the child traveled all this way just to warn us, brave as she has been," another, gentler voice interjected.

Cati turned to see Contessa standing behind them.

"Is there another reason?" Contessa asked.

"Well, yes, there is," Rosie said. "I came to ask for help. . . . Hadima is . . ." Rosie bit her lip and stopped.

"What is it, Rosie?" Cati said.

"Hadima is ruined!" Rosie blurted out. "The Harsh froze it from top to bottom. Everybody left is living on rooftops and in ice caves and stuff. We need help!"

"I don't believe this nonsense," Samual said. "I'm not even certain that Hadima exists."

"Of course it does," Cati said angrily. "Ask Dr. Diamond. He was there."

"The doctor has many fine qualities," Samual said, looking down his long nose at Cati and Rosie, "but he is easily taken in. No doubt you brought him to some filthy hamlet pretending to be a city in time."

"It used to be a city in time," Rosie said sadly. "It used to."

It took a while to get the story out of Rosie. It seemed that the Harsh, with the help of Headley and his men, the evil City police, had diverted the river that ran to the south into the City. There was panic as large areas were flooded. Cati was pleased to hear that her friends, the Dogs, had emerged from their tunnels and had helped many people. She explained to Contessa that the Dogs were homeless children who had formed themselves into a pack. They wore dog masks and took on qualities that were peculiar to dogs, like a good sense of smell. The Dogs were thieves and scavengers, disliked by most people. But when they were needed, their resourcefulness and knowledge of the secret places of the City had saved many. Contessa looked at Cati thoughtfully. She had heard a garbled tale about Cati running with a gang of children who acted like dogs.

Then, Rosie went on, the Harsh had unleashed storm upon storm. The waters froze, and froze again, rising every time so that all that was left of the City were the tops of the tallest buildings, protruding from the ice.

Cati gasped, thinking of her other friends in the City.

"Mrs. Newell is okay," Rosie said, seeing Cati's worry. "And Clancy and the other Dogs are keeping everybody fed."

"The Harsh have grown in power," Contessa said.

"They have," Samual said, "and they've grown in nerve too, sending their spies into the Workhouse."

"She's not a spy, I said." Cati's voice was low and dangerous.

"I know a thief and a liar when I see one."

"I'm not a thief!" Rosie said. "Well, only a little bit when I have to be. But I'd never spy for the Harsh."

"Will you vouch for her?" Contessa asked Cati.

"Of course I will," Cati said.

"Then we will leave it at that," Contessa said. "We don't have time for this."

Samual turned away with an expression of disgust.

"Excuse me, mister," Rosie said. Samual glared at her. "Can I have my hairpin back, please?"

Samual's face blackened. He looked at the hairpin in his hand. Then he raised the hand. Faster than the eye could see, the pin flew through the air and embedded itself in the tree trunk just behind Rosie's head. Samual stalked off.

"Be careful," Contessa said. "Samual is not to be trifled with. Cati, give your friend some food."

"I can work with the rest of you," Rosie said defiantly, then swayed on her feet and would have fallen had Cati not caught her.

"Feed her, then make her lie down, Cati. After that come back to work," Contessa said.

With her arm around Rosie's shoulder, Cati helped her into the Workhouse and down into the kitchens. Sitting in the warmth of the cookers, Cati spooned her out some gruel, which Rosie wolfed down as if she had never tasted anything better.

"Where are Owen and Dr. Diamond?" Rosie asked.

"There's a lot to explain," Cati said.

"Great food," Rosie said, licking the plate, "but what I really need is to fix the war paint."

Cati fetched a small mirror. Rosie took a look at herself in it.

"Blimey, not a wonder that bloke thought I was dodgy." She took out a small purse from under her coat and brushed and fixed her hair. Then she applied eye makeup and lipstick.

"A girl should never go anywhere without it," she said, casting a disapproving glance at Cati's face.

Cati grinned but didn't say anything. Rosie with her city fashion was so different from the Resisters, and it was odd, to say the least, to watch someone putting on lipstick with an enemy fleet practically on their doorstep. But Rosie, like all the Hadima folk, seemed to put her appearance before everything else. Cati looked down at her own faded uniform, feeling a bit tomboyish.

"I need to get back to work," Cati said. "Do you want to lie down?"

"Yes," Rosie said weakly. There was a little color in her cheeks, but she still looked exhausted. Cati went with her to one of the small bedrooms in the basement of the Workhouse. The sheets were clean and smelled of lavender, and Rosie didn't need another invitation to climb in. Cati sat with her for a few minutes.

"Cati?" Rosie said.

"Yes?"

"I was . . . when I came through the tunnel . . . there was a man . . ." Music soared in Rosie's head, and the thought was driven away. When Cati looked down again, Rosie was fast asleep.

She pulled the sheet up over Rosie's shoulder and tip-toed from the room.

By nightfall the Resisters were exhausted, but they had accomplished a lot. The Workhouse was no longer a tumbledown ruin but a mighty fortress. Much remained to be done, but the defenses were adequate for the moment. Sentries were set, and the Resisters ate a little before falling into an exhausted sleep. The Raggies had been given a turret to themselves for the time being and the young children's excited talk made grim soldiers smile as they marched to duty. Then the children were stilled and the Workhouse grew quiet. Yet here and there anxious eyes glanced toward the sky. Cati stood at the river, wondering where Owen was. At the cottage, Martha wrapped herself in a blanket and waited. And from the top of the Nab, Dr. Diamond sat motionless, his eyes open and unblinking as though he watched across the very seas of time for the *Wayfarer*'s homecoming.

Owen's plan might have worked for the Resisters, but it wasn't going very well for him.

The weather was the problem. The wind had risen and the *Wayfarer* was being tossed about on great crests, slowing her. Owen had to take in sail for fear that a gust would catch the boat and blow her over. The Harsh ships had no such problems. Their mighty hulls plowed through the waves, and they piled on sail. Looking back, Owen could see them stretched out behind him in a single, crescent-shaped line; the ships to his left and right were almost level with him. They made up the jaws of a trap, Owen thought, and any moment they would spring on him.

It was a magnificent sight, despite the danger: the crescent of white sails against the dark sky, the northern lights flickering behind them. But Owen could feel the *Wayfarer* laboring under him, and his blood boiled at the sight of her splintered timbers. He turned to the pursuing Harsh.

"You won't catch me!" he shouted. "Not ever!" But there was no reply from the black ships. They sailed on, gaining yard by yard.

Owen realized that he hadn't set the Mortmain on any particular course. Even if he did escape the pursuit, he didn't know where he was. He tried to think, but his mind was tired. There seemed to be no options. He could try putting on more sail, but he knew that he ran the risk of breaking the mast. He looked down at the magno gun. There were only three missiles left. The Harsh would laugh at him. He looked back. He could clearly see the Harsh queen standing in the bow of the center boat. And to either side the ships had overtaken and were moving in to form a circle around him. He was trapped.

It was then that he saw a strange thing—another boat, ahead of him. It was long and low and its sails were black and green, barely visible against the sky. She looked like a fast craft, he thought, about five times bigger than the *Wayfarer,* but she was moving slowly, often going crabwise, as though there were problems with the steering. The *Wayfarer* was gaining fast. As he got closer he could see that the boat was slim, with two masts and a row of gun ports on either side. There seemed to be crewmen and -women working at the stern, with a man wearing a tall hat directing them. As the *Wayfarer* approached, Owen knew that the man had to have seen her, but he would not look up. It was not until Owen drew alongside that the man finally glanced in his direction.

"It's a stormy day to be out, traveler." His voice was deeply accented. He had sallow skin and dark hair, and there were both laughter and darkness in his deep-set brown eyes. He wore a long black leather coat, studded with rivets, against the spray, and a pair of goggles was tied around his hat. His crew wore similar coats in all sorts of shapes and colors. They had the same sallow skin, and they moved nimbly on bare feet.

"Are you sinking?" Owen said, giving a nervous look around at the Harsh.

"After you, that lot, are they?" the man said, not answering his question. "They don't like us too much either. Looks like we're both in trouble. But I got an idea."

"What's that?"

"I got the fastest ship in the seas of time, but my rudder's busted, and I can't steer. You can steer, but with respect to your pretty little boat, she won't outrun the Harsh."

"What's your idea?"

"Lash the two of them together. You can steer, and the *Faltaine,* which is my craft, can give us speed."

Owen hesitated.

"Make up your mind, son. If the Harsh close that circle on us, we're all done for."

"Yes," Owen said. He didn't know if it would work or not, but he didn't have any other ideas.

The man smiled, showing brilliant white teeth.

"Captain Yarsk."

"My name's Owen."

"Right, lads," the man shouted. The crew swarmed all over the *Wayfarer* with ropes and grappling hooks. The crew wore the same tall hats, men and women, and under their long coats they had black breeches stuffed into knee boots. In seconds the two ships were lashed together tightly.

Owen didn't notice the slow withdrawal from the gun port nearest to him of a gun that had been pointed directly at his head. The port stealthily closed.

With the two boats tied together, Yarsk began to bark orders. His crew swarmed up the mast, and new sails billowed from the spars.

"Keep us pointed for that gap," Yarsk said. Up ahead the two lead ships had almost completed the circle, but there was still an opening between them. Owen could feel the *Wayfarer* begin to pick up speed. Within seconds they were tearing ahead. The tiller felt incredibly heavy with the weight of the larger ship attached, and it took all of Owen's strength to keep the boats aimed toward the gap. It was going to be close. Owen looked across at Yarsk. The tall man had lit a cigar and was puffing on it calmly.

"We're not going to make it," Owen shouted. The stern of the *Wayfarer* was dug in, and the bow was so high he could barely see over it.

"No, doesn't look good," Yarsk admitted, picking a

piece of tobacco leaf from his teeth. The two great ships ahead had lowered sails and were bow to bow. The boats were two hundred yards away, the ships gathered around them in a circle. The *Wayfarer* and the *Faltaine* were trapped.

"Looks like we'll have to fight," Yarsk said. "Better if we cut you loose, boy." Before Owen could object, the *Faltaine*'s sailors were onboard, cutting the ropes that bound the two vessels together. Meanwhile, the gun ports of the two Harsh ships in front of them fell open with an ominous clatter. The *Faltaine*'s gun ports opened as well, and Owen saw the polished barrels of her guns sliding into position.

"Wait!" Owen shouted. They were still just out of range of the Harsh guns, but Owen knew that the *Faltaine* could not outfight the entire Harsh fleet.

"Wait to die, or charge in glory," Yarsk said, flicking his cigar overboard and drawing a sword from his belt—a sword that shone with the fire of magno, Owen saw.

"No! I have an idea," Owen said. Yarsk turned to him and raised one of his narrow eyebrows.

"Hark at the lad," he said.

"Give me a minute," Owen said.

"A minute? I'll give you five." Yarsk sheathed his sword and sat down with his back to the Harsh, putting his feet up on a rail. He took an apple from his pocket and began to peel it—as if, Owen thought, the Harsh weren't there.

Owen urged the *Wayfarer* forward and she leapt clear of the *Faltaine*. Up ahead the Harsh guns were being run out. Owen steered straight for the queen's ship. As he did, the ship came round slightly to bring her guns to bear on the *Wayfarer*. Owen darted out of range again, then sailed close in. Once more the ship had to turn a little to point her guns at him. He did this four times. He could see the queen on deck, urging the helmsman to move faster. He seemed to be arguing with her. Owen could feel the cold power of her fury.

Once more he darted out of range, then back in, but this time he sailed as close as he dared, his heart in his mouth as the guns caught up with him. Anxiously he measured the distance to the hull of the ship. When he thought he had got it right, he leaned back and the *Wayfarer* came to a halt.

Owen ran up the deck and into the bow. He took off his helmet so the queen could see his face, and bowed.

"A message for her most gracious majesty, Queen of the Harsh," he shouted, "from her friends in the Resisters." He paused, then pursed his lips and blew the loudest and longest raspberry he had ever done.

The effect was instantaneous. The queen screamed, the icy blast tearing through the rigging of her own vessel, and her hand chopped downward—the signal to fire. Owen could see the helmsman reaching out to stop her, but it was too late. Owen glanced toward Yarsk, who smiled and touched the brim of his hat in appreciation. Then the guns roared.

For a second nothing happened. Then, with a tremendous hissing noise, thirty ice missiles shot from the side of the Harsh ship, directly at the *Wayfarer*.

But Owen had got it right. The *Wayfarer* was too close to be hit. The missiles passed over her masthead with inches to spare and flew on—straight into the side of the next Harsh ship.

With a mighty crash, the whole side of the ship seemed to disintegrate. One of her masts crashed down onto the helmsman. Fragments of timber and ice were thrown high into the air. Owen was flung from the bow as debris rained on the *Wayfarer*'s deck. Spray and steam filled the air. The *Faltaine* drew alongside.

"Follow me," Yarsk said. Owen jumped to his feet and grabbed the tiller. Steering the wake of the limping *Faltaine,* he found himself clear of the Harsh fleet. He looked back just in time to see the stricken ship crash into the side of another.

Yarsk leaned one elbow casually on the wheel of the *Faltaine,* looking for all the world as if he was out for a Sunday sail. A smile spread over his face as two more ships collided, their rigging getting tangled in the process.

"They won't be chasing anyone in a hurry," he said. Owen noticed that the *Faltaine* was moving closer to the *Wayfarer.*

One of the *Faltaine* crew approached Yarsk.

"Permission to board the prize, Captain?"

"What does he mean by 'prize'?" Owen called across the gap that separated the two boats.

"Prize?" Yarsk said. "Oh, yes. That would be you. You've been captured, you see."

"What?"

"Simple, really. You're ours now."

"What! You mean you're pirates?"

"I'd prefer the term *buccaneer*, actually, but yes. You are, I suppose, more or less . . ."—here Yarsk paused to examine his nails—"our hostage."

"But I saved you!" Owen protested.

"I suppose you did. But you see, if the ships hadn't been chasing you, then we wouldn't have been in trouble in the first place."

One of the pirate crew leapt onto the deck of the *Wayfarer* and reached for the sail.

"Leave that alone!" Owen cried. He snatched up the magno gun and leveled it at Yarsk. "Tell him to stop."

"I don't think you'll shoot," Yarsk said with a faint, bored smile. "You aren't the type."

"Maybe I'm not usually, but there are a lot of people depending on me."

"Still," Yarsk said, "I'm right about these things most of the time. Take the sail down, Majellan."

The man moved to obey. Owen kept the gun trained on Yarsk, but the man was right. He couldn't shoot him in cold blood. Owen lowered the gun. But just then Majellan's eye fell on something.

"Captain, look!"

Owen groaned inwardly. The man was pointing at the Mortmain! If the pirates took it, he was done for.

Yarsk leapt across the space between the boats. He knelt to examine the Mortmain, then stood up.

"You should have told us," Yarsk said.

"Told you what?"

"Who you are."

"I never got the chance."

Yarsk bent again to examine the chart next to the Mortmain.

"It is a long time since these objects were seen. In those days, this place was full of ships, a prize every month. Then the ships disappeared and time itself ran dry. But that has changed. Time flows as it should. What is happening?"

Owen explained to him that the Harsh had stockpiled time and now had released it so that their fleet could attack the Workhouse.

Yarsk turned to his men. "We cannot take this ship as a prize."

There was a murmur of dissent among the crew.

"It's our first prize in a long, long time," a gaunt woman cried. Owen noticed that they were all quite thin.

"How long have you been out here?" Owen asked.

"How long since we last saw Port Merforion, our home port? In your time, about thirty years."

"Thirty years!" Owen gasped.

"We cannot return home without a prize. We've bought or borrowed or robbed supplies here and there, but no prize."

"So why not the *Wayfarer*?"

"The Navigator sailed with us for a time. We cannot take one of our own as a prize."

"The Navigator!"

Yarsk looked Owen up and down.

"Yes. Your grandfather, I would say."

"My grandfather—a pirate?"

"Buccaneer," Yarsk said. "It sounds so much more civilized. But yes. We taught him what we knew about the oceans of time, and in return he guided us to lots of prizes."

"Damn fine prizes," a grizzled crewman murmured, and they all smiled as if at a fond memory.

"Anyway, we have to let you go. We'll have time to slip off and fix the damage while the Harsh are sorting themselves out. Which is a pity, since if we were to haul sail now, we're at the exact spot in time for Port Merforian."

On hearing the name of their home port repeated, the pirates looked at each other sadly. From the other end of the *Faltaine,* someone started to strum a guitar. The sailors put their arms around each other, and the gaunt woman started to sing a lonesome song.

"What are they singing?" Owen asked.

"Oh, they're always singing about Port Merforian and so on. Oddly enough, they never sing about the stinking harbor barrooms where they spend all their time when they're in port." Yarsk started to sing softly along with them.

> *. . . to sail time's ocean wide*
> *In time and time's divide*
> *Till the book of the past*
> *Thaws winter's child at last.*

"What does that mean," Owen said, "'thaws winter's child at last'?"

"Haven't the foggiest. I think your grandfather taught it to them," Yarsk said, dismissing the subject. "It's about time we were all moving."

Owen looked around. The Harsh fleet seemed to be re-forming and putting on sail.

Yarsk jumped lightly back onto the deck of the *Faltaine* and took the wheel. The gap between the two boats started to widen.

"I don't know how to get back," Owen said.

"'Fraid I can't help you," Yarsk said. "I don't know where the Workhouse is."

The *Faltaine* was twenty yards away now.

"Wait!" Owen called. "Does Port Merforian have a symbol?"

"There's a lighthouse on the pier with a light in the shape of an eye. Next time bring us a prize, Navigator!"

In reply, Owen raised his hand, although he wasn't sure if Yarsk could see him. The *Faltaine* blended in against the sky and Owen could no longer see her, though he thought for a moment that he could hear a snatch of a mournful song as the sad pirates set out again on their quest.

Owen turned to the Mortmain. He scanned the symbols anxiously. It was there—a lighthouse with an eye in the center. But there was no corresponding symbol on the map. Owen went back to the map. Behind him the Harsh fleet had taken their damaged ships under tow.

Any minute now they would sail again. Frantically he reexamined the map. There was no lighthouse with an eye, but then it dawned on him. There was the symbol of a house, with a light in the window. It must represent the lighthouse. Owen was beginning to get an idea of how his grandfather's mind worked, and how he had drawn the maps. The symbols were on the Mortmain to begin with, and his grandfather had copied them and incorporated them into maps. The symbol for a place such as Hadima was easily found—there was no reason to disguise it. But the pirate headquarters of Port Merforian was a secret place, and so his grandfather had added an extra precaution and disguised the lighthouse as an ordinary house.

Owen spun the Mortmain until the Workhouse and the lighthouse were lined up, then grabbed the tiller. The *Wayfarer* responded, surging forward. Soon only the masts of the Harsh ships were visible on the horizon, masts crowded with sail as they too set a course for the Workhouse, a Harsh song of war and ruin rising from the fleet for those with ears to hear.

Rosie could not believe that the Workhouse was the same place that she had seen on her first night. Owen had bought time for the Resisters to finish building, and now it was a proud fortress, dominating the whole area around the river. Soldiers stood on the battlements and the Resisters' unadorned black flag flew bravely. Walls and trenches had been erected at the river, and these were constantly patrolled.

Inside, the transformation was complete as well. The corridors were crowded with men and women, and the huge kitchens were in full swing. Cati was often called away to meetings. Rosie found herself spending time with Rutgar's soldiers, who were a homely lot.

If she slipped into the kitchen and hung around until Contessa saw her, she would get an extra ration of bread and honey, or perhaps some soup.

"You've had a hard time," Contessa would say, "and you need building up."

Rosie was amazed by the amount of magno in the Workhouse—it was used for everything from lights to weapons. In Hadima magno was very scarce and precious, and often only found in its raw and dangerous state.

On the second morning she came out of the kitchen carrying soup and water and a hunk of bread. She backed into the corridor, balancing her food in one hand while trying to close the door with the other. She jumped two feet into the air when her heel sank into something soft and there was a yell. The soup spilled all down her front and she swore out loud. She turned to see a barefoot boy sitting on the floor rubbing his foot.

"What did you do that for?" she said angrily.

"What do you mean, what did I do?" the boy snapped back. "It was you stood on my foot with your stupid shoes."

"You shouldn't be walking around in your bare feet, anyway," she said. "It's not . . . hygienic. And I just got my dress cleaned and mended as well, and now it's all soup."

They glared at each other.

"Where do come from with your funny clothes and all?" the boy demanded.

"Hadima," Rosie said, "a big city. I'd say a country boy with no shoes has never seen a city."

Just then Contessa came out of the kitchen and saw them.

"Oh, good," she said, "I'm glad you two have met. Wesley, this is Rosie. You'll have plenty to talk about, both being friends of Owen and Cati's. Which reminds me," she said, looking worried, "has Owen come back yet?"

"I haven't heard," Wesley said. "I'll go to the battlements and look."

"I'll come with you," Rosie said, faintly ashamed of squabbling when Owen was in danger.

"Come on, then," Wesley said. His tone was less sharp and she wondered if he was feeling the same way.

Together they climbed to the battlements, Rosie pulling her coat tight around her. Wesley seemed immune to the cold.

"Do you live in the Workhouse?" Rosie asked, trying to be polite.

"No," Wesley replied shortly, then added, "us Raggies live in the warehouse down by the sea. But Dr. Diamond, he reckons there's a big attack coming and we wouldn't be able to defend ourselves, so we had to come to the Workhouse."

Wesley gave a longing look toward the sea, and Rosie's heart softened toward him. She was starting to miss her home in Hadima.

"Wonder what the doc's up to," Wesley said, looking up at the Skyward. Dr. Diamond had disappeared into his lab at the top of the brass tower a day ago and had not come out since. Rosie followed Wesley's gaze. The windows of the Skyward were steamed up, so you couldn't see in.

"I'd love to see him again," Rosie said.

"No disturbing the doc when he's working," Wesley said. "Look!"

Far below them, in the snowy fields, Owen's mother was leading a party of Rutgar's men from the shop. They were carrying what looked like a grandfather clock with great care.

"Wonder what they're doing with that old thing," Rosie said.

"Why do you want to know that?" a sharp voice came from behind. Samual had come up on them so quietly that they hadn't heard.

"No reason," Rosie said, "just wondering."

"I wouldn't do too much wondering around here if I was you," the man said, his thin lips drawn tight.

"She can do what she wants," Wesley said.

"You'd be well advised to stay out of this, Raggie," Samual said, his eyes fixed on Rosie. "I wonder how many of her rat friends from Hadima came through the tunnel with her and are out there spying."

It was more than Rosie could bear. She thought of how her friends had suffered during the attack by the Harsh and the misery that they were enduring in the frozen city. Without thinking she felt in her hair, and a long sharp hairpin appeared in her hand.

Samual's eyes narrowed and he took a step closer to her, his hand on the hilt of his sword.

"Drawing a knife on an officer of the Workhouse guard, that's a serious offense," Samual said.

"So is being rude to guests of the Workhouse, Samual." The voice came from above. Rosie turned to look. To her great surprise and delight, Dr. Diamond was standing on the top of the Nab staircase.

"And it's not a knife," Wesley said, "it's a hairpin."

"She's a spy," Samual snarled.

"I appreciate your suspicious mind, Samual," Dr. Diamond continued in the same mild tone. "In time of war and intrigue being alert could save lives. But I can vouch for the young lady. She helped and guided us bravely in Hadima."

"Hello, Doctor," Rosie said.

"Good afternoon, Rosie. I'm glad to see you, although I hear that things are not good in Hadima. Now put the hairpin away, and let's not see it again in the Workhouse—unless, of course you are showing it to one of the Harsh. Samual is a generous man, and I don't think he would bring charges against a refugee."

Rosie put her hairpin away, blushing. Samual snorted but took his hand from his sword.

"I would be careful whom you vouch for, Doctor," he said coldly, and then, with a dark look in Rosie's direction, he turned on his heel and stalked off.

"Bleeding twit," Rosie said.

"He's been a faithful soldier for the Workhouse," the doctor said, "and I did mean what I said. You have to be suspicious in times of war, sadly. But how are you, Rosie, and what are you doing here?"

Rosie opened her mouth to speak, and as she did so music mingled with pain swelled in her head.

There was a shout from Wesley. He had caught sight of a movement in the clouds. Far above their heads, but closing every second, the *Wayfarer* descended toward the Workhouse, Owen standing at the tiller, pale-faced and tired but defiant.

For a moment Rosie and Wesley stood openmouthed and staring. Then they started to jump up and down and wave their arms. Owen saw them and altered course. The *Wayfarer* soared toward them in a great curve. Just in time, he leaned back, and the *Wayfarer* came to rest on the snow-covered battlements of the Workhouse.

"Rosie!" Owen said, leaping out onto the ground and throwing an arm around her. "What are you doing here?"

He grasped Wesley's hand and grinned. Cati rushed up the stairs, followed by Contessa.

"I thought you were killed or something," Cati said crossly.

"Good to see you too, Cati," Owen said. Other people came onto the battlements: soldiers in red, and some Raggies who crowded around, wanting to see the marvelous boat that sailed in the air. Among them was Silkie, who gazed shyly at Owen.

"I would like to spend time on greetings," Contessa said, "but we have need of news. What about the Harsh, Owen?"

"Not far behind." He told them about the chase and his meeting with the buccaneers. Silkie beamed at him, then blushed.

"Tell me about the buccaneers," Dr. Diamond called from the Nab, and it seemed that he would have discussed the pirates all day, but Contessa cut him short.

"The attack is coming! Get everyone behind the defenses and close all gates! Owen, you look exhausted."

"I didn't get much sleep," he said, "and the *Wayfarer* didn't get much rest either."

Behind him, Silkie had approached the boat where it lay on its side.

"It's hurt," she said, touching the scarred planks where the Harsh missile had struck. She gave Owen a look of reproach.

"They attacked . . . I couldn't . . . ," he stammered, unaccountably embarrassed. But she ignored him and knelt to examine the timber more closely, then spoke quietly to one of the other Raggies, who went off immediately.

"I think I can make her better."

Owen looked at her, surprised, and then remembered how, when the Raggies had owned a craft that they referred to simply as Boat, it was Silkie who had maintained it.

"Please," he said, and she smiled at him.

In the Convoke, Owen told his story to Cati, Contessa, Rutgar, Samual, and Pieta.

"They are almost here," Rutgar said, and rushed off to prepare his forces.

"Someone has to speak to the Resisters before the enemy is upon us, to remind them of what they are fighting for and what is at stake," Contessa said. But Pieta and Samual had raced off to supervise the defenses. Owen swayed, and Cati took his arm.

"I think the Navigator needs some sleep," she said, and he did not protest.

Rosie didn't know what to do with herself. The corridors of the Workhouse were full of men and women in armor. The walls rang with urgent shouts and hammering and banging as last-minute defenses were erected. A crane had appeared on the battlements on the instructions of Dr. Diamond and large flat objects covered in canvas were being lowered into position on the front of the Workhouse. Everywhere she looked there were tense faces and few friendly words. War was upon them, and everyone seemed to have a task except her. She looked up to see Cati, whose face was white. *She's scared,* Rosie thought.

"Come with me, please," Cati said. Rosie followed her up the long stairway to the battlements. Cati's hand found her way into Rosie's. Men and women waited on other parts of the wall, but there was no one here, at the highest point.

"What are you going to do?" Rosie said. In reply, Cati let go of her hand and started to climb up to where the

Resisters' black flag hung. The footing was slippery with ice, and Rosie watched nervously.

At the very top Cati straightened. She looked down. Rosie thought that she looked very small and alone, but when she spoke, her voice was strong and sure.

"Men and women of the Resisters!" she called. The defenders of the Workhouse looked up in surprise, and gradually all noise ceased.

"This is the darkest part of our history," she said. "We have fought the Harsh many times and each time defeated them. But now a mighty fleet is thrown against us, and we all know in our hearts what that means."

Cati held one hand out in front of her.

"We hold the fate of the world in the palm of our hands. We dare not contemplate defeat, though defeat stares us in the face. We must fight with courage. And if courage fails us, then duty must sustain us. We must fight and if need be die for the world, without anyone knowing what we have done. That is the duty of the Resisters. We stand alone."

"Not alone," a clear voice said. Rosie had climbed onto the battlements. "Not while Rosie is here. Hadima stands with the Workhouse!"

There was a great roar from the Resisters, a wave of cheering that rose from the trenches and redoubts along the river and spread to every window and rooftop of the old building. Far below, Contessa turned to Rutgar.

"With courage like that, perhaps we can hold out."

"I'm afraid it might take more than courage," Rutgar said heavily, "but we'll do what we can."

On the battlements Cati felt a familiar deadly chill, one that swept over her in the presence of the Harsh.

"They are coming," she said, almost to herself, then out loud: "To war, Resisters. The enemy is on us!"

The skies darkened. With a howling such as none of them had ever heard before, the ice came. Afterward they described it to each other as sleet, but it was more like frozen knives than sleet, and when it hit, it exploded into white powdery crystals that found their way into every crevice of their clothing. The corridors of the Workhouse were filled with the white powder, and Resisters walked blindly in it, unable to call out to each other in the tumult and howling. Some lost their heads and would have run wildly into the white blast, but their comrades restrained them.

Dr. Diamond went among them with his face wrapped in cloth, wearing goggles.

"It isn't the attack!" he shouted. "Keep your heads down. It will be over soon. I can see into the mist with these goggles."

As he finished his sentence, the white hail stopped.

The Resisters looked at each other. They were half deafened by the noise and covered in the powdery snow, which hung in the air like fog. The Workhouse slowly emerged like a ghost building.

"What is this?" Cati asked, moving her hand through the freezing powder that swirled in the air.

"It's the cold that built up around the Harsh ships as they sailed through time. When they passed through into our time, the cold reacted with the moisture in the air," Dr. Diamond said.

"Never mind that," Samual snapped. "Where are they now?"

"Not far away," Dr. Diamond said, "not far away."

The lookouts on the battlements saw the ships first, as the icy powder settled on the ground. But it wasn't long before everyone could see them and stood in awe and fear. The Harsh ships had alighted on the ice beyond the shoreline at the harbor. A forest of masts towered above the town, reaching to the horizon, rank upon rank of cold, white warships, their gun ports open and pointing toward the Workhouse. And above them all, on the lead ship, flew the pure white standard of the Harsh.

"How many of them are there?" Rutgar breathed.

"Not as many as you think," Dr. Diamond said, "and I suspect that the crews are small. But still, what a sight!"

Rosie looked up at the Workhouse, the black banner fluttering defiantly above the strong stone walls. But how could they last against the might of the Harsh? On the battlements she could see small figures moving about—she recognized Dr. Diamond and several other men, struggling with a large object concealed under a tarpaulin. But she didn't have time to think about what they were doing. There was a sudden report from the ships, then another and another. A great whistling sound filled the air, and an ice missile struck the Workhouse wall with a mighty crash. The wall did not buckle, but Rosie saw how the missile left a scar on the stone.

Another missile struck further up. In minutes they were raining down on every part of the Workhouse. One crashed into the ground right in front of Rosie, sending stones and frozen dirt high into the air. Rosie ducked, then lifted her head to look at it, a jagged lance of blue-white ice. Rosie reached out but one of the soldiers grabbed her hand before she could touch it.

"Them edges are razor sharp!" he said gruffly. "And that's not ordinary ice. That would give you frostbite with the one touch!"

Rosie looked at it with new respect. Her hands had been badly damaged from handling raw magno before they had been cured with the ring given to her by the Yeati—a strange and magical creature they had rescued in Hadima. She had no intention of hurting them again.

Further down the river, the ice missiles slashed through the trees, sending broken branches high into the air. Rosie could see men and women duck down into their trenches and foxholes.

"How long can they keep this up?" Rosie said, almost to herself. Rutgar looked at her without speaking.

He looks worried, Rosie thought.

Deep in the bowels of the Workhouse, Owen heard a distant drumming, like rain on a roof. He clambered out of bed and went into the corridor. There was no one about. Frowning, he climbed the stairs. The drumming was louder now. You could feel it in the fabric of the building. He started to run.

Owen burst onto the roof just as a shower of the ice lances landed. The impact of the ice against the building was the cause of the drumming sound! A Resister soldier crouched in the doorway.

"Get down!" he shouted. "They're aiming at the roof!"

The slate roof had been torn up in places by the ice missiles, and giant pieces of ice lay everywhere.

"Why didn't somebody call me?" Owen said furiously. The soldier shrugged. Owen could see men lying on the ground around an object with a tarpaulin half covering it.

"What happened?" he demanded.

"They got hit in the first volley," the man said. "The doctor was doing something with them."

"The doctor?"

"Yes—" Before the man could elaborate, Owen was sprinting across the roof.

"Come back," the man shouted, "it's too dangerous!"

Owen dodged an incoming lance, which exploded

against the rooftop beside him. Splinters of ice and slate hit his right side, but he kept going. One of the men on the ground was moaning and moving his head from side to side. The others were still.

"Dr. Diamond!" he shouted.

"Over here," a weak voice replied. Owen saw a boot protruding from behind one of the big Workhouse chimneys. He scrambled over, slipping on the ice.

Dr. Diamond had found shelter behind the chimney. His face was white and he was holding his left arm.

"I think it's broken," he said weakly. "They got us with the first volley. Sheer luck. What about the men?"

Owen looked out from behind the chimney. "I don't know," he said. "One of them's moving."

"What about the Porcupine?"

"The what?"

"The Porcupine. Underneath the tarpaulin."

"Whatever it is, it hasn't been touched."

"Then get me over there," Dr. Diamond said, struggling to his feet. Owen was going to object; the doctor was in no shape to enter a fire zone. But one look at his friend's face told him that arguing would be useless.

"Come on." Owen put the doctor's good arm over his shoulder. As they rounded the chimney breast, a missile glanced off the top, shattering the chimney pots.

"I was ready for them," the doctor gasped, wincing. "I hope this hasn't done too much damage. . . . Grab the other end of the tarpaulin," he said, reaching out with his good arm.

Together they hauled the canvas off, and Owen found himself staring at a very strange machine. The center of it looked like a huge golf ball, from which tendrils of steam arose. Attached to it were dozens of what appeared to be vacuum cleaner extensions. It had a forlorn look, like something found in a junkyard. The extensions drooped and the enormous golf ball was dented and scratched. Owen ducked as another ice lance whistled over his head.

"Get out of there," a soldier shouted. "You're completely exposed, you fools!"

Dr. Diamond fished in his pocket until he found a remote control held together with tape. A car radio aerial had been attached to the top.

"You remember the last time they used the ice lances against us?"

Owen remembered it well, and how destructive they were.

"I put my thinking cap on," Dr. Diamond said unhurriedly, just as if they were out for an afternoon stroll. "What is ice made from?"

"Water," Owen gasped as a fusillade sailed over their heads and slammed into the roof behind them. "Dr. Diamond, do you not think maybe—"

"And then I thought, what happens to ice when it is exposed to heat?"

"It melts," Owen said impatiently as another barrage of lethal ice struck the chimneys behind them. "But Dr. Diamond—"

"Of course it does." The scientist beamed.

"Dr. Diamond," Owen burst out, "we're going to get killed here."

"Time to get the Porcupine going. Of course, it doesn't really look like a porcupine, but it reminded me of—"

The scene in front of them disappeared in a cloud of ice splinters.

"Dr. Diamond!"

"Yes, yes, yes. Now, where was I?" He poked a finger at the remote control and the golf ball started to move, slowly at first, rotating one way, then the next. The vacuum cleaner extensions waved wildly in the air.

"Yes. Very good. I think multitargetting is called for." The scientist poked at the remote again, selecting three of four buttons. The golf ball wheezed and spluttered, and steam jetted out from underneath it.

"No, not quite . . ." Dr. Diamond stabbed another button. Owen looked up to see another salvo of ice lances heading straight for them. There wasn't time to get out of the way. The Porcupine coughed again, wheezed, then spun around with incredible speed. First from one vacuum extension, then another and another, a white beam shot out, each beam striking an ice lance in midair. There was a hissing sound, then nothing except a cloud of vapor in the air. Owen looked at the doctor with his mouth hanging open.

"Nothing to it," the doctor said. "Jets of superheated steam. They melt the ice lances in midair. Once you establish the general principle, it's simple."

The Porcupine spun again as another salvo came in. The same thing happened. Dr. Diamond pressed another button. This time the ice lances never got near the Workhouse. They were stopped in midair over the town.

"That's the full range, I'm afraid," the doctor said. "Doesn't really melt them after that. But this is only the Mark One version, of course. I have a few refinements in mind."

"Well done, Doctor," Contessa said, bursting out from the stairs.

"Well, it stopped them for now," the doctor said.

Owen leaned over the parapet and inspected the scars that the ice missiles had left on the stonework. Then he looked up at the vast fleet moored off the harbor. Dr. Diamond caught his eye.

"I know, Owen," he said softly. "It is only a skirmish, and they've done much damage. And they will have other weapons. We cannot fight them and hope to win, so we must outthink them."

"And outlast them," Contessa murmured, "for the Workhouse is now under siege."

Johnston's feet crunched in the snow as he walked down the road. Otherwise the night was soundless. The Workhouse stood tall and proud over the river, sentries pacing the battlements, but he did not glance at it. He went as far as the town bridge and slipped over it, down onto the riverbank below. Moving lightly for so big a man, he reached the Hadima entrance and stood under it. He took a rope and a grappling hook from the bag he carried over his shoulder and threw the hook toward the entrance. It caught on the stone lip, and silently Johnston climbed up it, hand over hand.

The tunnel was dark, but he could see starlight at the other end. He emerged after a few minutes into the little courtyard surrounded by shops. Everything was frozen and still. When he opened the doors to the tunnel that led down toward Hadima, the creaking noise rent the silence. But Johnston was not concerned. He walked into the tunnel. He did not get far before he knew that he was not alone.

"Agnetha is waiting for me," he said loudly. Almost instantly he felt something hard and sharp and cold at his throat.

"Take your filthy fingernails away from my throat, Albion," he said, "or you will answer to the Harsh for it."

The shiny metal nails seemed to caress his throat for a moment and then were withdrawn. Johnston walked on, knowing that the darkness around him teemed with the creatures.

After a few minutes he felt hands push him toward the side of the tunnel. There was an opening there and he clambered through it, finding himself on a staircase that led upward. He emerged into a dark chamber, lit only by what starlight found its way through a gap in the ceiling. Enough light for Johnston to see Agnetha seated in front of him on a chair of black obsidian, her long black dress lying in folds around her. Her white hair shone in the starlight, but her eyes were pools of darkness. Her courtiers were gathered around her. Every pale eye in the chamber was fixed on Johnston.

He made a mocking bow.

"If it may please your ladyship."

"No false words, Johnston, in the black chamber." Her voice was low and musical, but the words were spat out.

"I saw Harsh ships in the night," she went on. "I saw ice rain on the Resisters."

"Just the beginning," Johnston said.

"They promised that we would stand in the light without fear," Agnetha said. Johnston could feel the Albions stirring in the darkness around him.

"And of course you will," Johnston said smoothly, "when you have played your part."

"Then we must talk," Agnetha said. She clapped, and the chamber was suddenly empty.

"Stand at the foot of the black chair," Agnetha said, and Johnston moved closer, his great teeth showing in the starlight as he grinned. The Harsh had given him instructions to pass on to Agnetha and the Albions.

It was dawn when Johnston left Agnetha. After he had passed on the Harsh message, he had been forced to listen to the Albion queen's lament, about how the creatures longed for the sunlight on their faces. She had reminded him many times about the promise made by the Harsh that they would walk in the light without pain. He did not go back the way he had come, but continued down the tunnel. He had work to do in Hadima, but the vessel that he had used to cross time had been destroyed. He would have to go on foot.

He came to the customs post that marked the frontier of the Hadima lands. The traffic lanes were empty and the great lights that kept the Albions at bay had been shattered. Of the customs officer who had once kept watch, there was no sign. Johnston wondered what the Albions had done to him.

The road descended into another tunnel, and now he could smell snow. After an hour's walk he came to the end. Inside the tunnel it was quiet, but he stepped outside into darkness and a wind that blew snow horizontally along the ground. The pine trees around the entrance pitched and groaned as if they might snap at any minute. Without hesitating Johnston put his head down and walked into the shrieking wind. Within seconds he was lost to view.

After the initial attack, there was little activity from the Harsh. Standing on the battlements, the young Resisters could see eerie white shapes moving around the ships and in the town.

"They don't seem in too much of a hurry," Cati said to Wesley.

"What hurry would they be in?" Wesley said. "They got us trapped here."

Martha bent close to the radio she had brought with her. From time to time she picked up weak signals of emergency broadcasts—appeals for food and for shelter. News reporters talked about the new ice age that had struck the world. Even at the equator, apparently, there was snow.

"One thing's for sure," she said. "There isn't any help out there. We're on our own, and it's getting colder."

It was indeed getting colder. Contessa gave the children a stern lesson on avoiding frostbite, and even Wesley was forced to accept shoes and a warm jacket.

Samual had been arguing in the Convoke for an attack on the Harsh, and many of the younger soldiers agreed with him.

"Are we just going to sit here while they freeze us to death?" he said, and the soldiers stamped their feet in agreement.

"What does he think he can do against them?" Owen wondered aloud. But Samual was determined, and on the third day he forced a vote in the Convoke. Contessa and Rutgar voted against it. Pieta didn't bother voting.

"If they say fight, then I'll fight. If not, then I won't," she said, shrugging, and went back to teaching her two children how to use the magno whip.

Samual won the vote. They would attack the Harsh. After the vote Rutgar came over to him.

"Guard the Workhouse well if I fall," Samual said.

"We'll guard it together when we come back," Rutgar said. "I don't agree with the attack, but I won't let you and your men go out alone." Samual nodded. Rutgar clapped him on the back.

"Come. We have to plan."

"You need to fetch the Yeati's ring," Contessa told Cati. "There will be casualties. Guard the ring well, Cati. It is, aside from the Mortmain, the most precious and magical object that we possess. Many people's lives will depend on it, I fear."

The Yeati, the wondrous bearlike animal with the light of the stars in his eyes, had given Cati his ring in thanks for releasing him from the cage in the Museum of Time in Hadima. It was a great gift. The ring could cure all manner of ills. Cati had already used the healing power of the Yeati's ring on those injured during the barrage of ice lances. The healing power faded the more it was used, and the ring took time to recover, so she had decided that she would use it only when there was no other option. She had told Dr. Diamond, and he had agreed. When she had tried to use it to mend his broken arm, he refused.

"Keep it for someone who needs it more than me," he said. He was now wearing a tartan-patterned sling to support a plaster cast, which he found very useful, he said, for writing equations on.

Cati went to her room. She kept the ring in a box in a locked drawer with other precious things, such as her mother's cornflower brooch—her only physical link to the mother she had never really known and the father who had given his life for the Resisters. She carefully unlocked the drawer with the key she carried around her neck and took out the box. Apart from its healing powers, she delighted in the feel of the gold ring, at once delicate and enormously strong, with a deep gleam that seemed to come from far within.

She opened the lid. The box was empty. The ring was gone!

Frantically Cati searched the drawer and then the

entire room. But she was sure she had put it back—it was the last thing she had done before she went to bed.

She raced down to the kitchens. She swung through the kitchen door, almost knocking over two bakers carrying trays of loaves. Contessa was counting legs of smoked ham hanging from a rack.

"Contessa," Cati shouted, "it's gone! The ring!" She skidded to a halt as she reached Contessa.

"Hush, child," Contessa said with a frown. "The whole kitchen doesn't have to know your business. Tell me what happened."

Blushing at being reproached, Cati told Contessa what had happened. Contessa followed her back to the room. To Cati's surprise she didn't look at the box at all, but examined the drawer and the lock very closely.

"I put it away safely," Cati said miserably.

"I believe you," Contessa said, "but who would take it, and why? Particularly before an attack is mounted, when there may be many casualties."

"I should have looked after it better."

"You looked after it responsibly. Blame the thief, Cati, whoever he or she is."

Contessa went to find Dr. Diamond in the Skyward. He looked up at her knock and beckoned her in. She told him about the Yeati's ring.

"And she spoke to you in front of the kitchen staff?"

"Yes. The ring going missing is bad, but the thought of a traitor . . ."

"Is bad for morale, I know."

"It is very cold," Contessa said, shivering.

"Yes. I wonder how much colder the Harsh can make it. We must think of what to do, Contessa. We can stand a long siege, certainly, but not forever."

"Samual's attack might succeed."

"I think we both know it won't," Dr. Diamond said, "but he has to be allowed to try. My job is to try to work out some way of getting his men back safely. But that is work for tomorrow. My feeling is that Owen is key to our chances of surviving, but I can't figure out why."

"Yes, he destroyed the Puissance and stopped time from going backward. Perhaps he can do something similar," Contessa said.

"That was different, though. We knew what we had to do—destroy the Puissance. This time we don't even know if there is anything we can do."

"We will find out," Contessa said, sighing and looking out the window toward the Harsh ships.

Owen, meanwhile, felt as if he might be better off facing the Harsh than the wrath of Silkie. The Raggie girl had got him to sail the *Wayfarer* to a quiet yard at the back of the Workhouse. She had brought all her tools to repair the vessel, and Owen stayed to help, a decision he was beginning to regret. Every time she asked him to pass her a tool he either dropped it or gave her the wrong one, and each time she let him know what she thought of him. In the end he didn't know what way was up.

"When I say a small chisel, I mean a small one," she said, "not one you could use as a spade!"

As Owen cast about for the right tool he saw Wesley looking down at him amusedly from an upstairs window.

"She's a hard driver, our Silkie," he said, "for all she looks gentle."

"You can say that again."

"Which bit? About the hardness or the looks? But don't mind the telling-off. She always cared too much, our Silkie. Ain't that right, Silkie?"

Silkie looked up at him, her face pink from her exertions and threads of fair hair falling over her brow.

"If you've got nothing better to do than hang out of windows talking about folk as can hear you loud as day, then you better go and do something useful." She pointed her chisel at him threateningly. Wesley held up his hands.

"I'm here with a bit of news, if you're interested."

"What news?"

Wesley told them about the missing ring.

"It's all over the Workhouse," Wesley said, "and fingers is being pointed as to who done it."

"What do you mean?" Owen asked.

"Us Raggies are being blamed by some folk."

"That's not fair!" Silkie protested.

"There's some folk never had a good opinion of the

Raggies. Some of Samual's men won't talk to us ones now."

"Whoever took the ring, that's what they want," Owen said. "To start us fighting among ourselves."

"Looks like they got what they set out for, then," Wesley said. "Us ones aren't going to sit around here and be insulted."

"Take it easy, Wesley," Owen said. "Samual doesn't trust me either."

"Maybe," Wesley said, "but you're the Navigator. The Raggies is just harbor trash to them."

Wesley turned on his heel and disappeared.

"Wesley!" Owen called. "Wesley!" But the Raggie leader did not answer.

"You're better to leave him be when he's like that," Silkie said.

"He shouldn't be so touchy."

"You think not?" Silkie said. "Then you're not the lad I thought you were. Have you never noticed the way some of the Resisters look down on the Raggies?"

"No, I haven't, because they don't."

"I think people's been looking up to you for so long, it's hard to see when they're looking down on other folk."

"That's not fair," Owen protested.

"If the cap fits . . . ," Silkie said.

"That's it," Owen said. "I'm off to find Wesley. I'm not letting this go any further."

Silkie watched him go, wondering why she was always

so hard on him and so short-tempered when he was around. And yet when he wasn't there, she remembered the way she felt when he smiled at her . . . She sighed and turned back to sanding the splintered wood of the *Wayfarer,* soon lost in her task, in the rhythms of working on the living timbers.

Owen asked all around the Workhouse, but no one had seen Wesley. He found himself in parts of the Workhouse he'd never seen before, going deeper and deeper into a warren of corridors and storerooms. The further he went, the drier and warmer it became, a dim magno light showing the way.

In one room he found strange and beautiful weapons—swords and spears with still-sharp magno edges. In another he found armor, and the finest of chain mail, not unlike the suits in the *Wayfarer*. Here and there hung portraits of Resisters of times past, men and women in strange, old-fashioned clothes—the men with pointed beards and the women with tall headdresses. Owen wondered how long the Resister struggle had been going on.

In another room were trunks and trunks full of old clothing—long dresses and embroidered tunics, moth-eaten and faded.

Then he found a set of tall oak doors. The handle was dusty and stiff. The doors swung open with a loud creak, and Owen found himself in a large hall. At one end was a huge stone fireplace, where the fire had not been lit for many years. There was a long table, with chairs lined along each side, but woodworm had attacked the timber, and the table had collapsed. On each wall hung giant tapestries. They reminded Owen of the tapestry he had seen in Hadima where he had first glimpsed the *Wayfarer,* but on most of these the color had faded, so you couldn't see what scenes were depicted on them. Disappointed, he sat down on the hearth. As his eyes grew used to the dim light, he could see that there was another tapestry, almost hidden in the recesses of an alcove on the other side of the room. He got up and went over, squinting up at it.

At first he could only make out dim shapes in the ancient fabric, but he found that if he stood a particular way, the light from a nearby magno torch caught the tapestry. A boy's face became apparent, a fair-haired boy, looking off into the distance. There was a terrible sadness in his face. Owen could almost feel the child's pain. There were other figures behind him. Were they the people responsible for his hurt? If Owen could just turn the tapestry a little toward the light, then he could make out their features. He reached up and took hold of the tapestry gently . . . but it was too much. Just as he glimpsed cruel cold faces behind the boy, the entire tapestry turned to dust with a soft sound and collapsed onto the floor.

Owen stared at it in horror, taking an involuntary step backward. As he did so, something snapped under his feet. He looked down. It was a pencil, and beside it was a notebook, also fragile with age. And beside that again was an odd-looking machine. It looked like an old-fashioned typewriter, except there were no keys with letters, just the little arms that would have had letters on the top of them. On the side of the box was a brass handle, and on the floor beside it an old and delicate wooden hoop, just about the size of a man's hand. Owen looked at it, puzzled. He picked up the hoop, and jumped, almost dropping it, as something pricked his hand.

The hoop was studded with tiny needles, hundreds of them. He looked down at the machine, and he remembered something he had seen on television—an old-fashioned machine for playing music, with cylinders with bumps on them. When a bump was struck, the machine played a note. What if this was something similar?

Very carefully, he placed the hoop into the machine in the place where the paper would have gone in a typewriter. Then he gently turned the handle at the side. Nothing happened.

He took the hoop out and reversed it, then turned the handle again. This time there was a whirring from inside the machine. The hoop started to move. For several moments there was no sound, then a wheezy crackling came from the machine. He looked at the hoop. It was too old. The little arms were striking the needles and stripping them away, making the crackling noise. He sat back in disappointment. He was sure there was something important on the hoop.

He heard a sound, and then another, and then, almost inaudible in the wheezing and crackling, but growing in strength—a child's voice, thin and eerie and somehow terribly familiar. . . .

> *. . . to sail time's ocean wide*
> *In time and time's divide*
> *Till the book of the past*
> *Thaws winter's child at last.*

The song the buccaneers had sung. And there was more. . . .

> *Her earth mistress pride*
> *More dead than alive*
> *In her hands his fate*
> *The boy she awaits . . .*

Owen listened eagerly for more but, with a tearing sound, the hoop came apart. The machine ground to a halt as the remnants of the hoop became entangled in the steel arms.

What did it mean? Owen had forgotten about the notebook, but he reached for it now. Only two pages had been written on. The first page was a hurried sketch of the tapestry, showing the boy in the foreground and what appeared to be the shapes of a small king and queen in the background. The adults' features had not been filled in.

The second page of the notebook had three words and a question mark scrawled on it.

The Long Woman?

Of course! Owen thought. He had met the Long Woman on his trek north. She had rescued Owen and Pieta from the snow and brought them to her strange underground kingdom.

Her earth mistress pride
More dead than alive

She had talked about being buried, and when Owen, shocked, had asked her about it, she had laughed. Owen was sure that something important was buried in the song and the images on the ruined tapestry, if only he could find it. Who had crouched in the same place, many years before, and why had they left the notebook and recorder? If he could just talk to that person . . .

He sighed and carefully tore the two pages out of the notebook. People would be missing him. It was time to make his way back to the others.

The Raggies had been quartered in an old barracks just behind the Workhouse. They had made it comfortable in their own frugal way. There was no driftwood, so they gathered wood for fires along the river. Contessa had provided them with dried fish and potatoes, as they only ever ate fish and chips, and they had brought their bedding with them. But still they looked longingly toward the sea, and nudged each other when a hungry gull flew overhead.

Wesley was in a bad mood when he got back, but some of the younger children ran out to greet him, and soon he had a group of them sitting round him, as he told them stories about the sea.

His storytelling was interrupted by a loud banging at the door. Wesley frowned.

"I'll have to finish later," he said, to a storm of protest from the children.

He went to the door and opened it. The red-faced lieutenant named Moorhead stood at the door, with a group of soldiers behind her.

"What do you want?" Wesley asked.

"Your tone isn't particularly friendly, young man," the lieutenant said. She had the look of someone who thought that the Raggies needed a firm hand to make them behave more like everyone else.

"You and them ones don't look as if you're here to make friends neither," Wesley said.

"We are here to conduct a search for the missing Yeati ring," the woman said, trying to sound important. "It is considered vital that it is returned in order to treat the injured from tomorrow's attack."

"Is it now?" Wesley said. "Well, I can tell you for nothing, it ain't here."

"My orders are to search."

"Samual don't give orders to the Raggies."

"While you are in the Workhouse, his rules apply."

"He's not even the leader of the Workhouse. Who are you, anyway, to be coming around here giving us orders?"

"Lieutenant Moorhead. Step out of the way, please." Wesley looked around. The brothers Uel and Mervyn were standing behind him. They were tall, quiet boys who didn't like to fight but were dangerous when any Raggie was threatened. They were also very good shots with the magno crossbows they now carried at their sides. Meanwhile Moorhead's soldiers had moved closer to her.

"Hold on a minute . . ." Moorhead's eyes narrowed. With a speed that belied her size she darted past Wesley before he could stop her. Her hand shot out and grabbed a little girl who had been watching from behind the door. She yanked the girl off her feet and pulled her back through the doorway, then held her up in triumph.

"What is this, then?"

Wesley looked. Hanging loosely from the index finger of the girl's small hand was the Yeati's ring!

Wesley knelt down in front of her.

"Where did you get the ring, Hannah?" he said gently.

The little girl looked up at him with big eyes. "I . . . I found it, Wesley."

"Where did you find it?"

"I did find it, Wesley."

"Stole it, more like," one of the soldiers muttered.

"I didn't! I didn't!" The little girl burst into tears and buried her head in Wesley's shoulder.

"Take the child into custody," Moorhead said sharply. Two of the soldiers stepped forward. Uel and Mervyn looked at Wesley. Wesley got to his feet. His face was white.

"The child said she found it," Wesley said. Hannah was sobbing uncontrollably now.

"That will be for the Convoke to decide," Moorhead said. "Take her."

Wesley stepped in front of the girl, but the soldiers were much taller than him.

"Wait." A voice spoke from behind him. He turned around in surprise. Uel had put his crossbow on the ground.

"I took it."

"What?" Wesley looked around, his eyes narrowing.

"I took it and I hid it in my stuff. Hannah must have found it when she was playing."

"Where did you get it?" Wesley said.

"The two of us done it," Mervyn said, stepping forward as well.

"You're not taking any Raggies out of here," Wesley said angrily. "I know what's going on with these two."

Moorhead reached down and snatched the Yeati's ring from the little girl's finger. Her sobbing got louder.

"Hush now," Uel said, putting his hand on Hannah's head. "We know you done nothing wrong."

Gently but insistently the two boys pushed past Wesley. The soldiers seized them.

"Don't fight them, Wesley," Mervyn said. "We don't want Resister fighting Resister."

"I know you two done nothing wrong," Wesley said despairingly.

"Aye, but there's more than one way to skin a cat," Uel said. "This'll have to be got to the bottom of anyway, so why not like this? Calvin," he said, addressing a sleepy-looking boy, "go and fetch Silkie. She can calm down the lass." He gave a meaningful look at Hannah.

"Come on then, you two," Moorhead said, and the soldiers grabbed Uel and Mervyn. Wesley saw Owen running toward them.

" . . . What's going on?"

"They say Uel and Mervyn stole Cati's ring," Wesley told him.

"Don't be stupid," Owen said to Moorhead. "Uel and Mervyn never stole anything in their lives."

"They're coming with me," she stated firmly. Owen moved toward Uel and Mervyn, but they turned and started walking away, followed by the soldiers.

"Wait," Wesley said, putting his hand on Owen's arm. "Uel and Mervyn are right. We got to do this the way they say. First thing is find out how that ring got here."

"You find that out," Owen said. "I'm going to talk to Contessa."

Owen had set out to find Contessa, but the first people he ran into were Samual and Cati.

"Samual got my ring back," Cati said, but she looked confused and worried.

"My instinct was right," Samual said. "Lieutenant Moorhead is escorting the two prisoners to the barracks."

"Mervyn and Uel no more stole the ring than I did," Owen said. Samual gave him a look that said that he thought Owen was well capable of it.

"It's not that I'm not grateful, Samual," Cati said, "but I don't believe it either."

"The two boys have confessed," Samual said. "We can't have thieving going on. We must have discipline in wartime."

"We cannot have summary justice either, especially in wartime," Contessa's cool voice said as she entered the room.

"You can't just let them go!" Samual exploded.

"I did not suggest that," Contessa said. "I was thinking of a trial."

"A trial has not been held for many years," Samual said, watching her closely.

"An accusation of theft has not been made within the walls of the Workhouse either," Contessa said.

"And who will conduct the trial?"

"The tradition is that the accused will be judged by all the Resisters."

"All right," he agreed. "A trial it will be. But with confessions . . ."

"With confessions, a conviction is certain, unless there is other evidence," Contessa said.

"But that's not fair," Cati burst out. "Uel and Mervyn didn't do it."

"That may be, Cati," Contessa said, "but if the two boys say they did it, then it is not up to the court to deem them liars." Her voice was steady but her eyes were sad. There was a barely perceptible smile on Samual's face.

"Let's go, Cati," Owen said. "We have evidence to gather."

Silkie was soon with Hannah. But no matter how gently she quizzed her, she got the same answer. She had found the ring lying on the floor and picked it up because she thought it was pretty. Cati and Owen joined them.

"Why did Uel and Mervyn say they did it?" Cati asked, puzzled.

"Because they are honest," Owen said.

"I don't understand," Cati said.

"They couldn't bear to see Hannah being took off," Wesley explained. "They put the blame on themselves."

"They have to tell them they didn't do it," Cati said.

"They won't do it," Wesley said, "not without new evidence."

"If they do take back the confession," Owen said, "then blame falls back on Hannah. Besides, people will say that they confessed and only took it back to save their skins. We have to find out who *really* took the ring."

"I need to talk to Dr. Diamond," Cati said.

"And Dr. Diamond needs to talk to you," a voice said. They turned to see the scientist standing in the doorway, his face serious.

The four friends and Dr. Diamond found a warm room away from the rest of the children. The doctor had brought fresh oatcakes and a steaming can of tea with him, reckoning, rightly, that the children had forgotten to eat that day.

"And you can't think on an empty stomach," he said. They ate the still-warm oatcakes with melted butter dripping from them, and drank hot, milky tea.

"Now," the doctor said when they had finished, "tell me exactly what happened."

The friends told him everything that had taken place. Sometimes he made them go back over a particular incident several times, and he cross-examined Cati closely about how and when she had returned the ring to its box. In the end, he sighed and sat looking into the fire for several minutes.

"Can you make head or tail of it, Doc?" Wesley said.

"I can, in a way," he said, "and it isn't good. The attack with the ice lances was only a disguise for the real attack."

Owen held his breath, thinking that the Harsh had some strange new weapon, but Dr. Diamond shook his head.

"I know what you are all thinking, but there is nothing new out there for us to fear, I think, apart from a long siege and hunger. No, the real weapon works from within, turning us against each other."

"What do you mean?"

"Look at the theft of the ring, what it has done. Everybody now suspects each other. And there is another part to it. Samual was always ambitious—he wanted to be the Watcher before your father got it, Cati, and now he wants to be leader of us all."

"What has this got to do with the ring?"

"He has a chance to look good in front of the rest of the Resisters by catching the culprits—and the Raggies are associated with Cati and Owen in everyone's minds. It will be a blow against the two of you."

"But surely the Resisters won't vote against the boys," Owen protested.

"They need to find someone to blame. Unless we find something new, then Uel and Mervyn will be judged thieves."

"I can't believe that the Resisters would turn on us Raggies like this," Wesley said angrily.

"Do not be too hard on them," Dr. Diamond said gently. "There is a deadly enemy at their door, and they are scared. Blame whatever clever mind brought this about, and forgive them."

Wesley's look was anything but forgiving. Cati jumped up.

"We need to find that evidence!" she said. Without looking around to see whether the others were following, she dashed out.

"I'll go with her," Wesley said.

Silkie got up and followed him out, but just as she got to the door, she looked at Owen. "You have to do something for them two boys," she said.

"Silkie expects a lot of you," the doctor remarked when she was gone. *As do many people,* he thought. He turned to Owen. "Now, Navigator, I can tell from the look on your face that you have a tale to tell."

"I found something," Owen said, "but I'm not sure what it means." He told Dr. Diamond about the tapestry and the recorder.

"A circletagram!" the doctor exclaimed in delight. "I haven't seen one of those in years."

"What does the message mean?"

"Obviously someone thought of it as being important. I wonder who it was. The fact that the notebook and circletagram were left behind suggests that they were disturbed. The reference to the boy . . ."

"Could they be talking about the Navigator—I mean me?"

"I don't know. Possibly. And what has the Long Woman got to do with it? I have to confess, I know little of her history. I have to think about these things. It doesn't really tell us what to do."

I think it tells me what I have to do, Owen thought, but he kept it to himself. The thought was only half formed. Besides, there was a chance that his friends would try to stop him.

Dr. Diamond went to the window and looked out at the Harsh ships in the distance.

"What are they waiting for?" he mused. "One attack and then silence."

"I don't know," Owen said, "and that makes me afraid."

"We'll meet again," Dr. Diamond said, "after Samual's attack tomorrow."

Owen nodded. Neither of them knew there was going to be no attack on the following day.

16

It was very quiet along the river. Even those small animals who hunted by night were forced by the int cold to stay in their dens. No one was watching Hadima entrance, and no one saw the Albions swa from it, so numerous they were like smoke flowi downward onto the ice, for they were all dressed entir in white to disguise them against the snow. With Agnetl at their head they moved swiftly up the river, gathering i the very shadow of the Workhouse defenses.

Agnetha pointed toward two large trees, whose shadow fell across the river ice. She knew that this area was not as well watched as the others, and it led only to the strong base of the Workhouse. In twos and threes the Albions flitted across the ice and disappeared into the shadow of the trees.

When they had all crossed they followed Agnetha to the base of the wall. She looked up and saw the Resister banner far above, hanging limply in the cold night air, and she bared her teeth and made a hissing sound. Then she made her way along the wall until she found what she was looking for.

The little ironbound door had been there so long that it had been forgotten about. If Agnetha had known or cared, the last person to use it was the person who had studied the tapestry that Owen had seen earlier. And that person had been careful to lock it and drop the key through the little barred window, so that it fell onto the floor.

The key had lain there for many years until that day, when a human hand had lifted it from the stone floor, inserted it, and gently turned it. . . .

Agnetha tried the door. It was old and stiff, but it was unlocked. She stood back as the others streamed in. With a swift look around in the moonlight, Agnetha followed them. The Albions were in the Workhouse.

Once inside they separated into teams, each with a mission. They ran lightly along the unpeopled corridors, deep in the bowels of the Workhouse. They ran through the hall where Owen had studied the tapestry earlier that day. They passed the door of the bakery, where men and women worked to make bread for the following day. They reached the base of the staircase. Agnetha nodded. Each team went its way.

Silkie had taken to sleeping on board the *Wayfarer*. The little beds were comfortable, and she felt that Owen didn't pay enough attention to the boat.

If he won't look after it, then someone better, she thought.

There was a gentle scratching noise on deck, and at first she thought there was a mouse on board. She rolled over, but the scratching continued. She thought she had better see what it was, before the thing ate a hole in her new woodwork.

Wrapping a blanket around her, she sat up and padded barefoot to the hatch. She'd carefully waxed the hatch slides with fresh beeswax from Contessa, and it opened without a sound. Silkie reached for the edge, then froze. Someone was on the deck!

Holding her breath, she stared, trying to penetrate the dark. There were definitely two figures standing at the wheel and looking down at something. *The Mortmain!* she thought. Owen had taken his grandfather's maps to the Den, but he had left the Mortmain.

She was lying across the half-open hatch, and she could feel the living wood of the *Wayfarer* under her. It was almost as if the vessel itself had tensed, knowing that there was something wrong. One of the standing figures straightened and she saw a blade glint. The figure bent forward again. *They're trying to cut the Mortmain out of its setting!* She didn't understand how she could have known this, unless somehow the *Wayfarer* itself had communicated with her. She looked around wildly for a weapon. If she didn't act, they would get away with it. But there was nothing, unless . . .

She pressed her face to the deck, words going through

her head over and over again, whispering to the *Wayfarer,* wondering if somehow the boat would *feel* what she wanted it to do. She could hear splintering sounds coming from the deck now.

Please, she thought. And then it began to happen.

Imperceptibly at first, the *Wayfarer* began to rise in the air. It moved so gently that whoever was on deck was unaware of what was happening, intent as they were on the Mortmain. Then she had another idea. She slipped back down into the cabin.

Up and up the *Wayfarer* went, and still the two at the helm had not noticed. Then there was a muted cry of triumph and one of the Albions held the Mortmain aloft. The cry was followed by a wail of dismay as the Albions realized that they were high in the air.

Silkie, wearing one of the chain-mail suits, slipped out of the hatch while they were distracted. She crept up behind them and grabbed the Mortmain out of the Albion's outstretched hand.

"I'll have that!"

The Albion wheeled with a squeal of rage. Silkie recoiled. She had never seen an Albion before, and its pale skin and pink eyes looked like something from a nightmare. She fell backward, and before she could move, a knife flashed.

She felt the knife strike the mail just below her heart, a blow like a sharp punch, driving the air from her lungs, but not penetrating. She squirmed out of the way as the knife fell again, and scrambled backward up the deck. As the other Albion moved round the stern to attack from the other side, he suddenly pitched over the edge and was gone—Silkie could have sworn that the tiller had moved and had caught him behind the knees, but perhaps he had just tripped.

She didn't have time to think about it. The second Albion was advancing on her, slashing at her face. Round the deck they went, Silkie getting more and more tired. The Albion slashed and struck home. She put her hand up to her face and it was wet with blood, although she had felt nothing. The Albion was grinning. She could see his lips stretched over sharp teeth and bright red gums. She slipped again and this time he stood above her.

Throw it, a voice inside her head said. *The Mortmain— throw it!*

Without thinking she threw the Mortmain with all her strength. It flew past the Albion, who cried out and dived after it. He almost caught it, but his knee struck the rail. He toppled and fell. But Silkie's eyes were on the Mortmain. As it flew through the air it flashed and shone, and then started to describe a curve in the air. It was flying back toward her! She raised her hand and the Mortmain landed with a gentle thud in her palm. She fell back against the hatch and patted the deck beside her. She peered over the edge. Far below she could see the Albion. He had crashed through the ice on top of one of the Workhouse water tanks, and was trying to get out of the freezing water.

"I don't know what's going on," she said out loud,

"but I think you and me better stay up here." Her face burned where it had been cut. She gave the *Wayfarer* another gentle pat and fainted.

Meanwhile, Dr. Diamond was involved in another struggle, and it wasn't going well. He had awoken to the sound of crashing. Leaping out of bed, he ran toward the Skyward. It was full of Albions, who were busy pouring chemicals onto the floor and smashing everything they could lay their hands on. Grabbing a brush in his good arm, the doctor had run into the middle of them. Such was the fury of his attack that they fell back. But soon they realized that they had nothing to fear from a man who wore flannel pajamas with the sun, moon, and stars on them and who carried only a brush for a weapon. They pressed forward.

Dr. Diamond found himself pinned in between two filing cabinets. He managed to keep the Albions at bay with the brush, but the end of the wooden handle was hacked with many knife cuts and was starting to splinter. It must be a strange sight, he thought, the pajama-clad, one-armed man struggling with the Albions in white, moonlight illuminating the ruined lab.

Illumination! Of course! The Albions couldn't stand light. But he couldn't reach any of the switches. He looked up to see that the light fittings had been torn from the ceiling in any event.

The door opened. Rosie!

"Go back, Rosie!" he shouted.

"No way, Doc!" she yelled, fumbling in her hair for a pin. The Albions turned away from the doctor, thinking that the little girl was an easier target, but two of them fell back at once, nursing arms pricked by Rosie's long hairpin.

"Never mind the pin, then. Get on top of the cupboard—the big one!" the doctor cried.

"Not Rosie. She doesn't run from trouble."

"It's not running—it's a plan. Go on, quick!"

With a dubious look at the professor, Rosie jumped onto the sink, and then to the top of the biggest cupboard in the room. The Albions howled at her.

"Shut up," she snapped at them. "Doc, there's hardly room up here for me with all these jars."

"That's the idea. Find sulfate of zilphandium."

Rosie went through the labels of the tall jars stacked on top of the cupboard.

"Got it!" She held up a brown jar.

"Throw it onto the floor."

Rosie threw the jar down. The Albions jeered as it shattered without hitting any of them.

"Now, nectar of polvphanate."

Rosie repeated the process. The yellow polvphanate mixed with the zilphandium. An awful stench rose from the floor.

"Cor, Doc, it don't half pong," Rosie said.

"Quick," the doctor said desperately. The brush handle was getting shorter and shorter. "Throw the xerros oxide into the middle!"

"Stungart phosphate, no . . . dobocybin . . . ," Rosie murmured.

"Rosie," the doctor shouted, sharp blades flashing in front of his face.

"Xerros oxide. Here we go." Rosie tossed another brown jar onto the floor. It struck the other two compounds. The effect was instant. The room was bathed in a burning silver light that made Rosie flinch and put her hands over her eyes. The Albions wailed in pain and terror. The light died away, then pulsed even stronger.

"Blimey," Rosie said. The Albions, blinded, fought with each other to get to the door. The light died and pulsed, died and pulsed again. Screeching, the Albions jostled each other on the winding stair leading down the Nab from the Skyward. It got worse when they got to the bottom. Pieta was leaning casually against the side of the Nab, her magno whip uncoiled in her hand.

"Well," she said, "what do we have here? A bunch of little night rats, by the look of it." The end of the whip licked the air.

The Albions that Contessa and Rutgar discovered in the kitchen fled without putting up a fight. Samual and his men found a group trying to get into the rooftop storehouse where the doctor had put the Porcupine, and drove them off without too much trouble. Martha came across two of them trying to take down the Resister banner, and chased them with the help of some Raggies who had been woken by the commotion. Martha ran to check on the grandfather clock from Mary's house, the clock that was really a doorway into time. She had brought it to the small room assigned to her, hidden away in the upper stories of the Workhouse. It seemed to be intact.

Owen had taken to sleeping in the Den. No matter how cold it got outside, his hideout stayed reasonably warm. He liked to go there in the evening. It gave him a chance to be on his own and to think. He heard nothing of the tumult in the Workhouse. Instead, he woke to low voices just outside the entrance to the Den.

He sat up and slipped out of bed. There was no light in the Den, but some moonlight penetrated through the perspex in the roof. He peered through the bush that hid the entrance. Albions! They had attacked Owen, Dr. Diamond, and Cati on their way to Hadima, and Owen remembered their sharp talons and cruel violet-ringed eyes. But what were they doing here? The sickening realization dawned on him: *The Harsh must have recruited them.*

"Her said it was here," one said.

"Aren't no entrance here," another replied.

"May be you never listened right," the third one growled. He held a knife in his hand.

"Her won't be happy. Her said slit throat and be damned."

Owen felt his blood run cold. If the Albions attacked him in the confined space of the Den, he would not be able to fight them off.

But he had always been careful to disguise the entrance to the Den, and his caution had paid off. He could hear them scuffling around, obviously unable to work out what to do. Then it occurred to him that if the Albions were here, then perhaps they were in the Workhouse as well. His friends were there, and the *Wayfarer*, with the Mortmain still aboard! Suddenly he was desperate to reach the Workhouse. But how was he to get past the three Albions?

He needn't have worried. There was a shrill whistle from the direction of the Workhouse. Without a word, the Albions fled.

Owen left the Den and moved cautiously along the path, as much to avoid being speared by a jumpy sentry as anything else. When he arrived at the Workhouse, it was in an uproar. The Albions had fled into the lower reaches of the Workhouse, pursued by Rutgar, but the Resisters milled everywhere, demanding to know what had happened and how the Albions had got in. Owen saw Wesley in the crowd.

"What happened?" Owen asked.

"Albions got in and wrecked Dr. Diamond's lab. We don't know what else they done." The two boys looked at each other.

"The *Wayfarer*!" Owen said.

"Silkie! She's been sleeping there!"

The *Wayfarer* had drifted back to earth, and they found Silkie lying on the foredeck, a pool of blood gathering beneath her injured cheek. Wesley knelt beside her and felt for a pulse.

"Alive!" he said. Owen felt his knees go weak. He stooped down and brushed her hair away from her face. She opened her eyes and smiled up at him.

"They never got the Mortmain," she whispered. "Me and the *Wayfarer* stopped them."

Wesley made to lift her, but Owen brushed him aside and gathered her into his arms. She seemed to weigh almost nothing as he carried her down to the Convoke hall.

There were many injured in the hall and Cati was moving among them with the Yeati's ring. Most had cuts or stab wounds from the Albion knives, and it soon became clear that many of the blades had been poisoned. It was all that Cati could do to bring some of the injured back. She felt the power of the ring waning.

"You must do something about that wound," Contessa said, looking with concern at the long cut on Silkie's face. "Where is Cati with the ring?"

"No," Silkie insisted, "there are other wounded who need it far more than I do, and there will be more tomorrow. Just put a bandage on it." Wesley tried to insist, but Silkie would hear none of it.

Samual walked among the wounded, giving them encouragement. Owen could sense his popularity among the soldiers. Samual went over to Rutgar and spoke for a moment, then called Owen and Contessa. Wesley and Pieta came as well.

"We need to talk," Samual said shortly. Contessa turned to one of the young Raggies.

"Fetch Dr. Diamond for me."

As soon as they shut the door of a small anteroom behind them, Rutgar whirled around.

"This was a well-planned raid. They knew exactly where they were going, and now there is this!"

He held up the key to the old doorway. Rutgar had followed the fleeing Albions as far as the door, and had locked it behind them.

"This has gone too far," he said. "There is a traitor among us, maybe more than one."

"At least you know that Uel and Mervyn never touched the door, seeing as you have them locked up," Wesley murmured. Samual glared at him.

"What do you propose, Samual?" Contessa asked.

"Military law to start straightaway," Samual said. "No one to move from one part of the Workhouse to another without permission."

"Whose permission?" Pieta said dryly. Before Samual could answer, Dr. Diamond came in. He looked tired.

"What about the Skyward?" Contessa asked.

"They did a lot of damage," the doctor said. "Years of work destroyed. However, if they meant to destroy the Porcupine, they didn't succeed."

"Then I have the worst damage of all to report," Contessa said. "They got into the food stores and have spoiled over two-thirds of our food supply. The Workhouse starts on half rations tomorrow."

"That does it," Samual said. "We start military law tomorrow."

"I don't know, Samual," Contessa said. "The Resisters have always trusted each other and moved freely. It is part of who we are." Dr. Diamond looked troubled.

"We have no choice," Samual growled. "Another night like this one will finish us."

There was silence in the room. No one could disagree.

The attack on the Harsh had been postponed for another day. Most of the soldiers had been up all night and were exhausted. There were reports that at least some of the Harsh had left their ships. Sentries reported white shapes moving in the woods and the town. People were shaken—everywhere the Albions had gone, they had scrawled graffiti, which was almost impossible to wash off.

Wesley and Cati continued their search for the real traitor. They tried to visit Uel and Mervyn, but the guards would not let them. As they were arguing with the guards, they were surprised to see Dr. Diamond coming out of the room where Uel and Mervyn were being held.

"I wanted to talk to them ahead of their trial. To persuade them to change their minds. But they won't."

"Trial?" Wesley said.

"In two days' time."

"Surely Samual would not have done anything to the child, even if she had taken the ring," Cati protested.

"No, I don't think so, although Uel and Mervyn seem to think he would have harmed the girl. But since I can't do anything here, I'm going to have a look at the door where the Albions got in. Will you come with me?"

They went down into the lower reaches of the Workhouse. When they came to the hall of the tapestries, the doctor insisted on studying each one and spent so long on the broken circletagram that they had to drag him away.

They examined the door, but it told them nothing. Wesley and Cati resolved to try to speak to Uel and Mervyn again. Just before they left, Dr. Diamond stooped and picked up something. He slipped it into his pocket before the other two noticed.

They walked back up through the tapestry hall and into the main part of the Workhouse. Dr. Diamond left them to return to the Skyward. Wesley and Cati continued toward the kitchen.

"I'm starving," Cati said. "I hope they haven't started this half rations business yet."

"I don't know if there's anyone in the kitchen fit to say no to you." Wesley smiled.

But they were never to find out. When they got to the kitchen, they found two of Samual's guards posted at the door.

"Kitchen permit," one said stiffly.

"Don't be silly, Marlowe," Cati said. "You don't need a permit to get a snack."

"You do now," the man said, reddening. "Samual's orders."

Cati stared at him. Not all of Samual's men were like their leader, and she had always been fond of Marlowe.

"Please, Cati," the man said. "Don't make trouble." Cati eyed him. Trouble was exactly what she had in mind. But Wesley took her by the arm.

"Come on," he said. "Let's find out what's going on."

It was the same wherever they went. Sentries posted everywhere. Demands for permits. Cati blew her top several times and Wesley had to intervene. They decided to go to see Dr. Diamond, but before they reached the Nab they met Owen coming the other way. His face was grim. They told him what had happened.

"I know," he said. "They've tied up the *Wayfarer!*"

They followed Owen to the *Wayfarer*. A heavy chain had been attached to the anchor point in her bow, and the chain was fastened with a strong padlock to a ring set deep in the stonework of the wall. Cati was outraged.

"I'm going to have it out with Samual right now!"

"No," Owen said, "we've got to be cleverer than that. We need to talk."

"What about Dr. Diamond and Contessa?" Wesley said.

"I think we'd better keep it among ourselves for the time being," Owen said. "Contessa thinks that Samual is tough but fair."

"And the doctor doesn't always tell you what he's thinking," Cati said.

"Exactly. If we need to do something, then we all need to act together," Owen said, "and the fewer people who know about it the better."

"Even your mother?" Cati said.

"Especially my mother," Owen said. "I'm not sure if some part of her wouldn't approve of the *Wayfarer* being tied up. Keeps me out of danger."

"Where do we do this talking, then?" Wesley asked.

"On board the *Wayfarer*," Owen said. "I told Rosie."

They climbed on board the little ship and slid down into the cabin. Cati was surprised to see Silkie there. She was very pale and a large bandage covered one side of her face.

"How's my brave Silkie?" Wesley said.

"No bother, Wesley," Silkie said stoutly, but Cati's heart went out to her. The cut on her face was a serious injury. Cati had tried the Yeati's healing ring on it that morning, but the ring was drained of power and would take time to regain its strength. By then it would be too late. There seemed to be some quality to the Albions' blades that made the wounds resistant to the ring's power after a while. Cati feared that Silkie would be left with a scar for life.

They had just settled down around the little table when there came a knock on the hatch, and Rosie's head poked through.

"What's up?" she said cheerfully.

"Come in and sit down," Cati said, "before some oaf of a soldier stands guard on the hatch."

"They're all over the place," Rosie said. "But they weren't up to old Rosie. I got plenty of practice avoiding the Specials. Hadima police," she went on, in response to a questioning look from Wesley. "Not a very nice lot."

She reached into a pocket and produced a handful of still-warm biscuits.

"Where did you get those?" Wesley wanted to know.

"Er, borrowed them from the kitchen," Rosie replied.

"No more of that, Rosie," Owen said. "Food is short for everyone."

"Of course, of course," Rosie said, sharing out the biscuits, her face a picture of innocence.

"So what's the plan, then?" Cati said.

"Plain as the nose on your face that we can't just sit here," Wesley said. "The weather's getting colder and food is short. They'll starve us out in no time."

"But I can't see Samual's attack getting anywhere," Cati said.

"No," Owen said, "particularly if he's using his soldiers to stop people getting about the place."

"So what do we do," Wesley said gloomily. "Throw snowballs at them?"

"No," Owen said, "we're not going to stop the Harsh by force. We have to find out where they get their power from. If we don't, then they'll keep coming back. I mean, who are they? They must have come from somewhere. Maybe my dad had figured it out before he . ... before he died."

It was the first time Cati had heard him speak about his father like that. She leaned over to put her hand on his. But Silkie's hand was already there.

"How do we find out?" Wesley asked.

"I've got some clues," Owen said, thinking that the snatches of song he had heard and the crumbling tapestry didn't really amount to clues. "Enough to tell me the person to ask: the Long Woman. I'm sure that she's part of the solution."

Cati looked at him with a raised eyebrow. But Wesley was more thoughtful.

"The Raggies hear tell that the Long Woman is very old, maybe as old as the Harsh. You might have the right of it, Owen. She might know something to help us."

"But the *Wayfarer* is tied up," Cati said, "with a chain and lock—" She stopped. Rosie was examining her fingernails modestly. When it came to locks, there weren't many that Rosie couldn't pick.

"Even so," Cati went on, not knowing why she felt she had to object, "you don't know enough about time, about the maps . . ."

"I think what the lass is saying is that the people's fond of the Navigator," Wesley said. "Everything's gone strange and the Harsh is at the door, and if you're not here, who's to stand up for the rest of us?"

"As long as these walls stand," Owen said, "the Harsh

will not take the Workhouse. You and Cati and all the rest have to make sure that the Resisters are not beaten from within. I have to do—"

"You're not going on your own," a small voice said. They looked around. Silkie was standing up. And although her fists were clenched, her face was still pale and bandaged.

"Don't look at me like that," she said angrily. "I'm hurt but I'm not asking for pity. The *Wayfarer* listens to me, and I know how to handle her and how to fix her. She'll sail for me, I know. How is Owen going to sleep or rest or fix her when she goes wrong when he doesn't know nothing about boats?"

"I don't know, Silkie," Wesley said. "You're bad enough hurt, and you don't know what's out there or anything—"

"If the Raggies can spare her," Owen cut across Wesley, "Silkie is the best person I could hope to have with me."

Silkie stood proud and tall and her eyes flashed. She reached up with her right hand, took hold of the dressing on her face, ripped it off, and flung it to the floor. The gash on her cheek looked angry and swollen.

Rosie made a sound.

"What?" Silkie turned on her.

"Nothing," Rosie said, "I didn't mean nothing. I thought I saw . . . on your face . . . a rose . . ." She rubbed her eyes, looking confused.

"Well?" Silkie said, turning to Wesley.

"If Owen thinks you're the right one, then I won't stand in the way."

Silkie grinned. Owen and Cati cheered. Only Wesley noticed that Rosie wasn't joining in.

The attack on the Harsh was to take place at dawn on the following day. All evening there was the sound of weapons being prepared and of soldiers practicing drills. Owen moved about the Workhouse as best he could, in spite of Samual's guards. The soldiers were on extra rations and he helped Contessa serve the men and women. Some of them shook his hand. Others asked him what they might expect from the Harsh, but he had no answers.

Cati slipped past several lots of guards to get to the Skyward. Dr. Diamond was working at his desk. He had cleaned up some of the mess as best he could with his broken arm, but the Albions had done a lot of damage as well as scrawled their graffiti everywhere. When she came in, he stood up with a smile, but she thought he looked tired and worried.

"What are you working on?" Cati asked.

"It was supposed to be a helmet that the soldiers could wear to protect them from the Harsh breath, but the Albions destroyed the original plans and the model that I built."

"Why is Samual attacking them?" Cati burst out. "They're far too powerful. He'll be wiped out."

"Samual is difficult, but he isn't stupid," the doctor said. "Think about the Harsh attacks. They can use their lances and Harsh breath and the cold itself against us, but they have always had men and women to do their fighting for them."

"Where do these people come from?" Cati asked.

"Time is full of strange people. There are wanderers, mercenaries—bands of fighters for hire. Samual is hoping that he can target the Harsh ships and damage them. He also hopes to deliver a victory to give heart to the Resisters."

"He's trying to take over, isn't he?"

"Samual is doing what he thinks best. If we don't agree, then we have to show him that he is wrong. After the damage the Albions did, a lot of people agree with him."

"But blaming the Raggies—that's not fair!"

"No, it isn't, but people will always point at somebody different when things go wrong. It's the way the world is. Now, I have something for you." He held out a card.

"What's that—a pass?" Cati asked.

Dr. Diamond smiled wearily. "Yes. Samual is doling them out to a selected few. Contessa is setting up a field hospital in the Convoke hall. If there is any power left in the Yeati's ring, then that is where you will be needed. I persuaded him to give you one. It took a lot of persuading."

Cati went back to her quarters. She sat on the bed and thought for a while. It was almost two o'clock in the morning, but she could not sleep. She took out the pass that the doctor had given her, almost of a mind to tear it up. The words on it read: *The bearer and all who accompany her are entitled to access to the Convoke hall.*

Wish it could get me into the kitchen, she thought, idly

rubbing her thumb across the words. She was about to put it away, but something on it caught her eye. Instead of saying *Convoke hall*, it now said *kitchen*. Amazed, she tried it again. This time she rubbed her thumb over it and thought of the Starry, and the word changed to *Starry*. Dr. Diamond had given her a pass that would get her anywhere!

Thanks, Doc, she thought, and then realized something: if the doctor had given her a pass, then he intended for her to use it. She opened the locked drawer where she kept the few treasures she owned, including the cornflower brooch that had belonged to her mother. Taking up the length of the box was a magno gun and a belt of the bulbs of magno that it fired. She strapped the belt around her waist and slung the gun over her shoulder. She stood up, her tiredness lifted. She was the Watcher, and there wasn't going to be any fight unless she was in it. She closed the box, then changed her mind. She opened it again, took out her mother's brooch, and pinned it carefully to her tunic. It was time to face the Harsh.

She walked down the corridor, but didn't get far before a strong hand grasped her shoulder. She gasped. She was jumpier than she thought—it was Wesley. His shrewd eyes took in the magno gun and the brooch.

"Oh no you don't," he said, "not on your own."

"Then come with me," she said, knowing it was useless to argue with Wesley. He looked at her for a long time.

"You know," he said, "I've a mind to see a real battle."

"I can get us through the checkpoints," Cati said eagerly.

"Then what are we waiting for?"

Cati had no trouble with the sentries. They all knew her, and most of them had known her father. Wesley drew a few looks and there were mutterings behind him, but he ignored them.

Outside it was still dark and bitterly cold. Campfires were not allowed, so men and women huddled in trenches and tried to keep warm with the constant stream of hot drinks sent from the kitchen by Contessa. Cati spied Rutgar pacing at the head of his troops.

"Don't let him see us," she hissed. "He'll only send us back."

In the distance they could see the mast tops of the Harsh ships, but, unlike the previous night, there was no sign of the Harsh in the town or in the trees.

Half an hour before dawn, just when they thought they could bear the cold no longer, the Resister banner was raised at the front of the army. Men and women rose to their feet and fanned out along the river. The whispered order was given, and the Resisters began to move out.

High above them on the battlements, Owen watched them go, shadowy figures against the snow. His heart misgave him. There were so few of them. It was too far away to see Wesley and Cati, or he would have been even more worried. He went down the stone stairs toward the Convoke hall and the kitchen. As he took the last step he saw a small dark figure move swiftly down a side corridor and disappear. He quickly followed.

The corridor led toward the dank basements that lay in the damp ground alongside the river. Owen felt ice crackling under his feet, and could barely make out where he was going. But he heard footsteps ahead of him: a faint clack of high heels on the stone floor. He recognized the sound, and wished he didn't. What was Rosie doing here at this time of night?

The corridor opened out into a disused laundry. Rows of stone tanks and pipework ran across the ceiling. There were only a few tarnished magno lights in the laundry, and the light was very dim. Somewhere water dripped onto a stone surface, drop by drop. The footsteps had stopped. Owen crept forward, then froze in his tracks. The room filled with sound—an eerie, moaning, echoing noise in which he thought he could make out words, or at least sounds that might once have been words. The noise stopped as abruptly as it had begun, and he heard Rosie talking, her voice quick and urgent, but too low for him to make out what she was saying. Rosie stopped and the moaning noise started again. Forcing his feet to move, he crept forward. He rounded the end of one of the mangles to see Rosie crouched on the floor beside a large pipe. The sound was coming from the end of the pipe!

Owen watched, holding his breath. The sound stopped, and Rosie put her mouth to the end of the pipe.

She was using the pipe to communicate in secret with someone elsewhere in the Workhouse!

He inched forward, trying to hear but her mouth was too close to the pipe. She gave a furtive look around, spoke once more into the pipe, then stood up and walked back toward Owen. He pressed himself against the machine as Rosie passed him, close enough to touch. Owen waited five minutes, then followed. As he reached the top of the staircase he could hear a commotion—the unconscious sentry had been found. There was no sign of Rosie, but a window to the outside lay open. Owen climbed onto the windowsill and slipped through. Footprints led away outside—the footprints of someone with a dainty foot, wearing shoes that weren't meant for snow.

The small Resister army led by Samual and Rutgar advanced across the snow, the first cold light of day in the eastern sky. Behind them came teams of men pushing magno cannons on sleighs. And behind that was a large sleigh with the Porcupine mounted on it. Alongside the Porcupine, Pieta strode easily. She had always fought on her own, but this time she was not alone. On either shoulder walked her children, Aldra and Beck, tall and silent and each carrying a magno whip. At the very rear Wesley and Cati moved stealthily, still afraid that someone would see them and send them back.

There was no sign of the Harsh when they reached the outskirts of the town. Here and there a roof had collapsed from the weight of the snow. The Resister soldiers spread out and moved cautiously, checking empty buildings one by one and covering each other as they went forward.

"This is spooky," Cati whispered. The buildings hid

the harbor from view, and beyond the harbor, the Harsh fleet.

"I just thought of something," Wesley said.

"What's that?"

"The Hadima entrance. Somebody needs to check it out. The Albions came through it."

"It's daylight," Cati said. "The Albions can't stand the light."

"Who says the Albions are the only people that side of the entrance that don't like the Resisters?"

He was right. But Rutgar and Samual were far ahead and probably would not have appreciated the advice anyway.

"We'll go as far as the harbor and cut back," Cati said. "We'll have a look at it then."

On they went, through the deserted town. From one of the buildings, a thin dog ran. One of Rutgar's men tried to call it, but the dog ran away, howling in despair. "Harsh must have got to it," one of the soldiers murmured.

The sky was heavy with snow and strange mists rose every few hundred yards, obscuring their progress. At last they emerged onto the harbor road and crested the rise above the harbor. They stopped, awestruck. Not only were the Harsh ships moored on the ice in their dozens, each one looking bigger than the Workhouse, but beside each had been built a ice mansion.

"Igloo," Cati breathed as she and Wesley caught up with the leaders.

"Some igloos," Wesley said. The mansions were the domed shape of proper igloos, but there were many windows and great doors of ice.

"Set up the magno cannons along the ridge," Rutgar said. "They are not expecting us."

"All snoring in their beds, I expect," one soldier snorted as they hastened to do as they had been told.

But the Harsh were not snoring in their beds.

"Look." Rutgar pointed to the windows of the giant igloos, where they could now see the barrels of ice cannons.

"Not houses," Samual said, "castles."

"But why don't they fire?" Rutgar said.

"I don't know," Samual said, "but it's time we got dug in along the ridge. We can mount sorties from there."

"Now is our chance," Wesley said. He pointed toward the river and the Hadima entrance, but Cati could see his eyes were drawn toward his old home in the warehouse.

"We'll look at the warehouse afterward," she said, patting him on the knee.

Back at the Workhouse, Owen stood with Martha on the battlements. They were each consumed with a feeling of foreboding.

"I've been checking radio stations for the past twenty-four hours," Martha said. "People around the world are still broadcasting, but the signals are getting weaker. I think the Resisters are the only people who understand what is happening."

"Did . . . did my dad know that this was coming?"

"I don't know. The Harsh seem to have always been a threat, but never as bad as this. You know, there are people who say he made the whole thing worse. He opened the gate to Hadima."

"The Resisters closed it, then I opened it again—is that what they're saying?" Owen said bitterly.

"Yes, Owen, it is what they are saying."

"But if I hadn't, the world would have been destroyed last time!" Owen burst out.

"People forget," Martha said. "You can't just do a good thing and leave it at that. You have to keep meeting each bad thing as it comes along."

Owen stared moodily out over the river. The wind blew his hair back, and Martha saw as if for the first time how like his father he was: the strong line of his jaw, the steady unblinking gaze. And yet he was different from his father. Not as impulsive, nor as secretive.

"Did my dad ever say anything about the Harsh? I mean, I get the feeling that he was in a hurry on his way back from Hadima to here. There must have been a reason why he was rushing."

"No, not that I can think of," Martha said, "but I was frozen with the Harsh breath. I may have forgotten. There was something he said a few times that was strange. It just didn't seem like him, if you know what I mean."

"What was it?"

"He said that it's the child in us that is the most dangerous."

"The child? Why would a child be dangerous?"

"I don't know."

There was a great crash from the direction of the harbor, and the air above the town filled with white mist.

"It has begun," Martha said.

"I have to go!" Owen said. "There's no time to waste!"

"No!" Martha said. "Do you still not realize that the Navigator is the great hope of the Resisters? They look up to you. If they saw you fleeing in the *Wayfarer* during the battle, it would crush them."

"I wouldn't be fleeing," Owen protested.

"I know that," Martha said, "but they might not."

"I don't want to be looked up to that way," Owen said unhappily.

"Responsibility ends up on people's shoulders whether they want it or not," Martha said, putting her hand on his shoulder.

Down at the harbor, the barrage from the Harsh had come without warning. The soldiers were busy digging foxholes when the gun ports of the ships fell open and the ice cannons were run out. At the same time, Cati could see the gun barrels in the ice castles elevate as if they were being aimed.

"Get down," Samual shouted. Cati and Wesley threw themselves full length on the ground as the ice cannons roared. The Porcupine spun wildly, shooting the ice lances from the air, but there were too many this time.

The lances smashed into the snowy earth around them. Once again there was a volley, and Cati pressed her face to the ground as the lances whistled overhead.

"Bring our cannons to bear," Samual ordered, his voice calm. Cati risked a look upward. Soldiers worked around the magno cannons, heedless of the deadly hail that fell on them. Another volley—this time Cati thought they were targeting the Porcupine. One by one jets of steam roared from the Porcupine, and each time a lance dissolved. But then the Porcupine coughed and stopped.

"It's sucked snow into the intake," a soldier shouted. "Clear it!" But there was no time. An ice lance flew higher than the rest, soaring over the harbor, then dropped, gathering speed as it did. Helpless to do anything, Cati and Wesley watched it head straight for the strange weapon.

"We're rullocked without that Porcupine," Wesley murmured. The men tending it threw themselves aside. It was then that Cati saw Pieta, standing parallel to the Porcupine, the magno whip swinging lazily in her hand. She drew her arm back and lashed upward with all her force. The whip struck the side of the lance, and shards of ice crackled in the air as the whip drove the lance sideways, by inches only, but enough. There was a heavy thud, and the lance stood quivering in the ground beside the Porcupine.

"Fire all guns," Samual shouted. Blue flame shot forth. The rigging of the lead ship blazed up momentarily but the fire was soon quenched. A turret of one of the ice houses tumbled to the ground. The Porcupine spluttered back into life, just in time to meet a new shower of ice.

The sleds that had been in the rear were brought up, and the tarpaulins thrown back. Cati wasn't close enough to see clearly, but each carried a few dozen gray objects, stacked one above the other, and tilted toward a chute at the back. As she watched, a soldier stepped forward with a magno torch. He pulled a lever and one of the objects shot toward the chute. As it left the end of the chute, he struck it hard with the magno torch and it burst into blue flame. The device scuttled off across the snow looking like a fiery mouse with a long piece of heavy electrical cord hanging from the back like a tail.

"The mouse! The mouse!" The cheer went up from the soldiers as it hit the frozen surface of the sea and built up speed, careening toward the Harsh ships. It changed direction every few seconds, like a mouse desperately trying to escape a cat. The Harsh cannons began to fire, but the mouse was moving too fast and erratically for them to hit it. It had to strike a ship eventually, and when it did a sheet of blue flame roared up the side of the stricken vessel.

Another was released, and then another. Soon the ice was covered with them, and three ships were ablaze. Through the smoke the Resisters could see the ghostly shapes of the Harsh crew escaping across the ice. The Resisters reserved a special cheer for the moment when a Harsh ice lance, seeking a mouse, was fired right through one side of a Harsh ship and out the other side.

"Time to go," Cati said. The two friends slipped off

when everyone's attention was on the Harsh fleet. They ran back toward the center of the town, made for the bridge, swung over the parapet, and climbed down onto the frozen river. They rounded the corner and halted.

"I don't like the look of this," Cati said.

19

The Hadima entrance had been totally transformed. Before, it had been a simple hole in the wall, high above the ground, looking more like a drain than anything else. Now there were steps leading to the river, and it was fortified at ground level. But more disturbing than that was the fact that, lined along the river bank were what seemed like hundreds of armed men wearing a uniform that Cati recognized.

"Specials!" Cati hissed, ducking behind a low wall. "How did they get here?"

"Specials?" Wesley crouched beside her.

"They're the police in the City of Time—Hadima. Everybody hates them. But how did they get here, and what are they doing?"

"By the look of it," Wesley said, "they're about to attack the Resisters from behind. Our lot won't know what hit them. They'll be cut to ribbons!"

As he spoke, the first wave of Specials began to climb the riverbank. In Hadima they carried whistles and blew them as they went, to put fear into the inhabitants. But now they moved in silence. Cati looked up at the entrance and her blood ran cold. Two men stood there. One was the chief corsair and leader of the Specials, Headley, a smile on his cruel face. The other was Johnston. Somehow he had got to Hadima and recruited the Specials. The Harsh needed an army of men to complete their siege on the Workhouse, and here they were!

"What do we do?" Cati said, desperation in her voice.

"Run!" Wesley said. "Run like the wind!" They leapt to their feet, not caring who saw them, and scrambled back over the bridge. Downstream the Specials were swarming into the street. Cati and Wesley put their heads down and ran. Behind them they heard booted feet.

Cati pulled ahead of Wesley, but the Raggie boy had more stamina and he caught her at the edge of town. They could no longer hear footsteps behind them, but that didn't mean the Specials would be far behind.

"Faster!" Wesley cried. They could see the battle up ahead, smoke rising from the burning ships and ice particles flung high into the air. They reached the rear positions of the Resisters.

"The enemy . . . ," Cati gasped, "behind . . ." But she was out of breath and the Resisters were too caught up in their own battle to react to her. She seized one of the magno cannons and tried to turn it, but it was heavier than she could handle.

"Hey, what do you think you're doing?" It was Moorhead, Samual's lieutenant. "What is this," she bawled, "more sabotage?"

Cati felt like kicking the woman, but Wesley grabbed her arm.

"Pieta . . . we need Pieta."

The Raggie and the Resister ran headlong into the middle of the battle. A sortie of Resisters had got onto the ice but had been beaten back by ice lances. The flaming mice still scuttled on the frozen surface, but they were less effective against the ships further out.

Pieta and her children stood at the front line, using their whips to protect groups of Resisters from the ice lances. Wesley and Cati dashed up to her.

"Pieta," Cati called. "Come!"

"What is it?" Pieta said. "Quick!"

"Specials," Cati said, "attacking from the rear."

"Men from Hadima," Wesley put in. "We're not joking. The Resisters are finished if them Specials get in among them."

Pieta didn't hesitate. "Aldra, Beck, follow me."

Mother and children sprinted toward the town. As she went Pieta called to men and women. *She knows her fighters,* Cati thought, as each person followed her without hesitation.

It was almost too late. The Specials were in among the wounded who had been carried to safety. Those who tended them were trying to fight, but the Specials clubbed them viciously to the ground. Many of the

Specials carried heavy crossbows, tipped with a variety of ugly-looking bolts and explosive devices.

But they were not prepared for the onslaught of Pieta and her small band. With angry cries they were beaten back while still more swarmed up from the town. Pieta kept the area in front of her clear with great sweeps of her whip, while Aldra and Beck used their whips to concentrate on the crossbow bolts and other missiles. The Specials threatened to sweep around them, but other Resisters were now turning to the threat to their rear.

Soon, desperate battles were going on, the Resisters struggling hand to hand with the Specials. There were no more mice, and ice lances were raining down, far more than the Porcupine could cope with.

"Fall back," Samual shouted, downing a Special with the hilt of his sword. "Fall back to the Workhouse!"

The Resisters manning the magno cannons had to abandon them.

"The Porcupine," Rutgar yelled, "to the Porcupine!" He and his men formed a phalanx around the device and started to haul it back toward the Workhouse.

Cati had stayed behind the soldiers, helping with the wounded, while Wesley fired her magno gun, until the barrel was too hot to touch. She looked up through the heat and smoke of battle. Someone was staring at her, eyes narrow with hatred. Not twenty yards away stood Headley, the chief corsair.

Headley pushed toward her, knocking Resisters out of his way as if they weren't there. Cati ran backward but tripped over a shattered magno gun and went sprawling onto her back. Headley looked neither right nor left. A fragment of an exploding crossbow bolt left a gash in his forehead, but heedless of the blood, he pressed on. Only Pieta saw what was happening. Calling her children, Pieta sprang in front of the corsair, the long whips driving him back. With a snarl Headley seized a crossbow from his back and leveled it at the fallen Cati. Just as he did so an ice lance landed beside Pieta, and she staggered sideways. In one swift movement Headley aimed, cocked, and fired the bow. A deadly exploding bolt flew toward Cati, aimed at her heart. In desperation Pieta threw out the hand that held the whip, attempting to block it. She was off balance, and the blue flame of her whip did not fly true. The bolt glanced off it and exploded close to Pieta. Cati was saved, but Pieta was down, the snow beneath her stained red.

The retreat to the Workhouse was a nightmare, the Resisters under constant attack. Aldra and Beck carried their mother but in the end had to hand her over to others, and fought with a fury that none could resist. But they were only two. Samual fought bravely, many times going to the rescue of stragglers.

"Stay together," he urged, "fight for each other, don't run!" But Rutgar pointed to the figure of Owen standing on the Workhouse roof under the black banner of the Resisters.

"The Navigator! The Workhouse and the Navigator!"

The Resisters looked up, saw Owen, and fought with fresh heart.

It took them more than an hour to cover the ground between the town and the Workhouse, every inch fought over. Even close to the defenses, the harassment did not stop, and it looked as if they might fall within sight of home. Then a shout rang out. Dr. Diamond charged from the gate, leading a motley assortment of kitchen staff with knives and gardeners wielding hoes and spades. From the battlements Owen, Martha, and the Raggie children rained magno bolts on the attackers, and when they ran out, threw the very stones of the battlements onto them. Given fresh energy by the sight of the workers coming to their rescue, the Resisters turned on their attackers and drove them back. The small figure of Rosie darted among them, pricking the attackers in the legs with a hairpin. In the end, despite Headley's curses and threats, the Specials broke and ran.

The Resisters had fought their way home, but at a terrible cost.

20

Weary beyond measure, the Resisters threw themselves where they could. Those with minor hurts had to tend to themselves, for there were many with grievous injuries. Contessa worked calmly for many hours, Cati beside her, painfully aware that the ring had never been given a chance to recover its full power. Several times Cati had asked after Pieta, but Contessa had merely shaken her head.

Owen met Rutgar, who had put his exhausted men back on duty and was now looking for food for them.

"It's not good," Rutgar growled. "More than half of our fighting men are injured. And we've lost a good part of our magno cannons."

"What about Pieta?" Owen asked. Rutgar shook his head and ran his hand through his graying hair.

"She'll live, they reckon, but she may not fight again. She has lost her right hand."

Owen looked stricken. He could not imagine Pieta

without the whip flickering restlessly in her hand. And the Workhouse needed her!

"It's a bad day," Rutgar said. "We can't afford to do that again. I reckon they knew we were coming. The Specials were going to take us in the rear. If Cati and Wesley hadn't spotted them, we wouldn't have stood a chance."

But that was not the way that others saw it. Hours later Owen heard Samual in the Convoke hall, encouraging his soldiers and claiming a victory.

"We burned six ships," he said, "and we showed the Harsh that we haven't bowed the knee to them."

Yes, but we have lost over half of our fighting power, Owen thought. He felt torn: anxious to be gone in his search for the Long Woman, and reluctant to leave the weary and frightened Resisters. He could see how their eyes followed him as he passed. He felt like crying out, *I'm not the one. I don't know how to save you!*

Then Wesley was beside him, talking urgently. He'd overheard Moorhead talking to another soldier, and related the conversation.

"We could have beaten the Harsh for good if that Navigator hadn't opened the Hadima entrance. First the Albions came through it, and now these Specials. We would be free now if it wasn't for him and his Raggie friends," she had said, spitting out the word *Raggie*.

The next words made Wesley's blood run cold.

The other soldier said, "Every time he goes off in that boat of his, he brings more trouble."

"That's true," Moorhead said, her eyes shining.

"If somebody put a flame to it, then he wouldn't go nowhere, would he?"

Owen looked at Wesley. That settled it. He wasn't going to leave the *Wayfarer* to the mercy of resentful soldiers. "There's something else," Owen said.

"What?"

Quickly he told Wesley about Rosie and the pipe. Then a cry rose from the battlements. Owen and Wesley raced up the stairs to find Dr. Diamond at the parapet.

"What's going on out there, anyway?" Wesley said, peering into the darkness. Torches were approaching across the fields.

Dr. Diamond narrowed his eyes. "Johnston," he said shortly.

Soon they could all see that it was indeed Johnston, surrounded by Specials. Johnston stopped just out of bow range.

"Good evening, Resisters," he boomed. "That was a fine skirmish today, excellent. Most refreshing. I have to say you singed a few of the Harsh. They're in a right old snit about it. You know what the Harsh are like—no sense of humor."

"What do you want, Johnston?" a voice called from the trenches.

"Sorry about going on," Johnston said, not one bit sorry. "I know you must all be tired. And maybe a little bit hungry as well? I won't detain you. The Harsh are only here for one thing. A wrong has been done to them and they want to right it. Most reasonable, I think." He lowered his voice confidentially. "And we all know that

the Harsh can be *verrry* unreasonable." He resumed his normal tone. "As I say, they only want one thing: justice. They want to put the killer of their king on trial in their own court. Hand him over, and they hand you back the world. Simple as that. If you don't hand him over, then I'm afraid we'll have to starve you out. It won't take very long." He chuckled. "I hear the Albions did some very naughty things in your food stores. No morals, those Albions—you can't do a thing with them."

Still laughing to himself, Johnston turned away, then, as if he'd forgotten something, turned back.

"By the way, I hate to sound like a bad film, but of course you have forty-eight hours to consider the offer. No, I take that back. I actually *like* sounding like a bad film. Sleep tight!"

Shaking his head and smiling to himself, Johnston walked off into the night.

Owen was white-faced.

"The dog," Wesley said. They could hear a murmur rising from the troops in the trenches below.

"He has caught them at a low point," Dr. Diamond said. "He is very clever."

Owen looked over the battlements. Moorhead was moving among the soldiers. She spoke to a group of them, and afterward they turned resentful faces toward the battlements. There was a noise behind them. It was Samual. Ignoring Owen, he walked to the battlements and stared down at his men.

"You know what they are saying, of course?" Samual spoke without looking at Owen or the others.

"That I should surrender to the Harsh? That the Workhouse would be saved?"

"Yes."

Wesley made a disgusted noise and spat on the ground.

"But the Workhouse wouldn't be saved," Owen said, "would it, Samual? They would not spare it, even if I did surrender to them. If I thought that I could save everyone, I would give myself up to Johnston now."

"And if I thought that by sacrificing you I could save the Workhouse, then I'd throw you over the battlements myself," Samual snarled, spinning round to face them. "You're right. The Harsh won't stop at that. But stay out of my way, boy, or I'll hand you over anyway!"

Samual strode across the roof and down the stairs.

Wesley was livid. "Don't that man know what you done for this place?"

"I don't think he really understands," Dr. Diamond said. "He has a soldier's mind."

"It's time to set sail," Owen said, "long past time."

"I agree," another voice said. It was Martha. "I only said that you should wait until the soldiers had returned safely."

"One minute the Resisters are looking up to me, the next they're blaming me for everything. Which is it?" Owen said in despair.

"I didn't say to expect gratitude, did I?" his mother said gently, embracing him. "Go now, and bring back hope."

So it was that the five friends met on the deck of the *Wayfarer*. The air was thick with smoke from the burning

200

town, and the sky was red from the flames. It felt like they stood at the end of the world. Without a word Cati put her arms around Owen. Wesley stood back, but Silkie took his hands.

"Don't be daft, Wesley," she said, "give us a hug." Rosie grabbed Owen and gave him a bear hug, the top of her hat just reaching to his nose.

"Take care of yourself, Navigator," she said, looking playfully into his face. He wondered what secret was concealed behind those eyes.

They were silent for a moment. None of them needed to be told of the danger the Workhouse was in. They were only at the beginning of a siege by a deadly enemy, and already they were exhausted and short of food, with beds full of wounded. If that was not enough, the Resisters were rent by suspicion and mistrust and were about to embark on Uel and Mervyn's trial. If Owen succeeded in his mission, would there be a Workhouse to come back to?

Reluctant now that it came to parting, Owen stood at the helm. Rosie climbed up to the padlock and, feeling in her hair for a pin, had it open within seconds. Cati, Wesley, and Rosie stood in silence as the *Wayfarer* rose slowly through the smoke and then, with one last wave from Silkie and Owen, was gone. Cati felt tears on her face. Wesley put an arm around her shoulders, a warmth in the gesture that she hadn't felt from him before. She did not pull away.

"See you soon, Navigator," she murmured, but no answer came from the dark and smoke-filled sky.

From high above the Workhouse, Owen could see how bad things were. The silhouette of the Harsh fleet stretched to the horizon. The Hadima entrance teemed with men, their campfires fanning out in a semicircle facing the Workhouse. Fires smoldered in the ruins of the town, and the Workhouse rose from the smoke, still proud, but isolated, surrounded by enemies. And all around for miles, the world was white and frozen.

"Let's get the sail up," he said. "No time to waste. We have to find the Long Woman."

Silkie clambered onto the foredeck and loosened the ties that held the sail. More like shimmering air than cloth, the sail opened out in front of them. The scene below became misty and hard to see, and then it was gone. They were sailing on time.

Once he had seen that everything was going well, Owen lashed the tiller and went below. Cati had

done well on the food front. There were biscuits and hard bread, which would last for a long time. There was a full cheese and a side of ham, dried fruit, and pickles. There were even tea bags and a box of Dr. Diamond's buns.

They brought the food out onto the deck and ate together.

"I've never seen anything so beautiful," Silkie said as the northern lights shimmered around them. Owen flinched as the *Wayfarer* dipped her bow and a shard of icy spume stung his cheek.

"We need to get into the suits," Owen said. Silkie, looking about her in wonder, did not reply.

"Silkie," he said gently.

"Yes . . . I'm coming," she said. As she rose to go down below, he saw the scar on the side of her face, and his heart filled with pity for her.

After they got the suits on, Owen, to Silkie's delight, gave her the helm. The *Wayfarer* was sailing well, and there were no waves to think of. Carefully he lined up the symbol for the Workhouse on the outer ring of the Mortmain with the symbol for the Long Woman on the next ring. Each ring enclosed a smaller one, and as they got smaller they moved more, so the inner ones danced and twinkled.

Owen took the charts down into the cabin and spread them out on the table. It would seem that all he had to do was line up the Workhouse and the sign for the Long Woman on the Mortmain, but he felt uneasy: his instinct for direction told him there was more to it than that. On

the map there was a dark, shaded area between the symbols, and to either side red shading. What did it mean? At the bottom of the map he saw something he had never noticed before, it was so faded. A single word: *Legend.*

He knew from school that a legend was the part of the map that told you what the symbols and lines on the map actually meant. But below it was a jagged tear—the legend had been lost. Owen stared at the map for what seemed like hours, his eyes growing wearier and wearier. He had not slept the night before, and before he knew it, his eyes were closed.

He awakened to Silkie shaking him by the shoulders.

"Owen, wake up! Wake up!" He sat up. The *Wayfarer* was no longer gliding along, but rising and falling in great shuddering leaps. Owen got to his feet groggily and was thrown back against the cabin wall.

"It just started all of a sudden!" Silkie said. Owen pulled on his chain mail visor and climbed out through the hatch. The scene before him could not be more different from the one he had left. Angry and confused wave crests towered over them no matter which way he looked. Green lightning crackled on wave edges. The sky above them was black, streaked with ominous red. *Black and red,* Owen thought, *like on the map!*

He grabbed the helm, noting that Silkie had had the sense to lash it before she came below to wake him. He wrenched the helm around to guide them toward what looked like a calmer patch. Even with the visor on, he could see the fear in Silkie's eyes.

"It's all right," he shouted. "I've been in time storms before. The *Wayfarer* can handle it!"

But he had never been in a storm like this one. The cold was bitter. The waves were monstrous, and the storm shifted direction constantly, so every time Owen got the bow pointed into the storm, it came at him from another direction. Time and again the *Wayfarer* went over until it seemed that she would never come back, yet on she went. Owen sent Silkie below to get food, but all she could put together were some dry biscuits. The wind of time shrieked in the rigging. Owen had shortened the sail as much as he dared, but he could feel that the feisty little craft was at her limit, and there seemed to be no end to the storm. He touched the mast and felt it vibrate. Then with a loud twang, one of the stays holding the mast parted. Silkie looked at Owen, real terror in her face now.

"Take the helm," he shouted, thrusting the tiller into her hand so that she couldn't refuse. He dived into the cabin and grabbed the map he had been looking at earlier. He scanned it for the nearest place they could drop the sail and bring the *Wayfarer* out of the storm. When he saw what it was, he hesitated, but there was no choice. He climbed back on deck again and changed the setting on the Mortmain.

"What's happening?" Silkie shouted.

"Just keep her straight," Owen shouted back. "We'll be out of it in ten minutes."

Afterward he wondered how they had survived that ten minutes. Ahead of them there appeared massive jagged rocks. Sheets of time crashed up against them and were flung high in the air. The sea of time around them was a turmoil, and the harder Owen tried to turn away, the more it seemed that the helm fought him. He studied the Mortmain. If the course was correct, they would sail right onto the rocks, but if not . . . He glanced back at tossing angry waves. *Better the waves than the rocks,* he thought, and reached for the Mortmain to change the heading. But Silkie touched his hand.

"Trust the *Wayfarer.*"

The rocks towered above them now, slick and glassy with razor sharp crests. And then they were among them, unseen reefs suddenly appearing to the left and to the right. Silkie leaned over the bow and shouted back to Owen, but the noise of time crashing against the rocks made it hard to hear.

And yet the tiller of the *Wayfarer* felt light in his hand as she danced out of danger. The Mortmain rings moved at quicksilver speed.

"Owen—look!" Silkie shouted. Two great pillars of rock towered above them. Then he realized that they were not rocks but massive carved figures of men. The faces had been eroded, so you could only see something drooping and mournful, but the stone swords in their hands looked sharp as razors. There was a gap between them. He swung the tiller, but the *Wayfarer* seemed to move more quickly, and the little ship darted between the two pillars. Before them was a face of sheer rock. Owen looked down at the Mortmain again. The two symbols were exactly aligned.

"Silkie," he yelled, "the sails!" She dived across and grabbed the rope that lowered the sails. Just before they struck, the sail fell, and the wall of rock seemed to dissolve in front of them.

They found themselves high above a calm sea inlet. There were mountains to either side and ahead of them the lights of what appeared to be a town.

"We'll put her down in the water and sail toward the lights," Owen said.

"Where are we?" Silkie asked.

"Port Merforian," Owen said.

"Port Merforian? I never heard of it."

"No. Unless you were a pirate, you wouldn't have," Owen said.

He put the boat down on the water and gave the tiller to Silkie. His shoulders and his back were aching. Silkie sailed the boat well on water, with a sure touch. It was dark, but there were stars in the sky, and it was warm, so they had to take off the suits. Owen had forgotten what it felt like to be warm. He sat down on the rail and looked ahead. Fighting the storm had meant that he hadn't thought of anything else, and his head was clear.

The entrance in the rocks was obviously a way to stop intruders from getting into the pirates' world. The heat meant that the Harsh had not conquered here yet. But, despite the heat, he felt a sudden chill. The maps! He had never realized how valuable and dangerous they were! If the Harsh had the maps and the Mortmain, they would be able to make their way to all the hidden places in time. No one would be safe from them. The future of more than one world lay with him.

· Up ahead he could see the lights twinkling on the oily waters of a harbor. As they got closer they could see a crescent-shaped bay under a tall conical hill that looked as if it might once have been a volcano but was now covered in dense foliage.

"Look!" Silkie pointed as they drew near, her face shining. Large pink birds, like flamingos, roosted in the branches of the trees.

The harbor was crowded with ships and boats of all kinds: tankers and rusty coasters, elegant yachts and black-painted speedboats with a sinister look about them, and in between every kind of skiff and raft and canoe, many of which looked as if they would sink if you dared to take them to sea. People swarmed over the boats, some mending nets, others throwing boxes of fish up onto the quay. There were fair-haired fishwives and salty mariners with long white beards, swarthy ruffians smoking black cheroots, and pretty girl deckhands with bright red skirts and pistols at their hips. Along the wharf side he could see teetering piles of goods and barrels, and behind them crumbling buildings, some dark and some with garish signs—he could see a scorpion and next door a dancing woman, the lights on one leg broken, so she appeared to be dancing on one foot. Hawkers stood on the quay, fish sellers and buyers, kiosks selling a dozen different kinds of food. The air was full of rich aromas. People sat at battered tables eating their evening meal and drinking wine. And everyone was talking and shouting in such a jumble of languages and accents that Owen's head swam.

They rounded a tumbledown jetty, Owen keeping an eye out for anyone who resembled a guard.

"Sail her over there," he said. There was a jumble of smaller craft, not unlike their own. The *Wayfarer* would be well hidden among them. He scanned the harbor for the *Faltaine*, but there was no sign of Yarsk's buccaneer craft. Owen was sorry—even though they were pirates, they had been sailing the seas for a long time.

They sailed gently past a row of houseboats and heard a man and woman arguing. A one-eyed terrier watched them warily from the bow of another boat. From the wharf side came voices raised in raucous singing.

"Maybe I'll hear the song!" he said.

"What song?" Silkie asked.

Owen told her about the words he had heard sung by the crew of the *Faltaine*, and how he had heard more on the recording device in the tapestry hall.

"I'm sure it's important," he said.

"Sing it for me," she said.

"I'm not sure . . . ," he began, turning red.

"Please."

He hesitated, then shut his eyes and began.

> *To sail time's ocean wide*
> *In time and time's divide*
> *Till the book of the past*
> *Thaws winter's child at last . . .*

Owen fell silent. Then, faintly, he heard the song taken up. He looked wildly around, until his eye fell on a punt that was just rounding the end of the pier. The punt was being propelled by a man in a black hat, but it was the woman bent over a baby in the front of the punt who was singing the second verse of the song.

> *Her earth mistress pride*
> *More dead than alive*
> *In her hands his fate*
> *The boy she awaits . . .*

The punt slid around the end of pier, and the woman's voice faded away.

"That was spooky," Silkie said. She steered the boat easily between two rusty hulks sunk in the harbor mud. Owen stared after the punt.

"I want to tie the *Wayfarer* up and get working on her," Silkie said. "She took a battering during that storm." She stroked the rail fondly.

Owen looked around the *Wayfarer* and felt a pang of guilt. She looked battered and her stays and stanchions were stretched and broken in places.

Silkie eased the *Wayfarer* into the cluster of small craft. Owen climbed into the bow and moored her to the harbor wall.

"What do we do now?" Silkie asked.

"Let's get the *Wayfarer* into some sort of shape fast so we can keep going," Owen said. "If we can get that done, I can explore in the morning to find out how we get out of here. I don't fancy a strange town in the dark."

They set to, Owen tidying and cleaning and staying out of Silkie's way while she did the skilled work, her fingers quick and sure as she repaired the damaged rigging. Every time they slacked they both thought of their friends at the Workhouse, and worked even harder.

When they finally stopped, the quayside over their heads had gone quiet save for some late-night revelers. They were both exhausted.

"Time for food!" Silkie exclaimed.

"We have to keep working," Owen said.

"There's nothing more we can do in this light," Silkie said, "and we have to rest and eat."

They secured everything they could on deck, then went down into the cabin and locked the hatch. Owen found eggs and fried them up with some of the ham. It wasn't fish and chips, but it smelled delicious. Candlelight flickered in the small cabin as they sat down to eat. The *Wayfarer* felt safe and cozy, and for a little while they forgot about their troubles. Owen found himself telling Silkie about his lost father, how his car had gone into the harbor when Owen was only a baby, and had never been found. Silkie listened sympathetically. Then Owen realized what he was doing.

"I'm sorry," he said. "I'm babbling on about this, and none of the Raggies have . . . well, you don't have anyone, really."

"The children have Wesley, and me, I suppose." *But you and Wesley don't have anyone*, Owen thought. Silkie yawned and smiled.

"I'm sorry," she said, "I need to sleep."

"Me too," Owen said, weariness flooding his body. He could not remember the last time he had slept in a place where it was warm and secure, with no enemy camped at the gate. Silkie climbed into her bunk. Owen checked that the hatch was securely locked, then got into his own bunk.

"Goodnight, Silkie. We'll get up at dawn," he said, but she was already asleep. Owen lay awake for a while, listening to the gentle sound the waves made against the hull, then he too fell asleep.

When they woke the sun was shining and Port Merforian teemed with activity: ships and boats coming and going, cargoes being loaded, shipwrights and merchants thronging on the quay. Owen opened the hatch and emerged blinking into the sun. Fishermen were mending nets on some of the small craft beside the *Wayfarer*, but no one paid them any heed.

Owen climbed up onto the quay. Battered trucks wheezed along the quayside, with children running behind them. A man had set up a stall selling roast chickens. There were sailors everywhere, men and women, many of them scarred or missing limbs.

"At least I'll look at home here," Silkie said, appearing on the quay beside him. She touched the scar on her face. To his own surprise, and to hers, Owen found himself squeezing her hand.

Port Merforian looked like it could be a dangerous place for certain kinds of people, Owen thought. But for runaways and renegades and people who didn't want questions asked, it was ideal.

"We need to find a safe way out of here," Owen said.

"The boat's keel needs fixing first," Silkie said. "She can't be sailed in the state she's in."

"How long will it take?" Owen asked.

"Three or four hours. The keel piece has shifted. I need to take it out and plane it down. Then there's the fore stanchion and the aft guy rope . . ."

Silkie went on detailing the work. Owen burned to be on his way and to find the Long Woman. He knew how much the Workhouse was relying on him. But part of him hoped he might hear the rest of the song that the crew of the *Faltaine* had been singing. He was convinced that the song would supply answers to some of the questions that crowded into his head.

They had some breakfast and started in on the repairs. Silkie became more and more irritated with Owen, who was getting under her feet. By lunchtime she was exasperated.

"I can work quicker without you," she snapped. "Go

and see if you can buy some food. We need to keep up our stores."

"I haven't got any money," he said.

"For goodness' sake. There's money in the drawer under the table."

Owen hadn't known there *was* a drawer under the table, and indeed, it was concealed. He had to run his hands under the table to find it. There was a switch on it, and when he touched it, the drawer sprang open. Inside the drawer was an old-fashioned black leather wallet. When he opened it, he found a handful of gold coins. He stuck some of them in his pocket. Then, steering clear of the short-tempered Silkie, he clambered onto the quay.

He went over to the man selling roast chickens. The man was short with a potbelly and a graying mustache. Owen asked for a chicken, and when the man gave him one in a brown paper bag Owen handed him the coin.

The man stared at the coin.

"I can't take this," he said. "Steal it, did yer?"

"No, no. It was kind of . . . left to me."

"Askin' to get robbed, you is," the man said. "You'll get no chicken off me with this."

"Is it not enough?"

"Enough! Go to the bank. Thread Street. Go on, get off, out of here!" Muttering angrily to himself, the man waved Owen away in the direction of a nearby thoroughfare. Owen walked up it. It was broad and might once have been elegant, but there were weeds growing through the paving and junk dumped on street corners.

The buildings might once have been banks and great department stores, but now they swarmed with people, and washing hung out of their mullioned windows. To either side a warren of streets led off. Owen dared not leave the main street, even though it had its dangers. There was no pavement, and a motley traffic of trucks and rickshaws and broken-down cars weaved in and out of the rubbish and potholes, so he had to be alert.

Eventually he saw a street leading off to the side, which had rows of shops with *Money Changed* and *All Currencies, All Time Zones* signs, along with flashing images of coins and banknotes.

He went into the first shop on the street, which wasn't as easy as it sounded. When he knocked at the door, the man at the desk inside peered at him through what looked like a telescope, then spent what seemed like half an hour unlocking various bolts and chains and deadlocks on the door. Finally he frisked Owen with a homemade-looking metal detector before allowing him in.

He was a tall man with a sharp nose who wore a gray suit that was too short in the sleeves and legs. He sat down at the desk, which was too small for him, so his elbows and knees stuck out. He took a form from the desk drawer, put on a pair of black-framed spectacles, and looked up at Owen.

"Well?" he said.

"I was told I could change some money here."

"Of course, of course—there is a sign outside which says money changed. But where is this alleged cash, this mythical coinage?"

Owen put one of the gold coins on the desk.

The man stopped dead, his pen hand poised above the form. He stared at the coin for a long time. Then he stared at Owen. He coughed and stroked his chin. He picked up the coin as if it was something very fragile, and studied it. He sprang from the desk.

"Need to get exchange rate! Back in a second!" And he dashed through a door in the back and slammed it behind him. Owen was puzzled, and wondered if he had seen the last of his coin. He waited. There was an old black phone on his desk, and Owen saw a red light come on. Was the man on an extension phone in the back—is that how you got an exchange rate?

There was a large ledger on the desk. Unable to resist a look, Owen turned it around and scanned the most recent entries. He almost gasped when he saw the last entry. Someone called Yarsk had exchanged three thousand Milesian dollars. The *Faltaine* had reached port at last!

The door burst open and the man bustled back in again.

"Have you heard of a ship called the *Faltaine*?" Owen asked, trying to keep his voice casual.

"The *Faltaine*." The man fixed Owen with a curious look. "Of course."

"Do you know where she is?"

"You want to see the *Faltaine*?" the man said.

"Yes."

"Excellent—yes, of course, couldn't be better. She's at the rear dock. Allow me," he cried, shoving a wad of banknotes into Owen's hand and sweeping him out of the chair in one movement. Before Owen knew what was happening he was propelled through the doorway at the back, getting a fleeting view of piles of boxes and a very large safe. Another iron door in front of him was opened with a great clattering of locks and bolts.

"Just follow the alley down the hill. It's straight. You can't miss it. Thank you! Goodbye!"

Owen was pushed through and the door was slammed, locked, and bolted behind him. Owen looked around. He was in a dim alley and, when he looked in either direction, he could see no sign of the main street. But from the end of the alley came a faint smell of the sea.

Owen started walking and soon found himself in a very different part of town. It was quiet, for a start. Sometimes he would see a figure in the distance, but it would always disappear before he caught up. There were streets that seemed to be uninhabited, but there were also houses with high walls around them, and iron gates through which he could glimpse beautiful gardens and sometimes hear the sound of a fountain. Here and there a lizard basked in the heat of the afternoon sun. The streets rose, then fell again, so he was walking downhill. He was hot and thirsty and worried. Silkie would have missed him by now. Why had he not told her that he had gone to change money?

Then, in the distance, the song! His thirst and worry forgotten, he hurried forward. Two or three times more he heard the song, each time tantalizingly too far away to make out any words. He was almost running now.

Indeed, he was going so fast that he missed the end of a street and almost ran across the wooden jetty that lay beyond it and straight into what appeared to be a broad river.

He stared down into the limpid brown waters for a minute, then straightened—and found himself looking at the rakish hull of the *Faltaine,* moored alongside a row of warehouses.

She's here!

He rushed toward the elegant ship. Her gangway was down, but there didn't seem to be anyone around, so he boarded her. There was a smell of warm tar. She was badly in need of repairs and a coat of paint, but the crew were probably in the wharfside bars that Yarsk had talked about.

Owen went toward the rear of the vessel and the main cabin. He had heard the song, so there had to be someone aboard.

"Captain Yarsk?" he called out. "Captain?" The door to the cabin was ajar. He pushed it open. The interior was dark. He couldn't see if there was anyone inside.

"Hello?" he said. His eyes adjusting to the darkness, he saw that there was in fact someone there, sitting at the end of a dining table that ran the length of the cabin.

"Captain Yarsk?" Owen said.

"Good afternoon, shipmate." It was Yarsk's voice, but it was low and slurred. Owen went to one of the windows that looked over the stern and flung it open. Yarsk sat alone at the table. The cabin was oak-paneled, and gorgeous rugs and throws of oriental design lay everywhere. But it was not the rugs that caught his eye, nor the fact that the captain's eyes were glazed and his expression sleepy. It was the flask sitting on the table in front of him. Owen had seen one of those flasks before. But not here. Far away, in Hadima.

"Is that . . . ?" he said, indicating the flask.

"Horandum?" Yarsk said lazily. "Yes, indeed. Help yourself. Or perhaps not. Don't know how much is left."

"I don't want any," Owen said shortly. Horandum—a drink that enabled you to see time itself, to see its flow around you, its majesty. But it was a drink that ate at your soul, until you were hollowed out, until you belonged to it.

"Good, good," Yarsk said, his hands falling to his side.

"How did you get it?" Owen said. "You must have taken a ship as a prize."

There was a crash as the door that he had come through was slammed shut.

"From me, of course." The man who had been standing behind the door smiled coldly. "Make sure he doesn't spill it, Yarsk, like he did with mine."

"Black!" Owen gasped. Conrad Black, owner of the Museum of Time in Hadima, and Owen's enemy. The man who had betrayed them, who had imprisoned and tormented the Yeati.

"I do believe you're sailing around the place in my boat," Black said, stepping forward. He held a revolver in his right hand.

"My grandfather's boat," Owen said. "I bet you stole it!"

"As a matter of fact, I did, but we'll not go into that," Black said. "What matters now is that you're here."

"What happened, Captain Yarsk?" Owen turned to the forlorn figure of the captain.

"Took a prize at last," Yarsk said.

"Yes," Black cut in, "I fled the Harsh winter in Hadima in a passing ship. Captain Yarsk and his bunch of cutthroats captured the ship. But on the voyage home, the good captain developed a fondness for horandum. And of course, I am the only one who can provide it."

"Captain," Owen said desperately, "I thought you were a buccaneer, your own man, sailing through time!"

"He's still his own man," Black said with a cruel grin. "But I've persuaded him there's an easier way to make a living. The Harsh are hunting through time for one boy, and here he is! You're worth a fortune to us, Navigator."

"Captain, you sailed with my grandfather!" Owen cried.

"A fortune, that's what you're worth," Yarsk murmured happily to himself.

Black led Owen at gunpoint down into the bilges of the boat. Rats scuttled in the darkness. At the very bottom of the boat, rancid water swilling about their feet, was a cell of plain iron bars. Black motioned for Owen to enter.

"How did you know I was here?" Owen said.

"The money changer telephoned me." Black grinned. "After all, it isn't every day that someone tries to change a coin with his own face on it, is it?" He slammed the cell door shut and walked off, whistling.

His own face? Owen fished one of the coins from his pocket. He could just see it in a chink of light coming through the boards above his head. In the dim light he could see a face—not his, he knew now, although it was similar. The face belonged to his grandfather. He hadn't looked at the coin when he had taken it from the drawer on board the *Wayfarer*. He slumped against the bars of the cage. He was trapped on a pirate ship. No one knew where he was. And he was to be delivered into the arms of the Harsh.

Owen sat in the darkness, visions of the Workhouse in flames tormenting him. He thought about Silkie and her alarm when he did not return, about her alone in a pirate town. It was pitch black when at last he heard the sound of heavy boots and laughter from the deck. *The crew*, he thought, *coming home from the bars of Port Merforian*. There were good-natured shouts and, from the sound of it, someone trying out a hornpipe on the deck. Then suddenly, Black's voice rang above the commotion.

"Enjoy yourselves while you can. You're sailing in the morning. You'll be hauling your lazy hides out of your kips an hour before sunrise!"

The sailors fell silent. There was a lot of shuffling on deck, and then Owen could hear them coming below.

There was a low murmur from just above his head, which went on for a long time, and Owen fell into a fitful sleep.

When he woke again, it was to the sound of feet on deck, ropes being cast off, and sails being set. The gentle burble of water against the hull changed. The ship started to move under his feet. The *Faltaine* was under way! Owen sat up. He couldn't see, which meant it was still dark outside. *Silkie must be worried out of her mind,* he thought, wishing he was back on the *Wayfarer.*

He scarcely heard the sound of bare feet on the stair outside. There was a scratching noise and then a match was struck. Through the bars he recognized one of the crew: a small, wiry woman with teeth filed sharp, and an anchor tattooed just below her eye. She had a villainous look and was carrying a knife with a long thin blade. Owen flattened himself against the back of the cell.

But the knife wasn't for him. The woman put the tip of it in the lock and twisted it.

"We're bleedin' buccaneers," she muttered to herself, "not bleedin' child kidnappers. I don't know what's happened to old Yarsk."

"It's the horandum," Owen said. "It takes over your mind. Black is feeding it to him."

"There's a rotten villain for you, and no mistake," she said. The lock snapped open. "That's all I can do for you," she said. "You're on your own after this."

"Thanks," Owen whispered, but she had slipped away again. Cautiously Owen followed her past the crew quarters and out onto the deck. He crept to the rail and looked over. The *Faltaine* was in the middle of the river. The water was deep and fast-flowing. There was no escape after all. He looked up at the wheel. Black stood behind the pilot, silhouetted against the faint pink glow in the east. He couldn't see Yarsk. Owen was out of his cell but was still a prisoner. He crept around the side of the wheelhouse and toward the captain's cabin. He edged the door open. He could hear snoring. He tiptoed into the cabin. Yarsk was lying fast asleep in an armchair, legs splayed, the flask of horandum in front of him. Owen crept up and slipped the horandum off the table. Yarsk's eyes opened and fixed Owen with a black, fathomless gaze. Owen froze. But the time dreams consumed Yarsk again. Owen went to the window and dropped the flask of horandum into the river.

He went out on deck. There might be a lifeboat or a raft of some kind, and if he could slip it over the side . . . Suddenly he felt something hard and cold pressed against the back of his head.

"You really are an unpleasant boy," Black hissed. "If you weren't worth so much to me, I'd put a bullet in your head and toss you over the side."

"As you say," Owen said carefully, "you can't do it, so what's preventing me from just hopping over the side and swimming to shore?"

"Two things," Black said. "First, the river is too deep and fast. You'd drown. And the second thing is . . . this!" Black raised the revolver and brought it down hard on the top of Owen's head. Owen staggered and fell to the deck, stunned.

When he woke, he was tied to the mast. His head pounded and he could feel half-dried blood caked in his hair. It was almost dawn. There was a soft light in the east. He saw reed beds to either side of the river and heard the sound of wild birds. Black was arguing with the crew.

"Twenty minutes and we'll be sailing in time again. A day or so will put us in contact with the Harsh—their ships are patrolling everywhere. Hand the boy over and you'll be richer than you ever dreamed possible."

Someone must have mentioned Yarsk's name, and this time Black spoke with contempt.

"Yarsk is finished. I'm fond of a bit of horandum myself, but some people are just too greedy. The stuff has eaten away his mind. Forget about Yarsk."

Owen shut his eyes and sagged back against the ropes that bound him. There was a constant low buzz of pain in his head. Then he realized that the sound was not entirely in his head. There was another sound, something low and growling, like a powerful engine ticking over. He opened his eyes again and looked over the side. A long, black needle-shaped bow edged into view. One of the sinister black boats they had seen in the harbor. The bow seemed to go on forever as it moved alongside the *Faltaine*, but finally he saw a cockpit, and behind the cockpit, two massive engines. But it wasn't the engines that caught his eye, it was the pilots in the cockpit. One of them was an elderly man, smallset, wearing a motor-cycle helmet and goggles. He grasped the controls of the boat firmly and Owen could see muscles bulging in his forearms. The other pilot, features half concealed by another motorcycle helmet, was Silkie!

Owen made to cry out but stopped himself. Black didn't know they were there. Owen could see that the pilot was edging his boat closer to the *Faltaine*. Silkie was standing now, a knife in her hand. At a signal from the pilot, she put her knife in her teeth and leapt for the side of the *Faltaine*. Her hand wrapped around a stanchion and she pulled herself up.

Owen looked round. The crew's attention was on preparing to set sail, and Black was gazing eagerly forward. Silkie crept across the deck toward him. She winked and started to cut the ropes that held him. But they hadn't reckoned on Black. There was a sharp crack and a bullet thudded into the mast an inch from Silkie's side. She froze.

"I won't shoot you, Navigator," Black said, "but if your pal moves a muscle, I'll put a bullet between her eyes." He went to the side and looked down at the other boat.

"This is none of your business, Higgins."

"Everything that goes on in Port Merforian is my business. Particularly when someone tries to change a coin with my old friend's face on it." The man's voice was low and pleasant. Owen had the feeling that he was the type of man who never had to raise his voice to get what he wanted.

"Where's Yarsk?" Higgins went on. "I want to talk to him."

"Yarsk is unavailable," Black sneered. "He has an appointment with a horandum bottle."

"Yarsk is a Shipman Islander by birth," Higgins said, his voice cold now. "They have no tolerance for the stuff. Did you give it to him, Black?"

"I didn't have to press it on him, if that's what you mean," Black said. "Now take your little smuggling boat back upriver. I have a deal to do."

"Can't let you do that, Black."

"You can't stop me," Black said, pressing the barrel of the revolver against Silkie's temple. Higgins' eyes narrowed.

"Three minutes to the gate," one of the sailors said. Black grinned. Higgins glanced from Black to Owen and Silkie. There was nothing he could do and he knew it.

"Who gave that order?" a voice rang out. The crew stopped what they were doing and looked around. Yarsk was standing on the deck, using the rail to support himself. He looked awful. His face was pale and bloodless and his eyes were sunk in dark sockets. He kept passing his hand across his face as though terrible visions flickered in front of him.

"I said, who gave that order?"

"Black gave it, Captain." It was the woman who had freed Owen. "Do you want us to drop anchor?"

"Hold it!" Black threw Silkie to the deck. "There'll be no anchor!"

The first sailor spoke again. "Two minutes to the gate."

"This is my ship!" Yarsk's voice wavered.

"Not anymore," Black said, the revolver leveled at Yarsk. Yarsk straightened and stared Black in the face. Owen could see his hand grasp the rail. Moving faster than Owen would have thought possible, Yarsk grabbed a steel hook from the rail and flung it at Black. *He hasn't the strength,* Owen thought in despair as the hook hit the deck and slid along, dragging a rope behind it. It struck Black's foot and wrapped harmlessly around his ankle. Black smiled mirthlessly and squeezed the trigger.

The shot sounded louder than anything Owen had ever heard. A rose of blood bloomed on the front of Yarsk's shirt. The captain gasped and fell forward, but as he did, his left hand reached for a rope knotted around the rail. With one pull he loosened the knot. The rope streamed out. Owen looked up. One end of the rope was attached to a heavy block high up on the mast, and the block was now plummeting toward the deck. The other end was attached to the hook that was wrapped around Black's ankle. Black looked up at the plunging block, then down at his ankle. The rope snapped taut.

Almost faster than the eye could follow, Black was upended and flung high into the air by the rope around his ankle. He soared to the height of the mast, and then the rope parted. With a thin scream, Black flew through the air until he was far behind the *Faltaine,* then landed in the river with a loud splash. They watched the spot where he entered the water, but he did not resurface.

Owen shrugged off the rest of the ropes and ran forward to Yarsk. He knelt down. Yarsk opened his eyes. They were clear.

"Drop the anchor," he said. His voice was weak, but the crew ran to obey. "Come closer," Yarsk said, barely audible.

"Your grandfather used to say . . . time is . . . time is longer for a child than for a grown-up." Yarsk smiled and closed his eyes. The woman who had freed Owen knelt down beside them and felt for the captain's pulse.

"He's gone," she said quietly. Owen sensed the whole crew gathered around them in a silence broken only by the gentle sound of the river against the hull.

Owen and Silkie stood on the deck of the *Wayfarer* watching the *Faltaine* sail back toward Port Merforian, bearing the body of their captain. Higgins sat on the rail beside them, smoking a cigar.

"That's some sensible girl you got there," Higgins said.

"What happened?" Owen asked. "How did you find me?"

"Nothing happens in Port Merforian without me knowing," Higgins said, "and when somebody changes a gold coin with the Navigator's head on it, news travels faster than usual."

"When you didn't come back," Silkie said, "I went looking for you. I found the street with the banks on it. There was a . . . a row going on."

"I'd caught up with the crook that had taken your coin—he only gave you a tenth of what it was worth." Higgins grinned. "I . . . eh . . . persuaded him to tell me where you had gone."

"Mr. Higgins knew about us and the *Wayfarer*," Silkie said.

"She was seen the minute she came into the harbor," Higgins said. "Took me a while to realize that she really was the *Wayfarer*. That boat hasn't been seen here in many's a long year. Between one thing and another, we tracked you down pretty quick."

"I'm very glad you did," Owen said, his voice betraying his emotion. "All would have been lost without you and Silkie." He glanced at the Raggie girl. She had dressed the wound on his head, all the while scolding him for going off without telling her. But she was smiling now.

"You're the Navigator's grandson, and any enemy of the Harsh is a friend of mine." Higgins lifted up his trouser leg. The leg underneath was made of polished bone. "Frostbite. I was smuggling magno into Hadima, and the Harsh caught me. Took the magno and put me in prison. I tell you, it was cold in that prison, and many's the one froze to death in it."

"Smuggling?" Owen said.

"You get two types of people in Port Merforian, pirates and smugglers. I'm the latter. Retired now, of course, though lucky for you I kept the *Straight Flush*." He indicated the fast craft that had followed the

Faltaine downriver. "Would never have caught you without her."

"Wasn't such a lucky day for Yarsk," Silkie said.

"No," Higgins said quietly, "it wasn't."

In silence they watched the sails of the *Faltaine* go upriver until they could be seen no more.

23

Cati woke early. Owen and Silkie had left the previous day, and now Uel and Mervyn's trial was upon them. She got dressed and went searching for Contessa. She found her on the battlements. Contessa was looking out at the besieging forces, spread out in a great semicircle around the Workhouse, and beyond them the Harsh fleet. Smoke from campfires rose into the air, and men were getting out of tents. The urgency of the battlefield had settled into the long wait of a siege.

"I've never seen a trial among the Resisters before," Cati asked. "What happens?"

"Someone will be picked to be the accuser—probably Samual. Then the accused person can pick someone to defend him. The accuser puts his case and the defender puts his. Then the Resisters present—which won't be everyone, as the Workhouse has to be guarded—will vote on guilt or innocence."

"What happens if they are found guilty?"

"For a crime as serious as taking the Yeati's ring, there can only be one sentence. After all, people could have died if the ring wasn't there to save them."

"What is the punishment?" Cati said, feeling that she really didn't want to know.

"The long sleep," Contessa said.

"What's that?"

"To be put to sleep in the Starry and never woken again until time itself ends."

Cati looked at her, appalled.

"But there aren't any sleepers like that in our Starry, are there?"

"No. People given the long sleep will live for many decades in some cases. But something in the substance of them gives up hope. They all die eventually."

"That can't happen to Uel and Mervyn!"

"I have a feeling, Cati," Contessa said gently, "that Samual will do his best to make sure that it does happen to them."

Cati walked away from the kitchen, her mind in turmoil. She heard running feet behind her. Wesley grabbed her shoulder.

"The trial's set for one o'clock," he said. "Samual's the accuser."

"Contessa said he would be. Have they picked a defender?"

"They have."

"Who is it?"

"They picked you, Cati."

"Me!" She stared at the Raggie boy, shocked. "I don't know how to defend somebody!"

"Are you sure? People trust you, Cati. And they trust you to tell the truth, no matter what. You are the Watcher. And besides, they've picked you. You can't refuse. If it's any help, Dr. Diamond wants to see you."

Cati opened her mouth to speak, then closed it again. Wesley was right. She was the Watcher, and if being the Watcher meant anything, then it meant duty. Her heart raced.

"What time is it now?" she asked.

"About ten."

"There's no time! I have to think. Tell the boys I'll see them at the trial."

"All right." Wesley watched her hurry off, thinking that Uel and Mervyn could not have picked better, but that things still did not look good for them. Not with Samual in the mood he was in.

Cati ran up the steps of the Nab and into the Skyward without knocking. Dr. Diamond was waiting for her, his face grave. When she came out twenty minutes later, she walked slowly down the stairs, a strange, dazed look on her face. Several people greeted her, but she did not seem to hear them. When she got to the Convoke hall, she stopped and stared at the great empty space, then shook her head. There was very little time.

She went down to the sleeping quarters and knocked on Rosie's door, but the room was empty. Then she went to see the prisoners. Samual's guards let her in without argument. Uel and Mervyn were playing a game of chess. The small cell was sparsely furnished with two bunk beds, a table, and two chairs. It must have felt like home to the Raggies, she thought.

She sat down on the bed. The two boys looked at her calmly.

"I know that the two of you didn't do it," she said, "so why don't you withdraw your confession now?"

"If we withdraw, they'll blame the child again," Uel said.

Cati sighed in exasperation. "Do you know what the punishment will be?"

"The long sleep," Mervyn said. "Mr. Samual. He told us."

"We won't have them giving a young child the long sleep," Uel said.

"They won't do that to a child," Cati cried.

"Can you promise that?" Mervyn said. Cati was silent. With Samual in the mood he was in at the moment, there was no way that she could *promise*.

"So we done it," Uel said, "and that's all there is to it."

"But how can I defend you if that's the way you act?" Cati said in despair.

"You'll find a way," Uel said confidently, capturing a

pawn on the chess board. Cati looked at the two boys. There was a way, but she longed with all her heart not to use it. And even if she did, would it work?

The morning sped past. The Convoke hall started to fill with all the Resisters who could be spared from defending the Workhouse. The mood was somber. Many people would not meet Cati's eye as they filed into the hall. *Not a good sign,* she thought. She looked down the hallway and gave a start. Pieta! Gaunt and pale and supported on either side by her children. Her ruined arm was strapped to her side. Cati's eyes strayed to it, then she looked guiltily away. She didn't want Pieta to think she was staring. But Pieta walked past without looking at her and took her usual seat by the fireplace.

Samual strode in surrounded by six of his red-coated soldiers. Rutgar and Contessa took their places. Rosie slipped in just after them, giving Cati a quick wave.

Finally, when the hall was full, Uel and Mervyn were led in. They nodded to the Raggies gathered around Wesley in one corner of the Convoke. They were walked to the dais by Samual's soldiers, and there they sat down on plain chairs. The hall fell silent. Cati swallowed and felt that everyone could hear her. Contessa stood up, and the whole room stood quietly with her.

"This trial of the Resisters is convened," Contessa said. "Uel and Mervyn of the Raggies, you are accused of stealing the Yeati's ring, an object of great lifesaving power. This act was carried out in a time of war, which adds to the gravity of the offense. Are you guilty or not?"

"Guilty," Uel said quietly.

"We done it," Mervyn said.

Samual got to his feet. "I don't think we need to go any further with this matter," he said. "They've both said they did it, so let's get on with the sentence." There was a murmur of approval from Samual's soldiers. The rest of the Resisters looked troubled.

"The sentence is the long sleep," Samual continued. "We should proceed."

"Wait a minute," Cati said, standing up. "We should know something about the crime—for instance, why they did it. Why did you steal the ring?"

Uel and Mervyn looked at each other uncertainly and shifted in their chairs. They did not seem able to answer.

"They did it because they are thieves," Samual thundered.

"Or perhaps they can't say why they stole the ring because they didn't do it, and for some reason they are pretending to be guilty," Cati said.

"Nonsense," Samual snapped. "They are simple Raggies. They're not capable of such things."

"Maybe." Cati drew a deep breath. "But there is something else I want to say. I think that the thief of the ring is the same person who let the Albions in."

"That doesn't follow," Samual said, eyeing Cati suspiciously. "You're only trying to get them off."

"Put it this way," Cati said, every eye in the hall on her

now. "If I could prove who let the Albions in, would you think my theory was good?"

"No!" Samual said, but the Resisters were looking at each other. Cati felt that at least she had got them thinking.

"Besides," Samual went on, "you can't prove who let the Albions in."

"That's where you're wrong," Cati said. There was dead silence in the hall. Cati put her hand into her pocket and drew it out slowly. Slowly, because she wished that she was anywhere else rather than standing in front of the Resisters at that moment. Slowly, because things would never be the same again when she opened her hand and showed the Resisters what it contained.

But open it she did.

"This," she said, "was found on the ground by the door where the Albions got in. No one has any reason to be there, so it must have been left by the person who opened the door."

There was a pause that seemed to go on forever, then every eye in the hall turned toward a small figure sitting on her own. They all recognized the object in Cati's hand. There was no mistake. No one else in the Workhouse wore ornate pins in their hair.

"It's yours, Rosie, isn't it?"

Rosie's face was very pale. Her hands pulled at her hair, as if she wanted to pluck it out. She swallowed hard, then nodded her head. Wesley stared at her, his fists clenched. There were gasps from the other Raggies.

"They must be working together," Samual said.

"No!" Cati said. "Uel and Mervyn were trying to protect the little girl who found the ring. I don't know why Rosie acted the way she did—"

"I never trusted her anyway," Samual said. "And the sentence is the same as it was for the two Raggies. The long sleep."

"Wait," Contessa said. "If she is under some outside influence, then she cannot be held to account."

"Outside influence!" Samual sneered. "More like promised money when the Workhouse fell."

"Let her speak for herself," Cati said, her heart aching.

Rosie opened her mouth to speak, but as before, music swelled in her head, and this time the accompanying pain was excruciating. She buried her face in her hands.

"I call for a vote!" Samual said. Cati looked around the people in the Convoke. For the first time she noticed just how many red coats there were. Samual had obviously worked it so that Rutgar's men were doing guard duty. He hadn't left the vote to chance. There were enough of his soldiers to win any vote.

"Hands up, those who say the sentence should be imposed," Rutgar said. Immediately almost two-thirds of the Resisters in the hall put up their hand. Pieta's hand stayed down, as did Contessa's and all of the Raggies'. Many of the Resisters looked troubled. Cati looked over at Dr. Diamond. Very slowly his right hand rose into the air. He did not look at Cati.

"The vote is carried!" Samual cried. "Take her away."

Rosie, with a confused expression on her face, was hauled to her feet. Cati could barely watch as Samual's soldiers led the tiny figure away, her black hat tipped at an angle on her curly hair.

Wesley caught up with Cati on her way out of the hall. He grabbed her by the arm. "Did she really do it?"

"I think so. Dr. Diamond found the hairpin by the door. He gave it to me."

"I can't believe it."

"Neither can I."

"We've got to help her!"

"It looks like Samual wants to convict her anyway. To make an example or something. I don't know."

"When do . . . when do they do it?"

"Put her to sleep? Two or three days, I think. You're allowed some time. We need to think, Wesley, really think!"

Cati saw Mervyn and Uel watching her from the dais, where they still sat. There was no expression in their eyes, so why did she feel as if they were accusing her?

Samual's grip on the Workhouse was tightening. If not for the pass that Dr. Diamond had given her, Cati would have been unable to go anywhere. As it was, guards stopped her at every turn. Several times she set out to see Dr. Diamond but turned back at the last minute. She could not forget how his hand had risen into the air to convict Rosie. Nor, if she was honest with herself, did she want to be reminded of her own part in the conviction. She could not bring herself to go see Rosie. She remembered the Yeati in his grim cell, his fur matted with dirt. Having the free-spirited Rosie in a cell was just as bad.

The next morning she went down to Owen's Den. Part of her wished that he was there, thought that he would know what to do. Another part of her was angry with herself for relying on someone else. She couldn't bear the idea of Rosie sitting alone in a cell, even if she had betrayed the Workhouse. She took out Owen's tin of biscuits and munched moodily on one, and that was the way Wesley found her.

"Guessed as you'd be here," Wesley said, sitting down and helping himself to a biscuit.

"I can't help thinking about Rosie," she said.

"Same here," he said. "There's something well fishy about all of this." He thought for a moment, then burst out: "It's not right, Cati—she shouldn't be in there no matter what she done. We got to get her out."

Cati nodded. She'd had the same thought, unspoken.

"At least if we talk to her," Wesley went on, "we can try to find out what's going on in her head."

"I owe that much to her," Cati said miserably. "It's my fault she's in there."

"Would you rather it was Uel and Mervyn?" Wesley said gently. "You done your best, lass."

Together they slipped back to the Workhouse, staying off the pathways in case Wesley was stopped. They headed around the back of the Workhouse to where Rosie was being held. They went through the positions occupied by Rutgar's soldiers. The rough-hewn men and women had no interest in Samual's decrees and did not stop them.

Rosie was in an old storeroom under the high back wall of the Workhouse. There was only one approach to it, guarded by four red coats. Cati and Wesley studied it for a long time.

"Can't see no way past them guards," Wesley whispered. Cati's heart sank. What would they do?

"There's something else we can try," Wesley said.

"What's that?"

"We can find out who Rosie was talking to through that pipe. We might get some answers off them."

The corridors and tunnels underneath the Workhouse were deserted. Normally you would have found men and women coming and going, putting items into storage or looking for things that had been put away. But now that movement was restricted, the Resisters weren't bothering to seek the necessary pass.

Cati and Wesley had been lucky in evading patrols, but their luck was about to run out. As they turned a corner at the bottom of the stairs, they ran straight into Samual's lieutenant, Moorhead.

"What are you two doing down here?" she demanded.

"I've got a pass," Cati said. "I'm not answerable to you."

"You might have a pass, but your friend here doesn't, I bet." She glared at Wesley. "Just because we locked up that Hadima girl doesn't mean that we're not looking for other traitors. I think I should take the two of you topside and find out what you've been up to."

Cati and Wesley exchanged glances, then bolted past Moorhead. The woman made an attempt to follow, but she was puffing after ten yards.

"I'll be looking for you, Raggie," she shouted after them, shaking her fist. "You're a marked man from now on."

"Maybe that wasn't very sensible," Cati said as they slowed down.

"I don't care," Wesley said. "Raggies is fed up with all these rules and all. Down at the warehouse we done what we liked."

It might be a long time before you see the warehouse again, Cati thought.

Wesley showed Cati the pipe Rosie had used to communicate with her mystery accomplice. He examined it.

"Looks like an old ventilation pipe, keeps air moving down here. That's why the place is nice and dry."

"I wonder where it comes out."

"Must be in the air," Wesley said. "Somewhere on the roof. Hang on a sec."

Before Cati could stop him, Wesley had climbed into the pipe.

"Not too bad," he said. "A bit snug."

"Careful," Cati warned.

"There's rivets in here you can put your foot on," Wesley said. "I might as well just climb on up."

"No!" Cati said, but in seconds Wesley had disappeared from sight. She waited anxiously for what seemed like hours, then a weird low sound came down the pipe. The hairs on the back of her neck stood up.

"Wesley?" she said uncertainly into the pipe.

"Cati, can you hear me?" Wesley's voice sounded like wind blowing through a canyon, but she could make out his words.

"Where are you, Wesley?"

"Climb up and see." Cati looked dubiously at the shaft winding upward into darkness, then climbed in. It was claustrophobic, but surprisingly easy to climb. The rivet heads used to join sections of pipe gave good foot- and handholds—but it was dark and dusty and she sneezed several times. The sneeze echoed in the pipe like the call of some lonely animal. As she went up she could see other shafts leading off to the side.

At last she reached the top and felt Wesley grab her under the arms and haul her out into the fresh air. She stood up and looked around. They were on the very top of the Workhouse, standing on a roof ledge, looking down on the battlements forty feet below. Behind them, only the Nab was taller. Cati shivered. You wouldn't want to slip.

"No footprints or nothing," Wesley said gloomily. "Must have been fresh snow last night."

"You're right," Cati said.

"But there's one good thing," Wesley said, brightening. "I won't have to worry about old Red-face anymore. Far as I can see, these shafts go all over the Workhouse."

Cati realized that she had seen the pipes in every part of the Workhouse without ever wondering what they were.

"What's that?" Wesley frowned. There was something attached to the side of the chimney above their heads, a square red object that, Cati realized, could not be seen from the battlements. In seconds Wesley had scaled the brickwork, finding hand- and footholds, though Cati could see none.

"Looks like some kind of an aerial," Wesley said. "I'll take it down."

"No, leave it!" Cati said. "Whoever owns it will know that we've found it. Leave it."

"Might be innocent enough anyhow," Wesley said.

"I don't think so." Cati's eyes narrowed as she stared across the river valley. She could just see the chimney of Johnston's house, and there, attached to the side of the chimney, was a splash of red that looked suspiciously like the one above their heads. Somebody in the Workhouse was in contact with Johnston, but who?

"The rose," Wesley said to himself.

"What?"

"The rose. You mind when Rosie seen the red scar on Silkie's cheek? She said something about a rose?"

"Yes. The rose is Johnston's symbol."

"I know that. But Rosie shouldn't know it. Rosie never met Johnston. At least as far as we know," Wesley said grimly.

Owen sailed the *Wayfarer* into the reeds at the side of the river, with Higgins' fast smuggling craft in tow. Higgins had fresh ham and bread and fruit in the surprisingly sizable cargo area of the boat. They sat on deck in the light of the setting sun while the reeds rustled around them and the river whispered past. As they ate, Higgins told them stories of smuggling and piracy that were thrilling and terrifying in equal measure. Owen found Silkie edging closer to him as Higgins described a desperate pursuit by creatures he referred to as the wraiths of Neb.

When he had finished his stories (which may or may not have been true, Owen thought) he told them that the river they were on was in fact the way back into time.

"You're not too far," he said. "The river kind of . . . well, it falls off the edge of the world, if you like.

Put your sail up just before the end and off you go. Port Merforian only has one way in and out, for obvious reasons."

"I need to ask something," Owen said.

"Fire away, son."

"Is it just because we're against the Harsh that you're helping us?"

Silkie looked at him reproachfully, as if he had insulted Higgins, but Higgins laughed and shook his head.

"Nay, lass," he said. "I'm hard to offend, and it's a fair question. The answer is that, as I said, I knew your grandfather, and he did me a turn once, so I'm bound to help you."

"That's right, you said you knew him," Owen said excitedly.

"He was in Port Merforian for a few years."

"Captain Yarsk said he was a pirate," Silkie said.

"Well, I suppose he was. But the reason he was a pirate was that the Harsh were buying and stealing all the magno. He had to do something to get more—Hadima was dependent on it. If he could have bought it, he would."

"What was he like?" Owen leaned forward.

"Your grandfather?" Higgins chuckled. "He was a rogue, I suppose, but good-hearted and clever. He could never stay in one place very long. Couldn't sit still."

"Did he have Owen's dad with him?" Silkie asked suddenly. Like all of the Raggies, she was very curious about families.

"Not that time, no," Higgins said, "but a few years later he came through again. He had Owen's father with him then. He must have been about eight years old. He only stayed a few days, though. He was in a hurry."

"Why?"

"He never said. He was looking for an old book."

"What sort of book?" Owen asked eagerly.

"A child's storybook," Higgins said, with a glance at Owen. "I know, it is a strange thing. He didn't find it anyway."

A children's storybook? Owen and Silkie looked at each other. What could something like that have to do with the Navigator?

"Where did he go then?" Owen asked.

"He said he had to see the Long Woman."

"The Long Woman! That's where we're going," Silkie said.

"Are you indeed?" Higgins said.

"I have my grandfather's maps," Owen said.

"You may have his maps," Higgins said, "but do you have his mind? You have learned to sail across time. But to find the Long Woman you have to sail *through* time. And that is a different thing entirely."

"You found her before, Owen, didn't you?" Silkie said. "When the Harsh turned time backwards."

"That was different," Owen said, remembering back to when he and Pieta had been lost in the snow. "That time, *she* found *us*."

Owen showed Higgins the Mortmain and the maps.

"The Mortmain!" the small man cried. "The great compass of time! I haven't heard it spoken about for many years. And these maps . . . your grandfather was a genius, as well as being a rogue, of course. The maps are a great help, but to sail through time . . . that comes from *here*." He thumped his chest.

"Now," Higgins said, "it's getting dark, and time for me to go back to town. If I were you, I would stay here overnight and set off early in the morning. I'll make sure that there is no loose talk about you in the town."

Higgins shook Owen's hand. He turned to Silkie.

"If you ever think of coming back here, youngster, you'll make a great pirate with your spirit and that scar of yours."

Owen could tell that Higgins hadn't meant to be unkind, but Silkie reddened and her hand went to her face.

"Goodness," Higgins said, "sorry! I only meant to say that . . . I mean, I didn't . . ." Higgins looked so confused and unhappy that Silkie could do nothing except throw her arms around him.

When she let go, Higgins turned away and blew his nose on a large handkerchief embroidered with fierce-looking pirates. Then with a wave of his hand he climbed over the rail and into his boat. The powerful engines started with a roar, and he eased her away from the *Wayfarer*.

"I nearly forgot!" he shouted. He threw something

into the air. Owen looked up and could see the gold Navigator coin, cleaned and polished, turning and sparkling in the setting sun. He reached up and caught it. With a grin, Higgins gunned the engines. In a cloud of spray he shot off down the river and within moments was a speck in the distance.

Owen did not sleep well that night. His dreams were full of the northern lights and great crackling sheets of many-colored lightning. One moment he was looking up at the sky, which seemed to wheel around him; the next he was looking down into what appeared to be an abyss. When Silkie got up at dawn and came sleepily onto deck, Owen was already there with the maps and the Mortmain. After a quick breakfast, they steered the *Wayfarer* out into the current, which carried them swiftly downstream.

In three or four minutes they could see spray in front of them, like the spray from a great waterfall. As they got closer there was a roaring noise.

"Ready at the sail, Silkie!" Owen crouched at the tiller. It was hard to see through the spray to work out where the river ended. There were rocks as well, black and jagged, and it took all of his attention to prevent the *Wayfarer* from being holed. But finally the spray parted and in front of them the mighty river fell away.

"Now, Silkie!" he shouted as the current caught the *Wayfarer* and spun her around. Silkie worked frantically at the sails. Just when it seemed that they would be carried over the edge, the sails filled and the *Wayfarer* soared high in the air. Owen looked down at the turmoil of water where it disappeared into the void of time. Would he ever see Port Merforian again? He tore his eyes away and turned to the tiller. They had to find the Long Woman, and find her soon.

25

For two days they sailed across time. Owen had aligned the symbols for Port Merforian and the Long Woman on the Mortmain, but they didn't seem to close on each other. Studying the maps, he realized that the Long Woman symbol was enclosed within a fish shape on the map, drawn in green ink. At night when he fell asleep exhausted, his dreams were of the Long Woman's haughty, scarred face—a face that seemed to be laughing at him. During the day he ran through everything he knew about the Long Woman, wondering if there was a clue to her whereabouts: the underground kingdom, the dogs and sleigh that she kept. He remembered how her table had been set for strange guests, and that the food had been things of slime and mold. When he told Silkie about this she wrinkled her nose.

"You mean we're trying to find the Long Woman, not run away from her?"

Silkie meanwhile kept to herself. But Owen saw the pride she took in working on the *Wayfarer*. With Higgins' help she had repaired the keel. Now she set about polishing brass and touching up paintwork. Owen could feel the difference in the way the boat sailed, how taut she was, and how she responded to the tiller.

He was at the tiller on the third day, sailing under sky of shimmering green and bronze, when it came to him—the *Wayfarer* would show him how to get to the Long Woman, if only he could find a way to pose the question to the little boat. He asked Silkie to take the tiller and went down below. He opened all the cupboards and went through them. There were lots of old clothes and tools, but nothing that would help to find the Long Woman. Just as he had decided to go up onto the deck again, the *Wayfarer* gave a lurch that sent him sprawling onto the deck. Afterward Silkie swore that the sea had been calm and that she'd done nothing to cause the boat to move in the way that it did.

Owen felt his head where it had cracked against the table leg. He was about to get to his feet when he saw something gleam in the darkness under the bulwark. He reached out and touched a brass switch. He pressed it, and a long narrow drawer sprang open. Owen reached into the drawer and took out a polished wooden box the same shape as the drawer. He put it carefully on the table and opened it.

Inside, on a bed of black velvet, lay a slender, silver horn, delicately chased with gleaming scales, like those of

255

a fish. Owen lifted it up. It felt impossibly light and delicate. Gently he carried it out onto the deck.

"What is it?" Silkie stared at the horn.

"I'm not sure."

"It's beautiful. Are you going to blow it?"

"I suppose," he said, "though I can't see how music is going to help us."

"Go on," Silkie said. "I'd like to hear it."

He put the horn to his lips and blew, expecting it to sound something like a trumpet, but instead it emitted a long, mournful cry.

"What *is* that sound?"

Owen raised the horn and blew again.

"That was the sound the schooner made," he said.

"The schooner?"

"It's a kind of a fish that swims in time. I wonder why the horn was hidden away like that. Can't be that big a deal to sound like a schooner." He blew the horn again, then returned it to the velvet-lined box. He was about to bring it below again when there was a loud gurgling, boiling noise beside the boat.

"Look!" Silkie said in delight. A face had appeared—a face with black markings around the eyes that looked like glasses, long supple lips, and elegant whiskers.

"A schooner!" Silkie's eyes shone. "The horn must have called it."

She leaned over the rail.

"Can you help us find the Long Woman?"

"I don't think it can understand us," Owen said. But,

with a swish of its tail, the schooner dived under the *Wayfarer* and reappeared in front of the bow.

"Hold on a second," Owen said, grabbing the maps. He looked at the fish shape surrounding the Long Woman's symbol. It had the same distinctive double fin on the back.

"The fish on the map is a schooner!"

"Is it going to lead us there?" Silkie asked.

"Looks like it," Owen said. But it did not lead them. As Owen reached for the tiller to follow the great fish, the schooner leapt high in the air and, diving straight down under the surface, disappeared.

Owen and Silkie scanned the sea of time in every direction, but there was no sign of it.

"I really thought the schooner was going to show us the way," Silkie sighed.

"Me too," Owen admitted. He sat down on the hatch, feeling completely deflated.

"Wait. What's that behind us?" Silkie said. Owen jumped to his feet in alarm. There was something coming up fast behind them—a shape that was throwing up great sheets of spray to either side.

"I don't know," Owen said, his eyes wary, "but it's going to catch us pretty quick."

They stood at the stern, watching the shape approach. Owen felt Silkie's hand take his, and he squeezed it in reassurance. Then her eyes widened.

"Look, Owen," she gasped, "it's the schooner!" But not the schooner as they had seen it. The beast had its

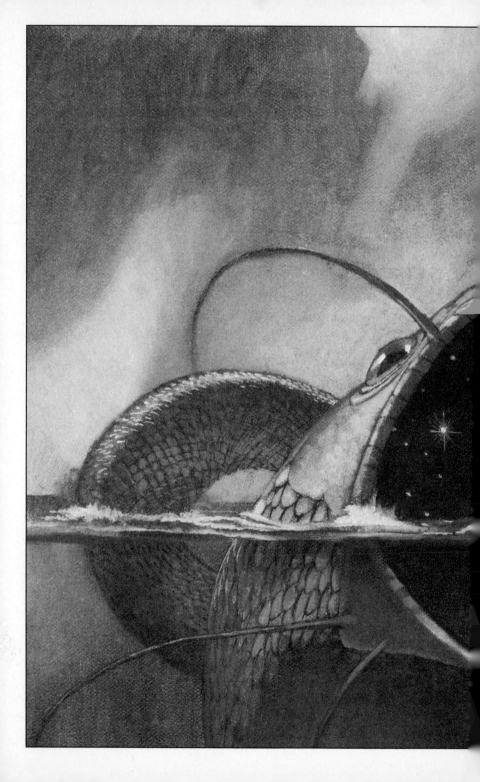

mouth wide open and in the massive cavity behind it, there was no tongue or teeth or anything you might expect in a mouth. Instead there was what looked like a night sky, a sky that glittered with a thousand stars. And just as it was about to catch the *Wayfarer*, there was a great whooshing noise, and what Owen could only think of as a silver wind came from the creature's cavernous mouth.

"It's blowing us along," Silkie whispered in awe. It was true. The schooner's breath filled the *Wayfarer*'s sails. As if a giant hand had picked them up, the *Wayfarer* was thrust forward with incredible force. Everything around them turned to a blur and there was a roaring in their ears. Silkie clung to Owen, and he thought he could feel her heartbeat through the chain-mail shirt.

"I'm frightened, Owen," Silkie said, "Take the sail down—we don't know where we're going!"

"No," Owen said, "we're safe." He could not say how, but he knew where they were going. In his mind's eye he could see the path they were following through time.

He didn't know how long the schooner's breath carried them. They barely noticed that the noise had stopped, that the world was no longer streaming past. Silkie clung tightly. Owen realized that he had his eyes closed. When he opened them the *Wayfarer* was motionless. Her sails hung limp. They were floating on a dark still pool of time. Everything around them was in darkness. When he looked down the two symbols on the Mortmain were shimmering slightly, perfectly aligned.

"Where is the Long Woman?" Silkie whispered, as if afraid to break the silence.

"There is one more thing to be done," Owen said, though he could not have told how he knew. He closed his eyes and thought hard about the Long Woman. Forced the image of her face to come into his mind, and emptied his thoughts of everything else. He heard Silkie gasp but he didn't open his eyes.

"We're sinking!" she cried. But Owen knew they were not. They were traveling downward through time, and he could feel time all about him as though he was immersed in clear cold water. And then it was gone.

He opened his eyes. The *Wayfarer* was floating in a lake in moonlight. In front of them was a small bare island. And on the shore a tall dark figure stood waiting.

There was no wind. Owen had to rig an oar over the stern and use that to propel the *Wayfarer* toward the shore. It took a long time, but the figure did not move.

"Is that her?" Silkie said fearfully.

Owen nodded. Silkie did not speak again, but kept her eyes fixed on the Long Woman as they neared.

Finally the keel grated on shingle. Owen leapt down, followed by Silkie. They walked along the shoreline until they reached the Long Woman. She towered over them in a long faded robe made of cloth that must once have been beautiful. She wore a tall headdress with a piece of ragged lace fluttering from the point. Her face was stern and her eyes were black and Owen could feel Silkie shiver when the Long Woman turned. Her skin was dark brown, the color of bog oak, and one side of her face was rent from temple to jaw, as if she had been struck by an axe. Without saying anything she bent down to Silkie, took hold of her face with a long elegant hand, and examined the scar. Then she let go, as if dismissing her. She turned to Owen.

"You have grown a little, Navigator, no? You find Long Woman all on your own."

She made a cawing sound that might have been laughter.

"So now you follow grandfather, and hope maybe a little bit to find father."

"Did my grandfather come here?"

"He did. Leave message for you."

"A message! What is it?"

"Long Woman not know. Come."

They followed her to the low hill at the center of the island. Owen didn't recognize anything. The last time he had been here, the lake had been frozen.

At the edge of the hill they entered a long dark tunnel. There was a dim greenish light and Silkie could see that the walls were covered in ferns and mosses, and from time to time something seemed to move behind the cover of the plants. She shivered and moved closer to Owen.

At the end of the tunnel was a large moss-colored

door. They had reached the Long Woman's house. She pushed the door open and they followed her in.

The house was lit with a dim green light that seemed to come from the walls, which were of rock and were slick with damp. Great ragged draperies stretched from the ceiling to the floor, shifting in the draft from the open door. Off in the darkness to the left something squeaked and scuttled away. There was a fish tank against the wall, but the glass was so covered in slime that you couldn't see much of what it contained, although Owen thought he saw a pair of bulbous eyes watching him.

As before, the Long Woman had fruit and nuts for them to eat. Silkie got a glimpse inside her larder before she closed the door. The shelves were full of things that glistened and slithered.

"The Harsh attack Workhouse?" the Long Woman asked.

"Yes," Owen said. "I don't know how long they can hold out."

"Navigator's work to stop Harsh. Why do you come here?" the woman demanded.

"I think my grandfather had an idea about stopping the Harsh. He was on the track of something . . . I don't know what, though."

"Time for you to see message then," the Long Woman said.

"Is it written down?" Owen asked.

"No. Is in Memorator."

"What's a Memorator?"

"Come, see."

The Long Woman brought them down a narrow staircase of tree roots, and then into a tunnel that appeared to be part of the living earth. More tree roots grew in and around it, and in the walls earthworms and beetles crawled. Silkie walked beside Owen, not taking her eyes off the Long Woman for a second.

At the end of the tunnel they came to a door made of bone.

"Memorator in here," the Long Woman said. Silkie looked at the door with fear in her eyes.

"Are you sure you should go in there?" she said in a shaky voice.

"You will see little mirror. Breathe on mirror, then step away. Touch no one in Memorator," the Long Woman said. "One touch, all die."

What did she mean by *no one*? Owen wondered. Who was in there? He stepped up to the door. Silkie gripped his arm. There was a pleading look in her eyes.

"I have to," he said gently. "I have to find out. But I need to ask something first." He turned to the Long Woman. "Why did you not give me this message when I first came here? Why wait?"

"Grandfather say not to give it to child. You were child then. Strong now. The Navigator!"

The Long Woman took a key from her belt. Silkie put her hand to her mouth. The parts of the key that went into the door and turned the lock were made from actual teeth.

The Long Woman inserted the key and bent to the lock. The door swung open.

"Go in."

Owen stepped through the door. It swung shut behind him. The light inside was dim and gray. He stood at the mouth of a series of tunnels. He moved further inside and saw that they were interlocking. He touched one of the walls. It felt like plastic, although softer and warmer, like a living substance. He remembered a biology book at school that pretended that you had shrunk and were inside a human brain. His surroundings looked suspiciously like that. It was brighter up ahead, and he walked toward the light.

His hands were shaking. A thousand questions ran through his head. What form would the message from his grandfather take? *Touch no one.* But whom might he touch?

He emerged into a large room, made of the same material as the tunnels. A mirror about twice the size of his hand was attached to the wall. It appeared to be mounted on rubber. He steeled himself and approached it. It looked like an ordinary auto mirror, something that had fallen off an old-fashioned car. He leaned forward and breathed on it. The glass fogged, then cleared. He looked into it and found to his surprise that he was looking at a light in the mirror. Peering into the glass, he saw that it was in fact a hall light with a shade. And as he got closer still he saw that the light was in a room, which had a sofa and a leather armchair. One wall was lined with books. The other was covered in maps. The floor was of polished wood. Then, to his utter surprise and amazement, the room started to *grow* out of the mirror. In the space of a second or less, the room had gone from a miniature in a mirror to a real room, right in front of him. Owen stared, then moved as if to step into the room.

"Hold it there, son!" A man's voice startled him. He looked up. A man had just entered the room from a side door. He had short gray hair and blue eyes and wore glasses with thick black frames. He was thin and tall and moved with a restless energy. He had a towel in his hands.

"Good thing I caught you," the man said. "I was just drying the dishes. Now, let me get a look at you."

"Granddad?" Owen said, his voice shaking.

"Yes, yes, of course," the man said, coming closer, but not touching Owen. "You are the picture of your father, I'm glad to say. I hope they had the sense to call you Owen."

"Yes . . . but you . . . you're alive!"

"Well, not exactly. Probably been dead for years at this stage. I wonder what got me. Probably something stupid. It's always the stupid things that get you." The man shook his head. "Well, at least the Long Woman kept her word. I was afraid the old trout wouldn't. She can be a bit tricky, the Long Woman. Pays to keep on the right side of her."

"I don't understand," Owen said.

"Well, it's one of these strange time things. A device called a Memorator. I'm still in my time—about thirty years ago—and you're still in your time."

"So in your time, I haven't been born yet," Owen said.

"And in your time I'm as dead as a dodo!" his grandfather explained cheerfully. "We have to be careful that we don't say anything that changes things in each other's times—that isn't allowed. But you can give hints." The old man gave Owen a broad wink. Suddenly there was a loud crackling sound, and the scene in front of Owen distorted, as though it was painted on a sheet of rubber and someone had stretched it. Then, just as suddenly, it returned to normal. The old man frowned.

"Dodgy batch of temporal alternators—Higgins, the old dog, swore they were fine." He turned to Owen, his voice urgent now. "We mightn't have much time with this machine. Tell me what's happening."

Owen quickly outlined the Harsh attack on the Workhouse and the larger world.

"I think you were on the track of something that would defeat the Harsh," Owen said.

"Not exactly defeat," his grandfather said. "It's more complicated than that. You know about the song?"

"Yes." Owen's eyes swam as the scene in front of him stretched and distorted again.

"The line you need is at the end." The old man began to sing, his voice quavering.

Time's child was left alone
Time's child fears the warm
The heart that's froze
Set cold kings ablaze . . .

"What does it mean?" Owen asked.

"It means the Harsh aren't who we suppose they are. We have to think differently about them." His grandfather was speaking urgently now.

"There is a book . . . ," Owen said.

"Yes," his grandfather said, "a book. I don't quite understand that bit myself, but it seems there is a book you must find. . . ."

But Owen wasn't listening. He had seen a door behind his grandfather open. A young boy wearing pajamas stepped into the room. He was rubbing his eyes sleepily, and looked to be at best half awake. There was a book with a bright cover under his arm. He squinted at the light, seemingly unaware of Owen, who instinctively stepped back into the shadows so that he wouldn't be seen.

"I woke up, Dad," the boy said. "I thought I heard voices."

"You must have been dreaming, son," the old man said. "There's no one here. Go back to bed."

Watching from the shadows, Owen held his breath. For years he had longed to see his father one more time, but he had never thought it would be like this. This sleepy boy with tousled brown hair was his father! And as he watched his grandfather lead his father to bed, he felt his eyes mist over.

In a minute, his grandfather was back. The old man rubbed his hands over his face wearily. "I do worry about that boy. Too like his dad, I suppose."

I always wanted to see him one more time, Owen thought, but he dared not say it. In his own time his father was gone, and it would not be fair to tell his grandfather. There was enough pain in his eyes already.

The room flickered again, and Owen heard the crackling sound, louder than it had been before. The whole scene disappeared, then reappeared, but shot through with static, so that he couldn't see part of the room.

"The book!" his grandfather was shouting. "Find . . . book . . . then . . . understand . . ."

His grandfather vanished, then reappeared, very close to him, a wolfish grin on his face.

"Good to . . . you," he yelled, ". . . proud of you!"

There was a final massive crackle and then his grandfather's room was gone for good. There was nothing except bare gray in front of him. Owen put his fingers to his face. His cheeks were wet.

Silkie had followed the Long Woman back to the fish tank room, not knowing what else she should do. As far as she could tell, the Long Woman had forgotten she was there, or simply didn't care one way or another. The Long Woman sat down at a dressing table draped with old and fragile lace with great holes in it. She took off her headdress and let down her hair—a wild and tangled mass that reached her waist. She picked up a hairbrush and tugged at the hair, but it was full of knots and burrs and thorns, and every stroke made her wince and hiss under her breath.

"Here," Silkie found herself saying, "let me do that."

Before the Long Woman could react, Silkie had taken the hairbrush from her hand. The Long Woman didn't move, and Silkie found that her hand was shaking. Nervously, she picked out a small thistle head and started to brush.

The hair was very fine, and the tangles fell out easily. Silkie felt as if she was dealing with a very old fabric. The hair appeared gray to start with, but as she brushed, strands of gold started to appear. Silkie had often brushed the children's hair in the warehouse, and she enjoyed it. And as she brushed she sang a Raggie song about a young man who met a beautiful girl on the beach one day. They fell in love and got married, but the young man was foolish and lost his bride back to the sea. Midsong she faltered. The Long Woman had grasped her wrist, hard enough to hurt, and had turned so that Silkie was looking into her eyes, into fathomless depths filled with strange knowledge that Silkie could not imagine. But there was something else, dancing just at the corners of her eyes. Perhaps not even a smile, just the memory of a smile. The Long Woman closed her eyes and released Silkie's hand, and Silkie brushed on and the hair grew finer and finer so that it seemed to fly about her in a golden cloud.

How long Silkie had been asleep she could not tell. She did not remember falling asleep, but when she woke she was curled up on a cushion on the floor. Owen was standing in the doorway. There was a strange expression on his face.

"How long have I been gone?" he asked.

"Hours, I think," Silkie said.

"It only felt like minutes."

"Have you been . . . ," Silkie stopped. She could see that his eyes were red. "I mean, what did you see?"

Owen swallowed. "It's not so often you get to meet your dad and find that he's younger than you are."

"What?"

Owen told her about everything that had happened in the Memorator. Silkie's eyes were as round as saucers when he had finished. Then she frowned.

"But he didn't really tell you anything that you don't already know," she said.

"I think he did, or rather my dad did without meaning to. Where's the Long Woman? We need to get moving."

"Where are we going?"

"Behind enemy lines."

They found the Long Woman outside, at her dog compound, where she kept the dangerous but beautiful long-muzzled dogs that drew her sleigh. The leader, Arcana, gave a sharp bark when he saw Owen, and Owen acknowledged the greeting with a smile.

"Does that mean he's pleased to see you?" Silkie asked.

"I think so. The Long Woman's dogs don't really go in for tail wagging and that sort of stuff."

The Long Woman turned from the dogs' feeding bowls. Her hair had been put up again, but Silkie could see glints of gold from under her tall hat.

"We need to go," Owen said, "but thank you for all your help."

"You find what you need?" The Long Woman raised an eyebrow.

"I think so."

"Then go quick. Fight Harsh. Maybe I fight Harsh too. Long Woman is too old to kill Harsh. Arcana go with you to boat. Too many dangerous things on island."

"Thank you for keeping my granddad's message," Owen said.

The Long Woman cackled. "Grandfather good man, better than grandson to notice what is straight in front of eyes!"

And with that the Long Woman turned her back to them.

"Goodbye, and, er . . . thanks," Silkie said. But the Long Woman did not speak again. Arcana looked at them expectantly.

It took longer than they expected back to the *Wayfarer,* and without Arcana they would soon have been lost in the dark.

"What did she mean by that last bit about noticing things in front of your eyes?" Silkie asked.

"I don't know," Owen said, slipping on a slimy weed. "Is it always dark in this place?"

The Long Woman . . . her face was different in some way . . . Silkie thought hard but couldn't work it out.

At last they reached the *Wayfarer*. Owen thanked Arcana. The dog bared his teeth in what seemed like a smile and loped off into the night.

"Light a lamp," Owen said. "I can't see a thing."

Silkie lit a magno lamp and carried it onto the deck, where she hung it from a nail on the mast. Owen looked up. His expression changed.

"What is it?" Silkie asked.

"Touch your face," he said quietly. She put her hand to her cheek. The skin was smooth. The angry scar had gone!

"Now I know what was different about the Long Woman," Silkie said. "She had another scar on her face, a small one beside the big one she always had.

"It must have been when I was asleep," Silkie added, feeling her cheek in wonder. "I would not have asked her to carry that burden for me."

Silkie turned and bowed in the direction of the Long Woman's house, and though she did not know it, the Long Woman's fierce, unblinking stare watched them from under the eaves.

"Get ready to let out the sail," Owen said. "The Harsh are waiting."

Cati and Wesley were at their wits' end. Rosie's sentence was due to be carried out the following day, and they had made no progress either in finding her accomplice or in figuring out how they would get her out of prison. Movement around the Workhouse was getting increasingly more difficult, particularly with Moorhead after them, and they barely would have been able to move if not for the ventilation ducts. The atmosphere was tense. The Albions had started creeping close to the walls at night, and several guard posts had been attacked.

Wesley and Cati had taken to escaping to the Den, which they reckoned was safe from the redcoats. Wesley sat on the sofa while Cati paced, stopping every so often as if an idea had struck her; then she would shake her head and resume pacing.

"Sit yourself down," Wesley said. "You're getting on my nerves."

"Never mind your nerves, I need to think," she snapped. Before Wesley could reply there was a noise in the doorway. Wesley leapt to his feet. It was only Martha.

"We don't have much chance of winning this war if friends keep falling out," she observed.

"It's Rosie," Cati blurted out. "We don't think it's fair, what's happening to her."

"We've been looking for a way to stop them putting her to sleep," Wesley said.

"If I can't work out a problem, I usually talk to the cleverest person I know," Martha said, sitting down. "Sometimes you only need to tell it, and then you start to see clearly."

"Who is the cleverest person we know?" Wesley turned to Cati. "Dr. Diamond. Got to be."

"Yes," Cati burst out, "but he voted for the sentence."

"Perhaps you should ask him why he did that, instead of judging him," Martha said gently. "We all owe our friends that, at least."

Rosie lay on the bunk in her cell, staring at the ceiling. The music in her head had become a lot more troubling, filling her mind so that she had difficulty thinking, and the stabbing pains were more frequent. She was often confused, drifting in and out of sleep, wondering where her friends were, and why she was in this tiny cell.

Twenty minutes later the two friends found themselves in a ventilation shaft, climbing upward toward the Nab.

"Martha's right," Wesley said. "We need to talk to him."

"All I can say is that his story better be good," Cati exclaimed crossly. Then she put her head to one side.

"What is it?" Wesley asked. He knew that since her time with the Dogs in Hadima, her hearing was very sensitive.

"Follow me." She started to climb down one of the side shafts. As they got closer Wesley could hear a peculiar high-pitched, half-strangled noise.

They clambered down until they were positioned just above a wooden grille. Down below was what appeared to be a guard's room.

"One of Samual's," Wesley whispered. There was a red uniform folded on the bed. There were pink fluffy cushions and photographs of kittens on the wall. The air was full of steam. They heard the strange noise again, and then Moorhead came into the room. She was wearing a shower cap and had a towel wrapped around her head. She had a large pink sponge in her hand, and as they gazed in wonder, she opened her mouth and started to sing.

"My secret love, I soar like a dove . . . ," Moorhead warbled.

Cati and Wesley fought back the giggles. They wriggled back into the main shaft, where they rolled around holding their sides, all of the tensions of the siege falling away. Afterward they sat in the dim lit shaft.

"I feel weak," Cati said. "My sides are sore."

"I ain't had a laugh like that this long time."

"Do you think we can beat them?" Cati said, now serious. "You know that time when the Harsh froze me? I couldn't bear that again, Wesley. I don't want to be a coward, but every time I even think about them I feel the cold in my bones. It's like death."

Wesley didn't say anything. Instead he reached out and took her hand. They sat like that for a long time, then without a word they started to climb again.

The shaft opened onto an old rusty grille on the roof. Wesley worked at the rotten screws with his knife until they were free. He put his head out cautiously and ducked back again.

"What is it?" Cati hissed.

"Take a look."

She peered out over the rim of the shaft. Ten yards away a group of Samual's soldiers stood around the base of the Nab, the brass tower that supported Dr. Diamond's Skyward. There was an immense tangle of barbed wire around the base of the tower. Dr. Diamond came out of the Skyward high above and stood on the staircase.

"Matt!" he shouted down. One of the soldiers looked up.

"Yes, Doctor?"

"Matt, for the final time, will you take a message to Samual?"

"I can't, Doctor. Orders."

"Orders, orders," the doctor muttered. "What happened to free will?"

"What's that, Doc?"

"Never mind," the doctor said irritably, and walked back into the Skyward.

"They're keeping him prisoner!" Cati said, slipping back into the shaft.

"Samual's getting rid of anybody might stand against him," Wesley said.

"I don't know." Cati looked uncertain. "In the end Samual is a soldier. And Dr. Diamond respects him."

"Don't matter anyhow. He's still a prisoner. Even if we get rid of the guards, we'll never get past the barbed wire."

"I have an idea," Cati said. "Follow me."

Cati plunged back into the shaft with Wesley behind her. They reached the spot where they had entered the shaft, but Cati kept on going. Down and down they went, deep into the bowels of the Workhouse, the shaft becoming darker, coated with the filth of ages. At last they emerged into what looked like the interior of a machine—there were giant brass cogs and pistons and pulleys, all covered in ancient grease.

"What is this place?" Wesley looked up at a brass cog that towered above him.

"Machine room for the Nab," Cati explained. "This machine puts it up and lowers it."

A grin spread across Wesley's face.

"I think I get you," he said.

Five minutes later, Samual's soldiers were standing around the brass shaft of the Nab when they felt a rumbling beneath their feet. The rumbling grew to a roar. They looked around in alarm as the shaft of the Nab began to vibrate. There was an earsplitting grate of metal against metal, then, with alarming creaks and groans, the huge brass towers started to shoot down into the earth, the sections telescoping into each other. The soldiers ran for cover as the shaft swayed this way and that and rolls of barbed wire were flung high into the air. With unbelievable speed, the Nab was swallowed by the Workhouse. As the Skyward drew level with the roof of the Workhouse, the soldiers saw Dr. Diamond. He was leaning on the rail of the Skyward, looking as relaxed as if he was out for a stroll and had stopped to lean on a bridge. With a smile he waved at them and then, with a tremendous clatter, the Nab disappeared.

Cati had covered her ears against the din made by the machine and the telescoping sections of the Nab. Looking up, she saw the Skyward speeding toward them. It seemed that it must smash into the ground, but just as it drew level with them it slowed and stopped. Dr. Diamond stepped off, brushing dust from his overalls.

"That was very clever, you two," he said.

"Why were they keeping you locked up like that?" Wesley asked.

"And why did you vote to sentence Rosie?" Cati demanded.

Dr. Diamond sat down on a large metal gear housing and sighed.

"I had no choice," he said. "Rosie has been working

for Johnston. I don't know how or why, but I had to get her out of circulation."

"You're talking about *Rosie*!" Cati was outraged.

"Take it easy." Wesley put his hand on Cati's shoulder. "Let the man speak."

"I know that, Cati, but her actions were putting the whole Workhouse in danger. I had to get her out of harm's way until I figure out what is going on."

"You don't have much time, Doc," Wesley said.

"I know that," the doctor replied. Cati and Wesley watched in puzzlement as Dr. Diamond gazed around the space they were in, then spotted what he was looking for: a ventilation shaft. He moved until he was standing right beside it.

"And there is something else," he said loudly. "She was talking to someone through the ventilation shaft. I am afraid she has an accomplice, and I think I know who that accomplice is."

In the still center of the Workhouse, Dr. Diamond's words drifted through dozens of ventilation shafts into empty rooms and stores and attics. And in one of those rooms an ear was pressed to the shaft, and a heart began to beat a little faster.

Rosie paced the earthen floor of her prison cell. She found it hard to believe that she was in prison, condemned as a traitor. She was confused. The immediate past was vague and far away. Her home in Hadima felt closer. She remembered how Owen and Cati and Dr. Diamond had arrived in the City, and how they had helped her secure the ransom for her brother, Graham, who'd been imprisoned by the Specials.

She tried to push away the thought that her friends might in fact believe that she was a traitor. She went to the barred window in the door.

"Shem?" she whispered. Shem was a young guard, not much older than Rosie. Most of Samual's men were stern, but Shem was different. He would slip her extra morsels of food, even though he didn't have enough for himself. And sometimes he would talk to her through the bars, even though everyone said that she had betrayed the Resisters.

"You'll have long enough without talking," he said once, and then blushed, realizing that he shouldn't have reminded her of what was in front of her. Instead of telling him off, she reached through the bars and touched his shoulder.

"Shem!" she whispered again.

"What is it, Rosie?" he replied. He was a tall young man with black curly hair, quick and alert in a way that reminded Rosie of the young people of Hadima.

"How long is left?" she asked.

"About an hour," he said. He looked both sad and frightened.

"Don't worry," she said. "Something will turn up."

"Something has turned up." Rosie heard a harsh voice. Moorhead. At a signal from her, four of the troops with her stepped forward. One of them opened the lock—which was on the outside and too far away for Rosie to have picked. The other three seized her. Shem stepped forward and grabbed her arm. Rosie was grateful. She knew he didn't want her to be alone.

"She has another hour," Shem protested.

"It's been brought forward—new orders," Moorhead said. Rosie was lifted from her feet and swiftly marched through the guardrooms of Samual's soldiers.

"Where is everyone?" Shem whispered to one of the soldiers.

"General alert," he growled. "Harsh is up to something."

Then they were in a corridor that Shem had never been in before. It led upward in a spiral. The walls dripped with condensation and the tramp of the soldiers' boots echoed on the stones. Rosie's mind worked feverishly. She had gotten out of many tough scrapes before, but this time she had no more ideas.

The soldiers stopped in front of an ancient wooden door. Moorhead opened it with a heavy key and it swung open with a groan. Inside was a small room with no windows. And in the middle of the room was a chair. There were metal bands on the chair and heavy cables ran from the bands to a large square iron box that took up almost one side of the room.

"What is it?" Rosie whispered to Shem.

"It's written on the side."

"I can't read, you twit," Rosie said.

"'Magno Generator,'" Shem read. Rosie stared at him.

"That's not for putting people to sleep," she said. Then two of the soldiers grabbed her.

"Shem, they're going to fry me!" she cried. But one of the soldiers forced a gag into her mouth, and the other men began to attach her to the chair using the metal bands.

"Something isn't right," Shem said. "There should be people here—Pieta, Dr. Diamond, Contessa. The law doesn't allow this . . . and that machine isn't for putting people to sleep. Rosie's right. You don't need magno for that."

"Shut up, boy," Moorhead snarled. One soldier looked uncertain, but the others put their hands to their magno guns. Shem stepped in front of Rosie.

"You'll have to go through me first."

"If necessary," Moorhead said. "Men!"

The soldiers started to advance on Shem. In desperation he grabbed one of the heavy lead-and-iron bands from the chair and snapped it around Moorhead's wrist. Then he ran to the machine and grasped the large brass lever protruding from the front.

"You think you can shoot me before I pull the lever and give Lieutenant Moorhead more magno than she can handle?" Rosie was struggling violently, but he ignored her.

"Put down the guns," he said as Rosie finally spat out her gag.

"You moron," she roared. "Shem! Look!" The other

cable was firmly attached to Rosie's leg. If he pulled the lever, then Rosie would get the same blast of magno.

"When I get out of this . . . ," Moorhead hissed.

"When you get out of this you will have me to answer to," an angry voice spoke out from the doorway. Rosie looked up. Samual. Behind him were Cati, Dr. Diamond, and Wesley.

"She's a traitor!" Moorhead cried. "Shoot her!" But the soldiers looked nervously at each other and did not move.

"There is only one traitor here, and that is you," Samual spat.

Cati slipped unheeded into the room.

"Rosie, do you remember the rose you were wearing when you first arrived at the Workhouse?" Dr. Diamond asked.

Rosie nodded. "Moorhead took it off me."

"Look," Dr. Diamond said. He produced the red rose from one of his pockets. He did something to the stem, then shook it. The rose began to unfurl, the petals opening out as if it were blooming into a flower of extraordinary size. But it wasn't a flower—it was a square of very fine red steel mesh with the stem running through the center.

"A transmitter," Samual said grimly. "Johnston used the Hadima girl to smuggle it in to Moorhead."

"And I bet if we look in Moorhead's room we'll find a receiver," Cati said.

Moorhead's plump face turned into a snarling mask.

She sprang at Rosie, her fingers like talons. Cati yanked the cable from Rosie's ankle and they leapt aside. Instead of Rosie's neck, Moorhead's grasping fingers found the lever of the magno generator. The others stood dumbfounded as Moorhead's despairing screech filled the room. There was a crackle and a gout of blue flame. Rosie turned her face away as Cati choked back a sob. Wesley looked pale. The soldiers were frozen but Samual's habitual grim expression did not change. The doctor was the only one to move, taking off his lab coat and spreading it over the prostrate Moorhead.

"A traitor," Samual said, "and she dies a traitor's death. But why?"

"I imagine," Dr. Diamond said mildly, "she was promised your job. After your death, of course."

Samual eyed the doctor. "And what about this Hadima street rat?" he growled. "What was she promised to betray us? She did steal the ring and plant it, and open the door to the Albions, did she not?"

"She did."

"Rosie!" Cati looked at her in dismay. Before anyone else had a chance to move, Dr. Diamond grabbed a sword from one of the guards with his good arm, and, spinning across the room, swung the sword at Rosie. Rosie leapt backward and reached into her hair for a hairpin. For a moment the Hadima girl and the scientist faced each other, poised for combat. Then Dr. Diamond put the sword up.

"Why did you reach for that hairpin, Rosie?" he said

gently. "This one is closer." He leaned over her and touched the tip of the pin at the front of her head.

"I . . . I don't know," she said.

"Take it out now."

Rosie took hold of the pin. But no matter how much she pulled, it would not budge.

"That's why you won't find any receiver in Moorhead's room," the doctor said. "Rosie *is* the receiver."

He took a small, odd-looking hammer from his pocket and put the twisted claw end around the pin. "Stay still, my dear. This won't hurt." He levered it against Rosie's forehead and pulled carefully. There was a creaking sound and the pin slowly slid out. Rosie looked at him in amazement.

"The music . . . in my head. It's gone!"

"What is it?" Wesley said, staring at the pin.

"A fugueometer," Dr. Diamond said. "Johnston could control your thoughts, or at least block some of them." Without warning, Dr. Diamond plunged the hairpin in the back of his neck. Cati gasped. But the doctor merely looked thoughtful. Then he started to hum a melody.

"Is that the music?" Wesley drew close.

"Yes!"

"Bach," the scientist said. "In very good taste, I have to say. Yes, I can feel Johnston's thoughts . . . he's reaching out to you . . . Ouch! Did that pain come with it as well?"

"Every time," Rosie said.

"Then you're braver than me." The doctor reached

for the hammer and swiftly levered the pin out of his neck, apparently without ill effects.

"Johnston captured me when I first arrived," Rosie said slowly. "I remember now!"

"He knew you were coming, probably from the Albions. He must have knocked you out long enough to insert the device—pretty easy to do, as you see. When Johnston wanted her to do something, he transmitted a signal. Equally, when he wanted to get an instruction to Moorhead, he sent it to Rosie."

"It was old Moorhead she was talking to through the ventilation shaft," Wesley said.

"Yes. And Johnston couldn't risk his signals not penetrating the Workhouse walls, so he needed the rose transmitter on the roof."

Rosie looked at the pin in wonder.

"Do you remember him talking to you?" Wesley said, staring at the pin in mingled wonder and disgust.

"No . . . no . . . just . . . just foul dreams. I don't want to talk about them."

"Your mind fought it," the doctor said. "You pulled at your hair a lot—you knew there was something wrong with your head, you just didn't know what. When you unlocked the door for the Albions, you must have been pulling at it so hard, you dropped another pin on the ground. Unconsciously, you gave yourself away."

"We only just got here in time," Cati said. "Dr. Diamond thought Moorhead might be listening through the shafts, so he pretended he knew who the traitor was to flush her out."

"So that's why she tried to get rid of the Hadima girl," Samual said.

"Without Rosie, there was no evidence," the doctor said.

"I don't have time for more of this." Samual glared at Rosie. "Count yourself lucky in your friends, girl!"

"I do," Rosie said quietly. "I do feel lucky in my friends."

Before anyone could reply there was a roar of engines outside. Dr. Diamond went to the window.

"More trouble," he said. Samual joined him, cursed, then ran for the door, followed by his men. The others followed. Only Cati paused to look down at the crumpled form of Moorhead under the lab coat. She had been a Resister too, fighting the enemies of time until corrupted by Johnston. Cati knelt and placed her hand for a moment on the woman's shoulder under the coat, then rose and followed the others.

The friends gathered on the battlements. The enemy encampment stood between them and the sea, but this time there was more than tents.

"What are they?" Cati said, in fear and awe.

"Q-cars," a hard, sad voice said from behind them. Cati turned to see Pieta, flanked by Aldra and Beck, her arm in a sling across her breast.

"I don't like the look of 'em," Wesley murmured. The Q-cars were pods, almost like aircraft fuselages, slung under four huge, thin bicycle-like wheels. Owen had been abducted by Johnston in one, and Pieta had rescued him. But these were different. Johnston's Q-car had not been armed. These bristled with gun barrels and weapons of every description, and there were dozens of them. They were manned by villainous-looking Specials.

And on the ground there was worse. The Harsh had equipped the Albions with bulbous dark glasses to protect their eyes from the light, and they were wearing dark suits to shield their skin. They looked like vicious insects milling around under the wheels of the Q-cars. In the distance near the harbor rose a cloud of white ice. There was to be no waiting for the Workhouse to be starved into submission. The Harsh were on the march.

27

All night they had battled against storms and squalls. The *Wayfarer* shouldered aside the seas of time gallantly. Owen sat at the stern without speaking, lost in thought. Silkie made food, tended to the *Wayfarer*'s rigging, and slept fitfully. When she awoke and came out on deck, Owen was sitting in the same position.

"What are you thinking?" she asked.

"I'm trying to remember a story," he said. He wouldn't say any more. She started to work around him, tightening sheets, tidying the decks, straightening out kinks in the ropes, doing all the little things that the craft needed to keep it sailing well. Gradually Owen became aware of her, first a sweet perfume with a hint of wood smoke that he had never noticed before, then her hair brushing against his cheek. She knelt to the deck to fasten a cleat and when she rose he found himself looking deep into her clear green eyes, which were flecked with gold in their depths. She smiled but said nothing, and kept on working around him. When she had finished she went and sat in the bow, and Owen realized that he would miss being on board the *Wayfarer* with her.

At last, as dawn broke in green and amber sheets of light, Owen stood up. He examined the Mortmain and adjusted their course.

"Nearly home. Get ready to drop the sail," he said. Silkie stood by, ready to act.

"Now!" he said. The shimmering sail dropped and they were in the clouds, the bitter cold burning their lungs. Through the cloud rushing past he caught glimpses of the scene below: The fleet of Q-cars poised to attack. The host of the Harsh moving inland from the ships, and the lone standard of the Workhouse raised against them. War and ice and ruin everywhere.

"And they look to me to end it," he said to himself, as if Silkie wasn't there. Silkie gazed at him. Her blood had run cold when she saw the forces arrayed against the Resisters.

Owen stayed in the cloud until they were well inland from the Workhouse, then dropped swiftly to treetop height. He turned back, speeding toward the gathering battle, using the shelter of trees and dips in the land to hide their progress wherever possible, handling the *Wayfarer* expertly.

In five minutes' time they were behind Mary White's shop, and Owen dropped the *Wayfarer* into the snow. They jumped down and ran into the shop. Without a word, he found a stepladder and climbed up to a trapdoor in the ceiling, disappearing inside it. Silkie went to the window. Her heart ached for her friends. Minutes passed, then an hour. Impatient, Silkie climbed the ladder. She found Owen sitting on the attic floor. There were books scattered around him on the floor, and he was reading intently.

"I can't believe you're up here reading," she cried, "and those Harsh are about to freeze everybody we know!"

The face Owen raised to her was serious. He held up the book in his hand. The once-bright colors on the cover were old and faded. The illustration was of a sad-looking, fair-haired boy with frost in his hair.

"What does it say?" Silkie asked, blushing. Owen remembered that the Raggies could not read.

"It's called *The Frost Child*," he said, "and I've just finished it."

"Is it for children?"

"Yes, that's it," Owen said. "It *is* a book for children!"

Silkie was puzzled. "What's it about?"

They heard an explosion from the direction of the Workhouse, and then another. The room shook.

"I don't have time to explain! Can you sail the *Wayfarer* on your own?"

"I . . . I think so. . . ."

"Come with me."

Silkie followed Owen outside to the *Wayfarer*. He spread out a map on the deck and spoke to her quickly and urgently. Then he adjusted the Mortmain. "Go quickly."

"But what about you?"

"I have to talk to somebody about something that happened long, long ago."

Silkie looked at him gravely, then took his hand and kissed him on the cheek. "Be careful."

"You too." He embraced her. He watched the *Wayfarer* take off and stood looking after her until she had disappeared into the clouds. Then, tucking *The Frost Child* under his jacket, he started to run.

He cut in behind the enemy encampment, keeping down so that he wouldn't be seen, although the camp was deserted. The Workhouse was hidden by a fog of ice, but every few moments there was an explosion followed by a gout of dull orange flame and dark smoke. He did not need to be reminded that his mother and all his friends were in there.

He followed the river toward the harbor. The Hadima entrance seemed to be unmanned, but he took no chances, climbing up onto the bridge and going through the town, or what was left of it. Blackened timbers and fire-scorched masonry covered in snow were all that was left of the town he had grown up in. Rage toward the Harsh welled up in him. They had taken so much. He could still see his father as he was in the Memorator, a sleepy boy in pajamas. There was another explosion from the Workhouse, a roar of triumph from the attackers, followed by a woman's scream. Tears of hatred pricked his eyes. He stumbled on something in the snow—a magno gun, dropped by one of the Resisters in their headlong retreat from the sea. He lifted it.

At last he reached the shore. The Harsh ships stretched toward the horizon, a towering ghost fleet covered in frost and ice, surrounded by their ice castles. He didn't see anyone on the ships, but he knew that he was being watched.

He made his way toward the ship with the banner flying from the topmost mast. As he closed he realized that the other ships formed a circle, centered on this one vessel. It got colder as he approached and the ice creaked and groaned. The sounds of battle were distant now. Was the noise muffled by the cloud of ice surrounding the Workhouse, or were the Resisters falling before the attack?

An ornate gangplank led from the deck of the ship to the ice below. As Owen mounted it, he noticed that the filigree carving and ornate detail was made entirely of ice. He touched the rail and it stuck to his hand. As he pulled it away, he hissed in pain. It had torn a patch of skin, and now red blood dropped on the snow-white gangplank as he walked, the cold draining his strength so only the heat of his anger kept him going.

At last he reached the deck. He did not have to look further. In front of the mast stood the frost child. Owen raised the gun. He knew that he need only pull the trigger and the Harsh would be destroyed forever. He thought of his father drowned. His mother and his friends battling for their lives. The people of Hadima buried under ice. He remembered Cati's father, sucked into the vortex of time created by the Harsh. His finger tightened on the trigger. Then he saw that the child was looking not at his face but at the book that showed from under his jacket, and there was an unimaginable longing in his eyes.

The boy spoke now, and the voice was that of a lost child, filled with loneliness. He said three words. Owen lowered the gun, his anger draining away. He could not fire. The child said the three words again.

"Read to me."

Owen put the gun down. He knelt on the deck and opened the book. The boy sat beside him with a grave, trusting look on his face. Owen read the story of a child born a long time ago, in another world, far from Owen's and from the Resisters'.

The child's parents could imagine things into being. That was their work. They imagined a forest and there it was. They imagined a new kind of animal and it appeared. But they were too busy at their work and they did not spend enough time with their son, leaving him alone in a garden under the stars. In his loneliness he began to imagine things to play with. At first it was just toys. And then he imagined a bear and a dog who would keep him company. But that was not enough. One day

when his parents had been gone longer than usual, the child was angry, and he imagined kings and queens of ice. And because he missed the warmth of his mother and father, the kings and queens hated warmth. And because he hated his life, they hated life as well. At first they did his bidding, but they were willful and were soon out of his control. They went abroad and did evil. And because he had imagined them, he could not unimagine them, and they kept him close to them so he could not escape.

When his mother and father returned from their journey, the garden was frozen and the child was gone. They searched all their days to find him but he was lost forever.

Is it true? Owen thought. *Could a child imagine the Harsh into being? Is that where they come from?*

"Did you imagine them?" Owen asked. "The Harsh?" The boy nodded.

"Can you stop them? Do you know how?"

This time the child shook his head and a tear rolled down his face.

"And that means . . ." Owen's brain hurt from thinking. "That you are frozen too."

The tear fell from the child's face. It was a drop of ice before it hit the deck.

Worse than that, Owen thought. *He is frozen and lost beyond his time. The Harsh are all he has. There has to be another way. I need to talk to somebody.*

Owen got to his feet. He was so cold he could barely move. He put the book back under his jacket. The boy watched him steadily.

"I'll think of something else," Owen promised, although he did not know what that might be. As Owen went down the gangplank, the tears ran freely from the child's eyes and fell on the deck like an icy rain.

28

The Resisters could not have prepared for the ferocity of the attack. A hail of fire from the Q-cars struck the leading defenses on the edge of the frozen river. Ice lances and magno rockets rained down. Frozen earth and ice were thrown high in the air, and the noise was deafening. The Porcupine could not shoot down half of the ice lances. And then the Q-cars started to advance. High on the battlements, Cati, Wesley, and Rosie watched.

"We ain't got a hope against that lot," Wesley said. Dr. Diamond, who had been watching the advance through binoculars, turned to them.

"Everything's been going much as I expected. I'm going to need each of you."

"I hope you got something special up your sleeve, Doc," Rosie told him.

"Have you ever practiced martial arts?" Dr. Diamond asked.

"What's that?" Rosie said suspiciously.

"A form of oriental combat. One of the principles is that you use your opponents' strength against them."

"How do we do that, then?" Wesley regarded the doctor dubiously.

"Look," Dr. Diamond said, handing Wesley the telescope. Beyond the lines of Q-cars, Wesley saw the ranks of the Harsh. They had formed themselves into pyramids, with nine or ten Harsh in each. Ice started to form about them.

"That's what they done before," Wesley said. "They put their Harsh breath together and make a weapon out of it, like a beam."

"Exactly."

"And then me and Owen brought out the dressing table, the one with the mirror. Boom!"

"Dressing table?" Rosie repeated, bewildered. "What dressing table? What are you talking about?"

"Do you remember those covered discs I hung over the parapet?" the doctor said. "They're mirrors."

"Brilliant!" Cati exclaimed.

"You're all bonkers," Rosie said. A low hum rose from the ranks of the Harsh.

"Cover your ears!" Cati warned. The hum grew in pitch and intensity, sounding at first like a bleak northern wind, a wind with lonely, wicked voices in it. Then it became an ear-piercing shriek. From each of the pyramids of ice a beam of absolute cold was hurled at the Workhouse.

"Quick!" Dr. Diamond said. "Use those ropes. Throw the covers off the mirrors!" They did as he said. The ice beams struck the Workhouse with a mighty crash. Chunks of masonry and ice were flung high into the air. Cati felt the ground under her feet vibrate with the power of the beam.

"Use the other ropes to raise and lower the mirrors," Dr. Diamond shouted above the mighty din. Cati looked down at the mirror below her, a polished disc of metal about four feet across. It was surprisingly light, and using the rope she could move it easily up and down. An ice beam was aimed at one of the corners of the Workhouse and it was eating into the old mortar and stone. Cautiously she lowered the mirror into the path of the beam. With an impact that nearly tore the rope from her grasp, the beam struck the mirror and ricocheted off into the sky.

"Well done, Cati!" Dr. Diamond shouted. "Now try to use the mirrors as aiming devices. Send the beams right back to them."

First Wesley and then Rosie intercepted a beam. Wesley's went upward but Rosie's sheared the top off a small copse of trees near the river, showering Samual with leaves and branches.

"Whoops!" She grinned.

Dr. Diamond was more successful. He managed to angle the beam so that it was sent across the battlefield, striking the left-hand wheels of the lead Q-car. It toppled slowly to the ground and burst into flames. There was a cheer from the defenders below.

Soon Cati and Wesley were sending their beams into the middle of the attacking Q-cars. Three of them had slowed to a halt, and another was in flames. But Rosie couldn't manage to direct her fire at all. In fact, the defenders below were more in danger than the attackers as ice beams struck at random among the trenches.

"Maybe you better stop, Rosie," Cati said anxiously.

"Just one more try . . . ," Rosie said, her face scrunched up with effort. An ice beam moved swiftly across the front of the building, tearing at the fabric with terrible power. Rosie closed one eye to aim and dropped the mirror right in front of the beam. It was turned back on itself, and shot across the fields, over the heads of the attackers and defenders alike, and crashed into the Harsh who had fired it. The Harsh structure began to vibrate. The Harsh inside threw their arms up, their mouths wide. With a mighty crash the structure exploded, ice raining down on the battlefield.

"Bull's-eye!" Rosie shouted, and a great roar arose from the defenders. From the left flank of the battlefield, Rutgar and his men appeared, taking the enemy by surprise. Two Q-cars turned in confusion, crashing into each other, their wheels becoming hopelessly entangled. The others fired wildly, in one case striking another Q-car. Rutgar pressed on. Gradually, and then in confusion, the attackers started to retreat, many flinging down their weapons and running.

It was this mob that Owen met as he came up from the harbor, the magno gun in front of him. But none of them spared him a glance, the Specials running without looking back, the bespectacled Albions squealing and crashing into things. For although they could now bear the daylight, the dark glasses meant that they couldn't see very well. Owen moved cautiously. Johnston could be anywhere, and would know him instantly.

But it wasn't Johnston who recognized him. A disciplined group of men came over the rise in front of him, moving quickly, and firing steadily at their pursuers. Owen tried to get out of their way, but it was too late. The man at their head spotted Owen. It was Headley, chief corsair of the Specials, who had flung Owen in prison during his time in Hadima. A wicked grin spread across Headley's face.

"Cover me, boys," he growled. "I've got business with this young gentleman here."

Owen tried to raise the magno gun but Headley's heavy baton dashed the gun out of Owen's grasp. The next blow came at Owen's head, but he ducked and caught it on the shoulder. The pain was sickening. Headley raised the baton again. Owen threw himself sideways in the snow and Headley missed, the baton sticking in the ice. Headley struggled to free it, Owen staggered to his feet and ran toward the Resister lines, evading Headley's men, but before he had got far he heard Headley bellowing in triumph. A shadow fell over him. He looked up and his heart sank. A Q-car stood over him, its front bristling with cannon. He turned to see Headley, baton raised. Owen fell to his knees in the snow. He could run no farther. He heard the baton descending with a whistling sound. He shut his eyes. But there was no blow, just a loud concussion and a shout of pain from Headley. He looked up. Uel was leaning out of the side window of the Q-car with a magno crossbow in his hand. Mervyn was at the controls. Headley lay in the snow, the baton in pieces.

Headley scrambled to his feet and Uel pointed the crossbow at him. Owen knew that Uel wouldn't pull the trigger. The two boys, for all their expertise, hated to fight. Headley backed away, a snarl on his face, like a wolf deprived of his prey. His men looked as if they might try something, but Mervyn swung the Q-car and brought the guns to bear on them. Like Headley, they sullenly moved off.

When the men were far enough away for safety, Uel lowered the ladder for Owen.

"Hop in," he said. "We'll give you a lift."

Owen climbed the ladder one-handed, his shoulder numb. He was delighted to see the Raggie boys. And with Mervyn waving from the window so that they wouldn't be attacked by their own men, they steered for the Workhouse.

29

When the defenders saw Owen, they cheered wildly. They had won a battle and casualties were light. Owen scrambled down the ladder and was surrounded by Resisters. He broke away when he saw Cati and Wesley pushing through the crowd. Cati grabbed him, half happy, half furious.

"I thought you were dead, you were gone so long!"

"Where's Silkie?" Wesley looked worried.

"Take it easy, Wesley," Owen said. "She's doing a job for me."

"Dr. Diamond says to come as quickly as possible," Cati said. "He keeps muttering dark stuff about just having won a battle, not the war, and for us all not to go silly celebrating."

"He's right." Owen and Wesley looked at each other.

"Don't start," Cati said.

Rosie pushed through the crowd.

"Camp traitor at your service, sir." She gave a mock salute.

"I can see there are more stories than mine." Owen grinned but wearily. "Let's go find the doctor—and some food. I'm starving."

They found the doctor in the kitchen, helping with the cooking while Contessa tended to the wounded. He kept getting in the cooks' way and insisting on fancy touches. They looked relieved when he spotted Owen and bounded towards him.

"Good man, good man," he cried. "What did you find?"

But Owen was looking past him to Martha, who was helping in the kitchen as well. She ran over. He could tell she was trying to be brave, but there was a tremor in her voice and tears in her eyes as she embraced him.

"You're back," she said, then as he winced, "You're hurt!"

"Only my shoulder—it'll be okay."

"Exactly what your father would have said." She smiled.

"We need to talk," the doctor said urgently. "The Harsh will not be so overconfident next time."

They all followed Dr. Diamond to the Skyward, which had stayed deep underground. Following the treachery of his lieutenant, Samual had abandoned his security. When they were all crowded in, Dr. Diamond put on the kettle.

"Now, Owen, tell us what happened."

Owen opened his mouth to speak but halted when Pieta came in, her hand swathed in a heavy bandage.

"Don't let me stop you," she said coolly, sitting down. So Owen told them about the voyage of the *Wayfarer*. The pirates and Port Merforian. The song he had heard that had pointed him toward the Long Woman. About the Memorator, and his grandfather. Although he was uncomfortable doing it, and thought that Dr. Diamond noticed, he left out the part about seeing his father as a little boy. There was something, well, *private* about it. He would tell his mother later. It was right that she should know first.

"The book, Owen." The doctor leaned forward. "Did you find the book?"

"I knew I'd seen it in a box of books," Owen said. "I thought it must have been my dad's."

They sat in silence as Owen told them the story of the frost child who had imagined kings and queens of ice. He took the book from where it had been stowed inside his jacket. He showed them the illustrations. The colors in which the blond child had been drawn had faded almost to nothing. But the drawings of the ice kings and queens were sharp and fresh.

"The Harsh!" Cati exclaimed, and shivered.

"Is it possible?" Pieta asked. "Can a child imagine another world so the world starts to exist?"

"Who knows what happens in realms other than ours?" Dr. Diamond said. "After all, Owen has sailed a boat on time itself. He has visited a city in time. He has seen the Long Woman, who should be dead and is not. May I see the book for a second?"

The friends sat in silence as the doctor examined the book, the only sound the ticking of Dr. Diamond's five clocks. Then he spoke.

"Have you looked on the flyleaf of this book, Owen?"

"No."

"Then come here." The doctor pointed to a faint inscription on the flyleaf. Owen peered at it.

"It's in French," Dr. Diamond said.

Ce livre a été fabriqué après des recherches
Sur l'histoire de l'enfant givré
Par J. M. Gobillard

He translated, "This book was made after research into the story of the frost child, by J.M. Gobillard."

"Gobillard!" Owen exclaimed.

"The man who had the shop in the Hadima court-yard!" Rosie said.

"He made the chest that could store the whirlwind of time!" Cati put in.

"And had my grandfather's maps in prison in Hadima," Owen said, and then, sadly, "and he died in the prison too."

"Yes." Dr. Diamond went on. "Did you ever wonder why the Harsh kept him in prison? He knew, or was close to knowing, the secret of their existence. They must have feared him. He made this book for a reason."

"But he can't tell us," Owen said. Owen had met

Gobillard in the Harsh prison in Hadima, but the man had been killed during their escape.

Dr. Diamond turned the book over in his hand. The paper dust jacket came away. There was a picture underneath.

"The tapestry," Owen cried. "That was the picture on the tapestry."

"So it must have been Gobillard who owned the circletagram and notebook we found by the tapestry," the doctor mused. "He pieced the story together bit by bit. How did you get the book, Owen?"

"It was in the attic," Owen said. He had told no one that he had seen his father as a child in the Long Woman's Memorator, with the book under his arm.

"I can help you there." Martha spoke for the first time. "Your father told me it arrived in the post when he was a child. He thought it was a present. He loved that book and talked about it often. He meant to give it to Owen when he grew up, but when he died I . . . I forgot . . ." She stopped. Owen took her hand. It was not her fault that she had spent much of his childhood lost in forgetfulness.

"Look!" Dr. Diamond exclaimed. Scrawled across the cover in pencil, the letters almost faded to nothing, was a single sentence.

"'*Quand ce livre sera détruit,*'" the doctor read, "'*l'enfant et ses créations seront également-tués.*' When the book is destroyed, the child and his creations will also be killed."

They looked at the book in silence.

"I think," the doctor said thoughtfully, "that the Harsh were after Gobillard. This message was written in great haste. He concealed it under the dust jacket and got someone to send it to Owen's grandfather, who thought it was a gift for his child and gave it to Owen's father."

Owen thought of the Memorator, how his grandfather had been looking for something that was under his nose the whole time.

"Then Gobillard was imprisoned by the Harsh," Martha said, "and kept a prisoner for many years."

"Why didn't Gobillard just tell Owen about the book when they met in prison?" Cati said impatiently.

"You are not thinking about the message," Dr. Diamond said sternly. "It is an instruction to kill a child. Would Gobillard have sent another child to do that? When it comes to it, which of us here now will destroy the book, knowing that a child will die?"

"But the Workhouse will be safe. The world will be free of the Harsh," Wesley said. They sat without speaking, each wrapped in his or her own thoughts.

"We can't tell Samual about this," the scientist said finally. "He will certainly destroy the book, whether we want him to or not."

"We should sleep on it," Martha said. "The young people must get some rest. Will there be another attack tonight, Doctor?"

"I don't think so. And you're right about sleep."

Owen didn't object. The pain in his shoulder was getting worse. He grimaced as he rose. Contessa was beside him straightaway. She made him lift his shirt so that she could see his shoulder. The skin had turned black and yellow. Contessa reached into her pocket and took out the Yeati's ring. She ran it swiftly over his shoulder.

"We should keep the ring for the seriously injured," Owen said, feeling a healing warmth.

"Your shoulder won't use much of the ring's power," Contessa said, "and we need the Navigator fit and well."

He was important to the Workhouse, perhaps their best hope. Owen sighed inwardly. He hadn't asked for this much responsibility.

Rosie, Wesley, and Cati walked back to the Den with him. As usual, Cati had raided the Workhouse kitchen, but the best she could charm out of them was some hard biscuit. It was better than nothing, and not bad at all with the hot tea that Owen made. At first they talked about the siege. But then their talk turned to other times they had spent together, and soon they were laughing and teasing each other, almost oblivious to the war outside.

And yet once the others left, responsibility settled on Owen again. More and more he knew what Cati felt, that grinding sense of duty. He lay down, but he could not sleep for a long time. And when he did he tossed and turned, dreaming that he pursued a shadow, a shadow that remained just out of reach.

Owen woke in the chill dawn and went down to the forward posts. Rutgar was glad to see him, but his men were nervous. The Albions had been active during the night, and several soldiers had narrowly avoided being stabbed or abducted. There was graffiti scrawled on the stones on the opposite bank of the river to show how close they had come.

"I don't like it," Rutgar said, rubbing his beard. Owen looked out at the smoke rising from the cooking fires of the attackers, and behind that at the ominous white mist that betokened the presence of the Harsh. Today would be another long battle. And the day after that, if they lasted. He *had* to find a way of disposing of the book without harming the frost child.

Both of them were right about the fight that day. Ice lances rained on the forward positions. The Q-cars fired at the Workhouse from a safe distance. They were obviously aiming for the mirrors. Although Cati and Rosie and Wesley tried to keep them moving so that they presented a bad target, by the afternoon they were dented and battered, and some had fallen from their ropes. A sneak party of Albions came up the frozen river and managed to get among Rutgar's men. Several Resisters were stabbed with poison knives. The Yeati's ring called them back from the point of no return, but still they hovered between life and death. Samual reluctantly gave the order to pull the soldiers back to the Workhouse. They were too few to defend the outer perimeter. Minutes after they had got the last Resister safely in the Workhouse, the Specials and the Albions swarmed across the river, whooping and crowing. A few Resisters aimed shots at them, but Rutgar stopped them.

"Save your ammunition. You'll need it."

After that there was only sporadic shooting. As night set in Owen found himself wandering alone through the Workhouse, avoiding the others. Something was gnawing at him, a thought that was just out of reach. If he stayed on his own, it might come to him. As he paced he realized just how few they were. There were a huge number of wounded who had been moved to the upper floors for safety, and those who were not too badly injured had been patched up and sent back to the battlements. Owen went onto the roof so that no one would see him. He spotted a shape moving beyond the river, and imagined he saw the gleam of huge teeth—Johnston. He'd been absent from the fight the previous two days. What was he up to now?

Owen's head hurt with thinking. What had happened to Silkie? Had her mission been a success? He missed her quick hands and ready smile. He worried that the Den might at this minute be swarming with Albions, although he doubted it. No one had ever entered the Den unless he wanted them to.

He stayed on the roof until he was frozen, then went to find his mother. She was in her room. Her face was pale with exhaustion. An unfinished meal sat on the table and in one corner stood the ingress. *It's good,* Owen thought, *that it's hidden away here, unknown to anyone.* He didn't know if Johnston or the Harsh could use it, and he didn't want to find out.

"Hello." Martha smiled.

He sat down and, without being aware that he was going to do it, told her the whole story of the Memorator and how he had seen his father as a boy. Her eyes filled with tears.

"Did he . . . did he see you?"

"No. I think he was still half asleep. He had the book of *The Frost Child* under his arm."

"Did he now?"

"I wonder if he ever worked out what it was—later on, I mean."

"I wish I knew. Your father could be a bit mysterious at times. And then of course toward the end, after we had been attacked by the Harsh, I wasn't really aware of what was going on around me. All I can remember is him pulling me away from them. They were attacking from all sides . . . they . . ." Pain darted across her face. "We were both wounded . . ."

"Stop," Owen said, seeing that it was torment for her to recall the injury inflicted by the Harsh. He struck the table. "We have to get rid of them!"

"Yes," his mother said gently, "but we must do it the proper way."

Just then there was a whistling sound outside. They ran to the window. A great ball of cold light hung in the air.

"They're here," his mother whispered. In an instant her face turned gray and her breathing became shallow. "Help me, Owen—don't let them come near me again."

Directly in front of the Workhouse, a multitude of Harsh had formed themselves into a shape like a cathedral of ice, and at the spire of it stood the Harsh queen. They opened their mouths and a shriek that defied all comprehension came from them, a shriek that might have been heard across all of time. A massive bolt of pure cold flew at the Workhouse. With a roar of falling masonry, a huge rent appeared. The wall crumbled. And from the fortifications below, Johnston led a band of Albions and Specials. The Workhouse was breached, and the enemy was in.

As the sounds of combat reached them, Owen started to race toward the door, but Martha grabbed his arm.

"Think! Owen. If you go down there . . . if you go down, you'll be able to fight but . . . but . . . we can't win. You're our only hope! Please don't be so like your father. . . ."

Owen brushed past her and bolted out of the door. As he took the stairs two at a time, her voice echoed in his head: *Like your father . . . like your father . . .* He hated himself for leaving his mother, and the hate turned to anger.

He ran past a mirror and saw his face in it. He stopped dead, and came back, staring at his face in the mirror. *In the mirror, of course!* How could he have missed it?

Down the stairs he went. At the bottom a knot of soldiers fought desperately with a group of Specials. They were outnumbered and almost overwhelmed. Owen slowed but forced himself on. He could see no sign of his friends, though he did spy Samual with several of his men, cut off from the other Resisters, fighting hand to hand with Specials while Albions danced about, thrusting with their knives.

He burst out onto the riverbank. On the other side the Harsh cathedral towered above him, but they were quiet, seemingly content with their night's work. The queen gazed on the sight before her with haughty satisfaction. *If she saw me*, Owen thought, *she mightn't look so pleased*. He raced on, grabbed a club from a fallen Special, and ran full tilt at three Albions who stood in his way. They didn't see him until the last minute and he scattered them with the club. Then he was on the path along the river, the trees that he remembered—the ash and rowan and alder—blasted to smithereens. As he ran he had a sudden flash of memory of how the path had looked in the autumn, the reds and the rusts stirred by the wind while the now still and frozen river brimmed over as it raced along.

Almost sobbing with effort, he reached the entrance to the Den. No one had been there. The air was still, as if it had lain undisturbed for a very long time. It felt at once familiar and strange, and the sounds of battle could not be heard. Owen stepped inside. The palms of his hands were moist, but he knew what he had to do. He went straight to the old truck mirror that hung on the wall, the one that had been there for so many years that he had forgotten where it had come from, imagining that

317

he had picked it up in Johnston's scrap yard long ago. He breathed on it. For what seemed like an eternity he waited for his breath to clear, then he saw, deep in the mirror, the Den, but the Den as it must have been a long time ago, without his sofa, or the mirror, or the perspex sheet in the roof.

It was a Memorator.

He stood back as the Den of long ago expanded into view. Owen stayed very still. A man stepped through the entrance, a tall man with long limbs and clear blue eyes. A flap of hair fell over his face, and he had to sweep it back with his hand. His father looked weary, hunted. He was pale and his hand kept going to his side. But when he saw Owen standing there a smile that was both tender and wistful flickered on his lips.

"I knew it," he said. "I knew you would grow into a fine boy."

"Dad," Owen whispered. He stepped forward, but the man moved back, raising a warning hand.

"Don't touch. You can't, you know, in a Memorator. There isn't much time. And all the time in the world would not be enough. You found the Mortmain? Of course you did."

"And the *Wayfarer*."

"The *Wayfarer*! Wonderful!" The man's eyes lit up, then he grimaced and clutched his side. "What about your mother? Is she . . . ?"

"She is very well now."

"Better and better. Listen, Owen, I'm not going to

beat about the bush. I was pierced by a Harsh dart saving your mother. There is no cure . . . but tell me this, the Harsh . . . ?"

"Are overrunning the Workhouse."

"Then there is no time. You found *The Frost Child*, the book? I was on my way to get it when we were attacked by the Harsh."

"I should destroy it—"

"No! You will kill the child—could you live with that for the rest of your life? I cannot tell you what to do. It would immediately nullify the Memorator, and this scene would never take place. But think, boy—there really is only one place for it. Think! It must be returned to time."

Owen's father coughed and held his side again.

"I can help you! The Yeati's ring . . . ," Owen burst out.

"You cannot," his father said sadly. "My fate is sealed. Were you not listening? You cannot change things in my time. It was a good old life, and I will miss you so much, you and your mother."

The scene around them began to stretch and distort. His father sighed.

"Those temporal alternators. Goodbye, son. I love you."

"You can't . . . just like that . . ." Owen reached out for his father, as though he might pull him through time into his world. But the scene was fading fast. His father smiled again.

"I am so glad we met like this . . . and not just like this." He lifted a bundle from behind the Den entrance. It was a baby. Not just any baby, Owen realized. It was him! And dangling from his father's hand were the keys to the Alfa Romeo, the car that had crashed into the harbor the day his father disappeared. A terrible dilemma seized Owen. If he tried to warn him, then surely it would be as if the scene they were in now would never have existed. If he didn't . . .

"Dad!" The word burst from him. But it was too late. His father was gone.

Owen did not remember starting to run, but he found himself on the path leading back to the Workhouse. He was dully aware of Albions in his path, but there was something in his face that made them stand aside. One whole section of the Workhouse was ablaze. Owen burst through the front door. He saw his friends fighting at the bottom of the stairwell: Wesley, Dr. Diamond, Cati, and Rosie wielding her hairpin. A great press of Specials stood against them, but Owen pushed through. Up he ran, his lungs about to burst. Everywhere there were screams, cries of triumph and despair.

At last he emerged onto the roof, and ran to the battlements. Down below he could see the battle, his enemies swarming over the riverbank that he had loved, now burning and despoiled. Flames leapt hungrily from the burning building below him. There was the roar of collapsing timber and masonry.

He thought again about the damage that the Harsh had

done. To his mother and father. To Cati, her heart frozen by them, her father snatched away from her. To the world itself, turned to ice and ruined. In his mind's eye he could see his father wince with pain as the Harsh poison worked on him. Below him the flames crackled. He took *The Frost Child* out from under his jacket, and held it aloft. He would throw it down into the flames and all this would end. Then he remembered that the Harsh child had once saved Wesley and Silkie. But no, it wasn't enough. Too much damage had been done.

He heard a sardonic laugh. Johnston leaned on the battlements ten yards away, leering at him.

"Owen!" A calm, commanding voice rang out from the other side of the battlements.

"It's over, Dr. Diamond."

"If you burn the book, the child will die. If you do the right thing, the Harsh will be destroyed—the child will no longer be frozen and will go on growing up and grow old and live life as was intended."

"Why should he have that? I never had the chance to live life with a mother and a father the way it was meant to be!"

"Only you can answer that," the doctor said.

Owen glanced down. In front of the main gate was a group of terrified Raggie children. A band of braying Specials surrounded them. But there, side by side and fighting like demons to defend the children, stood Cati and Samual. Blood streamed from many wounds on Samual's body, and as Owen looked, an ice lance struck the man. He threw his head back in agony, fell to the ground, and lay still. The Specials cheered, but Cati, grim-faced, looked up through the wreathing smoke, and her eyes met Owen's unflinchingly. *I have done my duty,* they were saying; *you must do yours.* And in his head he could hear his father's voice: *Think, boy—there really is only one place for it. . . . It must be returned to time.*

He ran for the staircase. He cleared a flight of stairs, then ran into a corridor that led into the burning part of the building. Acrid smoke made him cough but he kept going.

His mother's room was empty. Small flames licked across the ceiling beams and the walls were hot to the touch. Owen went to the grandfather clock, opened it, and found himself looking into the cosmos itself, infinite blue-black space that was at once present and far away beyond knowing. Owen held up *The Frost Child.* He looked into the face of the child on the front cover, the eyes faded almost to nothing. His own eyes clouded with tears. He thrust the book into the ingress and closed the door.

A few miles away, the Harsh child found his gaze drawn away from the battlefield to the thin band of light running along the horizon. He felt warmth flow back into his legs and arms. A pink flush spread across his cheeks and he smiled. And then, as if a gentle breeze blew across the deck of the Harsh ship, the Harsh child shimmered and was gone.

At the top of the Harsh pyramid, the queen shrieked. The other Harsh joined their voices to hers. Cracks ran across the ice that enclosed them, cracks that then ran through the Harsh themselves and they came apart like shattered crystal. Their voices rose to a crescendo, and all who heard it covered their ears and fell to their knees. Then the pyramid crumbled to icy dust as the Harsh voices faded away to a distant wail and were gone. The ice that bound the Harsh ships together started to melt, and the ships collapsed until all that was left were rotten hulks on the ice.

Owen saw none of this. He went to the door of his mother's room, but the corridor beyond was full of flame. He sat down on the edge of the bed, weary and full of sorrow. It was over. After a while he became aware of smoke all around him and flames licking at the bedsheets. He looked at the fire. *Some air would be nice,* he thought vaguely, and made his way to the window. The air was fresher, but he looked down and saw that there was no escape that way. *Ah well,* he thought. *At least I got to sail on time.* . . . Behind him flames scorched the door, and the bed ignited with a whoosh. He shut his eyes. Far away he thought he could hear the swish of the *Wayfarer*'s hull and sails as she crossed the oceans of time.

"Owen! Owen!" an urgent voice called. "Wake up!"

He opened his eyes. The *Wayfarer* hovered, six feet away. Silkie was leaning over the rail.

"Grab the rope!" she shouted.

The two Specials guarding the Hadima entrance gazed anxiously toward the battlefield. They hadn't noticed the spluttering mechanical noise behind them until it was too late. A battered truck burst through the Hadima entrance, with people clinging to every surface. They were small and sharp-eyed like Rosie and wore velvet jackets and rakish-looking hats. They carried a variety of hooks and cudgels and other homemade weapons. Behind them came a mass of Dogs—street children wearing dog masks, some of whom had taken on the characteristics of real dogs. The Specials fled in terror.

On the battlefield Cati had taken a blow to the head, and a Special had run a knife along her ribs. She had gone down once but the Raggies behind her had picked up rocks and pelted the Specials until she got back on her feet. She barely had time to glance at the collapsing Harsh cathedral before the Specials renewed their assault.

They were hardened thugs and not likely to be easily put off.

Elsewhere in the Workhouse, a blood-drenched Rutgar and a handful of men fought to stop the invaders getting into the Starry. A gang of Albions had started to loot, carrying away what they could and piling it up outside. They had pinned Contessa behind the great ovens in the kitchen, and she fought back with two large and sharp kitchen knives.

One of the Specials threw his cudgel at Cati. It hit her under the eye and she went down again, half blind with pain and blood. They were on her in a flash. One grabbed her hair and exposed her throat. A knife gleamed. Then he stopped, looking up in confusion.

Over their heads hovered a long black ship. The *Faltaine*! Lines fell from her sides, and a crew of villainous-looking men and women brandishing magno flintlocks and muskets and scimitars slid to the ground. A young man with a luxuriant mustache and a steel post in place of a left leg confronted the Special who held Cati's head.

"Doesn't look like fair odds to me, matey," he growled. Faster than lightning, he whirled and the steel leg flew through the air, striking the Special's temple. As his shipmates put the rest of them to flight, he helped Cati to her feet.

"Midshipman Dardanelle Smith from the *Faltaine* at your service, ma'am." He saluted.

There was a mighty commotion from the Workhouse,

and a crowd of squealing Albions ran out. Behind them came Pieta and her two children. The children carried swishing magno whips, but Pieta at first seemed to have nothing in her hand—that is, until a Special dropped a huge rock on them from a window above.

"Look out!" Cati yelled. Pieta looked up. Her right hand flashed, and the rock fell in pebbles around them. Cati could now see the metallic claw attached in place of her severed hand.

"Based it on the Yeati's claw," a disheveled Dr. Diamond said, staggering through the entrance. "I gave her an anesthetic to do it after you left. . . ."

"And forgot to wake me up!" Pieta gave Dr. Diamond a baleful look. "No time for talk. Fight."

The Albions regrouped with Agnetha at their head as a body of Specials ran up from the river. The friends were pressed back against the Workhouse wall. The magno whips flashed again and again, and Pieta's claw carved the air, but the weight of those behind pushed the front attackers forward. The pirates had joined the Resisters but were distracted by fire from two of the remaining Q-cars, which had struck the *Faltaine* amidships with ice cannon. The pirates had climbed back into the ship and moved off to deal with the Q-cars.

"It's too much," Cati gasped.

"I don't think so," Dr. Diamond said. "Look!"

In the east the sun was rising. Not just the dull red sun of past weeks, but a glorious ball of light, as if to celebrate winter's end. The Albions wailed and covered their eyes. They had been confident of victory during the night and had no dark glasses. They ran blindly toward the Hadima entrance. Only Agnetha stayed. Her eyes almost closed, flinching from the touch of the sun on her skin, she brandished her long, poisoned knife at Cati. Pieta raised her claw.

"No!" Cati exclaimed. She found herself feeling sorry for this deadly, beautiful creature, condemned to live in darkness.

"Put the knife down and go home," Cati said. "You don't belong here." Agnetha held her gaze, though she winced at the sunlight.

"We long for light," she said, "always. Always."

"Don't turn your back on her." A mocking voice spoke from above their heads. "She'll stab you as soon as look at you. Treacherous like a snake, them Albions."

Johnston leaned on the parapet above them.

"You lie," Agnetha spat. "You and Harsh say we will feel sun on skin."

"The dark's where you belong," Johnston said, showing his teeth. "Go back under your stone, you pink-eyed witch."

With a flick Agnetha's knife left her hand. Cati gasped. Johnston's hands went to his throat, where the knife lodged, quivering. Something fell from his hand and the doctor dived to catch it as Johnston toppled over the parapet and landed on his back with a thud, eyes open, great teeth bared in a lifeless grimace. Once more Pieta lunged to attack Agnetha, but the doctor stopped her.

He held up the object that had fallen from Johnston's grasp.

"A magno grenade. Primed. It would have killed all of us if it had hit the ground." Very carefully, he removed its fuse.

The sun cleared the horizon and Agnetha hissed, then turned and ran. No one tried to stop her.

"I smell something," Cati said, raising her face to the air. "Dogs. The Dogs of Hadima!" And indeed they could hear barking coming from the river, and the squeals of the Albions intermingled with the curses of the fleeing Specials.

"Pieta," Dr. Diamond said, "take your children and clear the Workhouse of the enemy."

"Land ahoy," they heard from above as the *Wayfarer*, with Silkie and Owen on board, skidded to a halt beside them. Wesley ran to Silkie and embraced her.

"Here's me thinking something happened to you . . ."

"Nothing except a lot of adventures! I went to find our friends, and get help. The Dogs and the Hadima folk are chasing the Specials and the Albions back into the tunnel. We could see them from the boat."

Owen got out of the *Wayfarer*, looking groggy.

"Silkie," Dr. Diamond spoke urgently, "get the buccaneer ship. You can carry water from the harbor to help put out the flames. Wesley, round up the Raggies and whoever else you can—find Rutgar. Now where is Cati?"

They found her kneeling beside the fallen Samual. Gently she closed his eyes and folded his hands across his breast.

"He fought beside me to protect the Raggie children. He fell because of us," she said in a small voice.

"He was proud and difficult," the doctor said, "but also brave and faithful. Do not cry too much for him, Cati. He would have thought of this as—"

"His duty. I know," Cati interrupted. The snow had been disturbed beside Samual's head, and Cati rubbed it with her hand until she could see grass—and something growing. She plucked a blue flower from the ground—a cornflower, the Resisters' symbol of remembering—and threaded it carefully through Samual's buttonhole. From the direction of the river, they heard a trickle of water.

"I do believe the thaw is on its way." The doctor smiled.

For the rest of the morning they fought the flames, Rutgar and Martha directing teams of firefighters while the *Faltaine* and the buccaneers carried water from the sea. By lunchtime they had it under control. They had managed to keep the flames away from the kitchen and the Starry, although a large part of the sleeping quarters had been destroyed.

The Dogs and the Hadima people roamed up and down the river chasing anything that moved back into the Hadima tunnel. Under the Harsh ships, the ice was melting with sharp cracks and dull booms, and the ice castles had collapsed.

Dr. Diamond took Owen back to the Den and insisted he lie on the sofa while the doctor made tea. Owen told the doctor about the Memorator, and Dr. Diamond examined it with great interest. But Owen was fatigued and listless, and the doctor was worried.

"You have defeated the Harsh forever, you know," he reminded Owen, but the boy's mind was on other things.

"My father. He was so pale, and in pain," Owen muttered.

Dr. Diamond shook his head.

"Do you mind if I take the Memorator back to the Skyward?" Dr. Diamond asked.

"If you want." Owen closed his eyes.

Back at the Workhouse, Cati sat on a piece of masonry. There was ash in her hair, and her face and clothing stank of wet, burned timber. She was exhausted, but still she leapt to her feet when she heard the pattering of feet. Clancy, the leader of the Dogs, loped across to her, followed by the other Dogs. They rubbed noses.

Rosie had spent the whole morning on board the *Faltaine* with Dardanelle Smith, the two of them generally getting in the way. But when she saw the Dogs and the hats of the Hadima folk, she asked to be put back on the ground.

"Ahoy, lubbers," she shouted, her hat askew, then shrieked in delight. "Graham! Graham!"

Her brother waved back from the ground. She tumbled head over heels over the thwart of the *Faltaine* and threw her arms around him.

"Where did you come from?"

"Silkie flew the *Wayfarer* to Hadima and told us that the Navigator needed help. We took the old road in that truck that was left behind the last time Owen was in Hadima. Silkie flew ahead and guided us."

"And us buccaneers met the *Wayfarer* on the way there." The woman who had freed Owen on board the *Faltaine* leaned on the rail, now wearing a captain's hat and grinning with her sharp teeth. "We was game for a fight."

They milled around happily in front of the Work-house, but Contessa watched them with sadness in her eyes. "The Workhouse is almost destroyed and the world is in ruins."

"Yes," Martha said, "but look at them. They are young and the future is theirs."

When it seemed that the last enemy was gone and the Hadima entrance was secured, the friends walked to the harbor. Owen and Cati followed Silkie and Wesley, eager to see if their warehouse had been spared. They were silent as they walked through the ruined town, and stood for a long time on the shore watching the rotten Harsh hulks, which had started to sink into the melting ice. When they got to the warehouse, they found Albion graffiti scrawled on the outside doors and walls. But the inside was dry and untouched, although cold. Wesley and Silkie were delighted, and they ran about making fires from stored driftwood. Cati and Owen went outside. He waited for her to interrogate him about everything, but she was quiet for a long time.

At last she said, "The Harsh have gone."

"I remember the first time I met your father," Owen said. "We heard the Harsh cry, and he said, 'It has begun.'"

"Now it is over," she said. She had turned her head away, but he could see the tears on her cheeks.

"Yes, it is over."

"It is over," another voice said. They turned to see Dr. Diamond coming up behind them. "But a new era has begun. Tonight we will bury our dead. Tomorrow we begin again."

Samual's redcoats had cut down trees and built a funeral pyre for him. When the time came they lit the pyre. As the flames leapt high, the Resisters sang a fighting song for their lost leader, but Cati and Pieta turned their faces aside and would not watch.

Late that night, as Owen lay awake in the Den, he heard Dr. Diamond calling from outside. He looked round the door. "I brought you back your Memorater," the doctor said.

"Thanks," Owen said. But he thought, *Couldn't this have waited until the morning?*

"I found something on it," the doctor said. "I think your grandfather must have intended it for your dad, and your dad recorded over it when he had to without ever having seen it. It's a kind of a ghost image, and you mustn't disturb it, but I thought you'd like it."

Dr. Diamond breathed on the mirror. An image appeared in the room. It was his grandfather's room, the same room he had seen in the Memorater at the Long Woman's house. The image was crackly and grainy. Sometimes it stuttered and went from color to black and white. His grandfather stood in the middle of the room. He looked troubled, and peered toward Owen.

"Are you there, Owen?"

"Yes," Owen said, "yes, I am."

"I wanted to say something. . . . You know I haven't been the best of fathers. I've been running about all over time, chasing . . . chasing shadows, if truth be told."

Owen realized that he thought that he was talking to his son, not his grandson.

"You wanted to save the world from the Harsh," Owen said.

"Was that what I was doing?" The old man looked thoughtful. "Maybe I was, and maybe I was a selfish old goat who needed saving from himself. But it's generous of you to say it."

"I was angry," Owen said.

"You have every right to be. Fathers have their own sorrows, but they shouldn't let their sons carry them. Can you forgive me?"

"I forgive you," Owen said. And then, before he could stop himself, "I miss you."

"I miss you too, Owen. But that's all right. Be something wrong if we didn't." The scene flickered and stretched.

"Those damn cheap alternators again. If there is one

lesson I can give you in life, it is don't be a cheapskate."
His grandfather's eyes wrinkled in a smile. "Goodbye,"
he said simply.

"Goodbye."

The scene flickered once more and then Owen found
himself in the stillness of the Den.

32

It was two months before the frost fully loosened its grip on the earth. During that time the Resisters were busy at the Workhouse, rebuilding the burned sections and fixing the building so that when the world did awake, it could more easily be disguised as a ruin. They had lost soldiers, but they were not as shorthanded as they might have been. The Yeati's ring had saved many of the injured.

It was a time of much coming and going between Hadima and the Workhouse. The truck traveled once a week. There was no sign of the Albions, and the road was safe. Hadima was gradually thawing, and the Specials' hold on the city was broken. A new city council was formed. Graham, Rosie's brother, was appointed. And to Rosie's delight, if not that of many citizens, Graham picked Clancy, the Dog leader, to sit beside him.

Owen spent as much time as he could on the *Wayfarer*,

sometimes alone and sometimes with Silkie. Every now and then he sailed off on his own and was silent about where he had been. Martha suspected that he had been to see the Long Woman.

Martha passed several hours each day scanning the airwaves on her radio, hoping to hear some signal, a human voice, that would tell them that the world had awoken.

Owen spent a lot of time with Dr. Diamond, talking about the future.

"Is time safe now?" he asked the doctor, half dreading the answer. For he did not want the Harsh to return, and yet he didn't want the Resisters to go back to sleep forever.

"Who knows," the doctor replied. "Perhaps somewhere, in another time and space, a lonely child is dreaming of another set of kings and queens and a new Harsh will be born. There will always be a threat to time."

"And what about the Harsh child?"

"I suspect that he was very old but was frozen in the mind of a child."

"What will have happened to him?"

"I imagine that instead of his being frozen in that moment of childhood, that moment passed and he went on living his life, had his own children, and died many, many years ago."

"That's sad." Owen thought for a moment, though as usual, thinking about time made his head ache. "If the moment passed, wouldn't that mean that the Harsh never existed at all, so none of this would have happened?"

"The moment passed in his time but not in ours." Dr.

Diamond stood up and stretched. He went to the window. It was a pleasant evening. There was still snow and ice on the high ground, but the river ran free, and the buds had started to form on the trees.

"When you threw the book into the grandfather clock, you were putting the child back to the place he came from."

"I still don't understand."

"Imagine time as one long story—a very long story, one with no ending and a beginning so far back it is lost. Then think of it written as a book. The Harsh child was a chapter torn out of that book. He was in the wrong place. That was the genius of Gobillard. He figured that out and wrote it down as a story. All we had to do was return it to the book—which is what you did when you put the book into the ingress. Once the story was intact again, everything was put to rights."

"The clock is gone."

"Yes, destroyed in the fire. Half of me is glad. No one should have access to such a powerful and dangerous object." He turned to Owen. "You and your friends must come to the Hadima gate tomorrow evening. There is something I want to show you."

Owen left the Skyward and went to find Cati. Anytime he looked for her now, she seemed to be at the warehouse with the Raggies. He had been spending some time there himself, swimming in holes cut in the melting ice and eating fish and chips around sweet-smelling driftwood fires.

He passed the dark Hadima entrance, still guarded by

Rutgar's soldiers, and wondered what it was Dr. Diamond wanted to show them. When he got to the warehouse, Cati and Wesley were lying on the roof watching the sunset. Silkie came up and sat beside them.

"Owen, we had a meeting last night," she said. "We decided that the Raggies needed a Watcher like Cati, and a Watcher in the real world like you. Wesley and me is scared when we're all sleeping and nobody watching."

Owen could see her looking at him in the dusk. He felt as if he was supposed to say something, but he didn't know what.

It was late when he got home, but his mother was still awake. The little room behind the shop looked bare without the grandfather clock.

His mother had her old battery radio on the table in front of her. Owen could tell that something had happened. He sat down.

"What is it?"

"I picked up a signal. Human voices! The world is awake again, Owen."

Owen sighed. He knew that he should be glad, but he would miss so much of the world that would go back to sleep.

The next evening Owen, Cati, Wesley, and Rosie went to the Hadima gate. Dr. Diamond met them at the foot of the stairs that had been built up to the entrance. They climbed in silence and walked along the dark tunnel, still covered in Albion graffiti. When they emerged into the courtyard, though, much had changed. Instead of the old graffiti-covered shops, there was smooth stone with complex astrological symbols etched on them. Owen and Wesley looked around in bewilderment, but Cati and Rosie knew immediately.

"Andromeda!" They rushed forward. The mythical Yeati stood in the entrance that led down to the Hadima road. They buried their faces in his white fur as Wesley looked on in astonishment and Dr. Diamond beamed.

"The Yeati don't really like to fight, so I couldn't involve him in our battle, but I asked him to do a job for me. Look."

The tunnel entrance had been fitted with a stone door carved with the same symbols as the walls. When Rosie and Cati let go of the Yeati, he showed them how it worked (though not without fixing his ruffled fur first— he was very vain). When the door was closed you couldn't see the join. The Yeati reached into his fur and produced a marvelous key, carved entirely from white stone, fine and light and delicate. He presented it to Owen and bowed deeply. Owen, embarrassed, stuttered his thanks.

"It is a grave responsibility," the doctor said. "The Navigator now has control over the Hadima entrance. Guard it well, Owen."

To Rosie and Cati's delight, the Yeati walked to the harbor with them. The Raggie children hid when they saw the fabulous beast arm in arm with Cati and Rosie. Together they strolled along the quay and over the ice bridge still joining the warehouse to the mainland, while Raggie children ran giggling in front of them. One very small girl was brave enough to present him with a piece of seaweed and received the same courteous bow that the Yeati had given to Owen.

But evening came time for him to go. Cati and Rosie hugged him again. He stopped in the tunnel entrance and his green eyes met Owen's. Owen felt as if he was looking across galaxies to the very source of time and space itself. The Yeati's eyes crinkled in what appeared to be a smile, then he walked off and was swallowed by the darkness of the tunnel. Owen closed and locked the door behind him.

That night there was a flurry of radio signals from the outside world. The next morning the Resisters started to prepare for their sleep. There was an air of departures and of leave-taking. The *Faltaine,* with Dardanelle Smith at the helm, arrived to take Rosie and Graham back to Hadima. Shem wouldn't even glance at the buccaneer ship, but just before they boarded, Rosie darted forward and kissed him on the lips. He looked stunned.

Rosie climbed on board. She stood on the bow, grasping the foremast as the *Faltaine* lifted off to cries of farewell, and disappeared into the cloud.

Owen looked everywhere for Silkie, but no one knew where she was. He couldn't understand why he was so afraid that she would go to sleep before he found her. He asked Contessa if she had seen Silkie, but she only shook her head and smiled in a strange way.

Martha was saying her farewells to Contessa, Dr.

Diamond, and Rutgar, and still Owen could not find Silkie. He met Cati and Wesley, walking along deep in conversation.

"Where is Silkie?" he asked, almost crossly.

Cati shook her head. "Silkie is the new Watcher in the world, you bonehead. Wesley is going to stay awake and watch with me, and she is to stay in the world. But she has nowhere to live and is afraid to ask you!"

"Why . . . what . . . ?" Owen's face was a picture of bewilderment.

"You know a lot about sailing through time," Cati said, "but you don't know much about girls!"

In the end his heart told him where to find her. The *Wayfarer* was in the garden behind Mary White's house. When he looked in, Silkie was asleep in the cabin. He looked down at her, at the curl of fair hair across her cheek where the scar had once been, now flawless. He shook her awake gently.

"The *Wayfarer* is great when you're sailing across time, but maybe you'd be more comfortable in the house."

She smiled up at him. He took her by the hand and helped her to her feet.

The next few hours were a blur of preparations for sleep, Dr. Diamond thrusting books into Owen's hands.

"them reading enjoy You'll," he said, then grinned. "Only kidding!"

Rutgar was gruff and unemotional with everyone.

341

Contessa was dignified as always. She shook Owen's hand, then to his surprise—and to hers, it seemed—she hugged him.

Cati hugged him and Wesley shook hands. They would be in touch with each other, but still could not contact Owen unless there was danger.

"You won't be so lonely, will you, Cati?" Owen said.

"What?" Cati asked innocently, but her eyes flickered in Wesley's direction.

"You don't know much about boys either." He grinned, and Wesley blushed.

Silkie went to the warehouse to help put the children to bed, and when she came back her eyes were puffy.

And then it was time to leave. Owen, Silkie, and Martha climbed the two fields on the far side of the river. When they got to the top they turned to see all the Resisters standing in the windows and on the battlements of the Workhouse.

"The Navigator!" they shouted. "The Navigator!" And there was a great roar from every throat. Owen waved back, unable to speak. Silkie and Martha each took him by the hand and they crossed the top of the hill, the Workhouse no longer visible.

They ate quietly together that evening, and when they were finished Silkie went to bed. Owen knocked on the door to his mother's room. It swung open, and he gasped. For a moment he thought that it was Rosie or one of the other Hadima folk standing there, wearing a long dress and an elegant stovepipe hat in velvet. Then he saw his mother's face under the hat, a mischievous gleam in her eye, and caught a glimpse of who she had been when his father had met her, an elegant citizen of Hadima, the great City of Time. She was taller as well, for she was wearing stiletto heels. She smoothed down the dress and cast a critical eye at herself in the mirror.

"I wore this on the way back from Hadima with your father," she said. "I'm amazed it still fits."

"You look . . . brilliant," Owen said.

"Do I? I must have, then. Your father certainly thought so. Perhaps someday we'll travel back to Hadima."

"I'd like that." He hesitated. "I have a lot to tell you. About fathers and grandfathers and . . . things."

His mother smiled and kissed him on the cheek. "I know. But now—to bed." She turned to the mirror for a last look, then took off the hat and laid it on the bed.

Owen slipped out of the room. He went outside to check the *Wayfarer,* then made his way to bed. He woke several hours later, to see moonlight streaming through the window. He got up and slipped on a jacket and a pair of shoes.

Outside the fields were awash with silvery light, but the shadows under the Workhouse were dark and impenetrable.

"See you soon, Watcher," he called out. He waited for a long time but there was no reply. He sighed. The Harsh were gone. Johnston was dead. It was over. He remembered the first time he had seen the Workhouse. He had been so much younger then. How strange a thing time was, that his first glimpse should seem not just years but worlds ago. He turned and made his way to the brow of the hill. As he did a girl's voice rang out, clear and loud in the night air, a call that could have been a farewell, or a summons.

"From the shadows, Navigator!"

He smiled. "See you soon, Cati," he murmured, and walked toward the lights of home.

ABOUT THE AUTHOR

EOIN MCNAMEE was born in County Down, Ireland. He is the author of *The Navigator,* a *New York Times* bestseller, and *City of Time,* the first two books in the Navigator trilogy. He is critically acclaimed as a writer of novels for adults, the best known being *Resurrection Man,* which was made into a film. He was awarded the Macaulay Fellowship for Irish Literature and has also written three adult thrillers under the name John Creed.